NIGHT WIDOW

CAROL DAVIS LUCE

Sudalu Media

Dedicated with love to Tatum,
the baby girl of the family—now all grown up.

Acknowledgments

Many thanks to my supportive friends, family, and readers. J. Carson Black for leading the way in the electronic world and making it look so easy. My brother, Harry Davis, for keeping my books in the public eye. Fred Rayworth, for striking out the 'and' and 'buts' — but not all of them. K.C. May, author extraordinaire.

A special thanks to A. L. Shaw for her diligent assistance throughout the many drafts of this novel. For her valuable contribution of the Hollywood haunts, movie biz, and film editing material (if there are any errors in these areas, they are mine alone). Above all, I thank her for her treasured friendship. She kept me honest and made me work harder.

A big thanks to my husband, Bob, who never stopped believing in me. And my mother, who on her 90th birthday, when asked if she had a favorite author, replied: "Carol Davis Luce." Thanks, Mom, couldn't have done it without you.

CHAPTER 1

Where Are They Now? *Washed up? Hiding out? Dead?*

SYBIL SQUIRE….

Not dead yet. This stunning platinum blonde will be forever ingrained in our hearts for her femme fatale role in the 1950 Oscar win, The Shady Lady. One flash of her pale blue eyes and men were putty. Seems she hasn't been hiding all these years. She surfaced briefly this year after police and paramedics were called out to her mansion in the Hollywood Hills. A housekeeper found the Golden Age screen idol unconscious at the bottom of her staircase with a blood alcohol level above .10.

Rehab again or the old folk's home?

—WashedUpStars.com

PIPER LUNDBERG RUSHED THROUGH the ultra-modern house with the last of her personal possessions. No time for sorting and packing, it was grab and dump into whatever was handy. Almost done, she couldn't get out fast enough. Gordon was supposed to be boarding a plane for Europe at this very moment, but knowing her soon-to-be ex-husband, she wouldn't be surprised if he canceled his business trip to ambush her in their Santa Monica home.

Through a front window, she saw her best friend across the street stuffing shoeboxes into the back of her SUV. Lee's Escalade was already stacked to the ceiling with Piper's clothes, books, CDs and laptop.

Sweat beaded on her forehead and upper lip. Her heart raced. It was a race to be free. Rounding the corner with the cumbersome recycled carton, Piper slipped on the polished hardwood. The box caught the edge of the doorway between the living room and dining room, spewing its entire contents across the floor. She groaned in frustration, wiped her sweaty palms on the front of her jeans, and dropped to her knees to retrieve the dozens of old video cassettes, DVDs, and mementos. Of all her possessions, this collection meant the most. As her fingers wrapped around a cassette, a black leather dress shoe pressed down on her hand, pinning it and the cassette case to the floor.

Piper jerked her head up. Gordon looked down on her. She expected to see that sanctimonious smirk that had, over the years, come to define him. His expression was hard, stony. When she tried to free her hand, he increased the pressure. She should've known it wouldn't be easy. Gordon didn't play fair.

"In a hurry, are you?"

She yanked her hand out from under his sole.

Gordon kept his foot on the cassette. He turned his head to stare out the window at Lee who was still struggling to load the SUV.

"Brought the dyke for moral support? Or is it the muscle?"

She bit down on her lip. Gordon knew she hated it when he called Lee it. A transsexual, Lee had made the full male-to-female transition several years ago. Lee Sikes, formally Leroy, was Piper's first husband.

"I don't want any trouble." Piper tried to control her anger. "I don't want anything of yours. I just want to go."

Gordon pinched the fabric at his knees, lifted his slacks, then squatted down and picked up the cassette case. He'd just had a haircut. She could see the red skin above his collar where the electric shears had chaffed his neckline.

On his haunches, level with her face, he pinned her with his gaze. "You'll regret this."

Piper and Lee, with the help of Belle Vogt, had unloaded her belongings from the two cars and carried everything upstairs to the Vogt's guesthouse above the garage. Piper left Belle and Lee in the driveway talking shop and hurried upstairs. She wanted a few moments to herself in her new home. She crossed the room, dropped an armful of clothes on the pulled-down Murphy bed, and glanced around. Assured she was alone, she made a beeline to the northwest corner window.

The late afternoon sky, recently purged by the hot, dry winds of the Santa Anas, was clear of smog. A red-tailed hawk soared high above hills thick with vegetation, casting a sharp eye below to the yucca plants, greasewood and royal palms for signs of prey. The hawk continued upward, growing smaller, following the winding road to the top near Mulholland where Brando once lived. The hawk dove, disappearing into the thick brush.

The hawk held little interest for Piper. What *did* interest her was the Mediterranean mansion on the huge lot next door. That she would have a birds-eye view was beyond her wildest expectations. Closest to the six-foot property wall was the pool. A small rose garden in full bloom extended off a brick patio at the rear of the stately house. The house belonged to Sybil Squire.

She scanned the grounds, looking for a glimpse of the owner. Someone was in the pool. Piper leaned closer to the glass. The old woman with platinum hair executed a strong, yet graceful, backstroke across the rectangular swimming pool. Except for a pair of black swim goggles, she was as naked as a newborn.

"What's got your attention there, Piper? As if I didn't know."

Piper spun around.

Belle nimbly leapt over a pile of shoeboxes blocking the entrance. With her pale complexion and dark hair cropped close to her head, her root-beer-brown eyes, innocent and childlike, dominated her China-doll face.

"Busted. I was spying on our neighbor." Piper turned back to the window. "Did you know she swims in the nude?"

"Really? I can't see the pool from the house." Despite a quarter century of living in the US, Belle's British lilt infused her words. "Is she alone?"

"In the pool? Yes."

Belle wove her way through the boxes and bags to stand alongside Piper.

"Oh, my, not bad for an old babe, eh?" Belle peered down. "But those goggles...what is that? Sort of spoils the au natural effect, don't you think?"

"Um. Maybe she doesn't expect an audience?"

"Are you kidding? Everyone in these hills has a telescope, and believe me, they're not pointed at the stars. At least not the heavenly stars." Belle chuckled. "Bet you didn't expect to see her so soon, now did you? Or so much of her."

"I expected her estate to be a fortress, hidden behind towering walls and gates, like the one in her movie, *Black Ribbon.*"

Belle bent at the waist and picked through the carton of old video cassettes. "All of her flicks? Impressive. Some of these you can't even get on digital download."

"They were my grandmother's. Instead of the family flatware, I inherited her collection of Sybil's movies. I've had them all converted to DVDs, but I can't part with these original cassettes."

"You must have every film our platinum widow made."

"Not quite. Every one but *Judgment Day.*"

"That was, what, her last one?"

"Yes. It was pulled right after its release."

"Maybe out of respect for the loss of husband number three."

"Four. He was her fourth husband."

Belle sorted through the cassettes. "What is it about her, Piper, that you fancy so much?"

Piper took a moment to answer. "She helped my grandmother Ruth through a very hard time."

"Helped her how?"

"Sybil took her in after the fire. Gave her and my mother a place to stay when they had nowhere to go. Nana was a seamstress in the fifties there at RKO where Sybil worked."

"They stayed there, next door?"

Piper nodded. "It was a long time ago. My mother was eight. All she could remember about the house was the swimming pool. Nana thought the sun rose and fell on Sybil. Said she was her savior."

Piper looked out at the pool. It was empty. A trail of wet footprints darkened the concrete and bricks leading to the back door.

"Belle, has she been alone all these years, hiding out?"

"I wouldn't call living in the Hollywood Hills hiding out exactly. Of course, from the main house we have a different view than from here. And see there, her house sets cockeyed on the corner, so our front entrances aren't even on the same street."

"You live next door to her. You must know something about her."

"She fancies birds. Canaries. Keeps them in the sunroom, there ... off the patio. Dr. J tries to imitate them. It's not a pleasant sound." Dr. J, short for Dr. Jekyll, was the Vogt's twelve-year-old Goffin cockatoo.

Piper put her ear to the open window and closed her eyes. Yes, she heard them, a chorus of songbirds.

"Does she go out? Have people in?"

"I don't know, Piper darling. She keeps to herself and even if she didn't, I'm not one for coffee-klatches or chitchatting over the fence. Following the lives of tragic former leading ladies is not my bag."

Belle gathered up a half dozen cassettes. "Where do you want these?"

"On the bookshelf. Where's Lee?"

"She made her excuses and dashed."

"Manual labor is not Lee's bag."

With Belle's help, they tucked Piper's few possessions away in record time. She had taken only personal effects and things recently purchased with her own money. Anything bought with Gordon's money was Gordon's. She didn't want anything of his, only her freedom. Would he try to keep that from her as well?

The guesthouse matched the main Tudor-style house. The polished cherry wood cabinets, window casings, and hardwood floors enhanced the smooth lines of the ivory Kreiss couch and leather club chairs. Belle's love of feathered creatures was reflected in the hanging prints of exotic birds—cockatoos mostly—and throw pillows covered in a vivid bird-and-bamboo-patterned fabric. A cherry wood screen separated the living area from the bedroom area, which was a Murphy bed on the north wall.

In less than one day, Piper felt more at home here than she'd ever felt in Gordon's model-home-like house. For her, the comforting smell of old leather and the aged area rug overrode the aseptic odor of fresh paint, granite, and sharp angles. The guesthouse, once an office for Belle's husband, Mick, was now Piper's home. House-sitting while the Vogt's were in Hong Kong gave her a three-month time cushion to get her life together.

Belle brushed her palms together and looked around the studio apartment. "There, I've done all I can do. The rest is up to you."

"Belle, I can't thank you enough."

"Nonsense. You're doing us a favor," Belle said. "We'll see you at eight for dinner. Don't bother to knock. The side door will be open."

An unexpected wave of dizziness hit Piper. Belle, standing beside her, froze. Just then the floor beneath them came alive, vibrating. She knew instantly what was happening. Any resident of California would know. The metal handles on the built-in cabinets rattled, jingling like a wall of tiny bells. She grasped Belle's hand in a death grip and stood perfectly still, afraid any movement might make it worse. There was nothing she could do to stop it. Then, as suddenly as it started, it stopped. The floor became solid again. The metal handles settled against the wood.

"There, there, Piper, nothing to fear. A teaser." Belle disengaged her hand from Piper's and rubbed her fingers. She patted Piper's hand. "Sneaky buggers, those."

At a quarter past eight, Piper walked across the concrete driveway to join the Vogts and their guests for a small informal dinner party. A late-model car with tinted windows cruised up the street and slowed as it passed the Vogt's driveway. There were already two cars parked in the driveway and no room for a third. The car accelerated and continued up the hill.

Mick Vogt greeted her at the side door with a big hug, as though she'd come across town instead of across the driveway. Mick was a film producer. Four Academy Award nominations and an Oscar for his last picture had thrust him onto the fast track in the industry. Belle, ten years his senior, the most together person she knew, maintained their relationship like a mechanic maintains a high performance racecar. They were the perfect couple. Piper envied them their solid, twenty-year marriage, made more enviable by the fact that her own second marriage was down the toilet.

"One of your guests looks lost, or they're searching for a parking space," Piper said.

"No guests of ours. Everyone is here."

Belle was telling the story of James Dean and the lovesick jumper when they entered the living room. Rumor had it that in the fifties the Vogt's English Tudor belonged to a wealthy studio executive whose starlet wife, so distraught by the death of James Dean, dove from a letter on the Hollywood Sign, following Peg Entwistle's lead some twenty years earlier. The rumor, though never substantiated, was a lively conversation starter at all the Vogt's parties.

Belle stopped in midsentence. "Here's our dear friend, Piper."

A man Piper's age sat on an overstuffed chair. The unattached male. A flash of eagerness sparked when their eyes met. The floating male was Eric Billing. When he shook her hand, he held on with both hands until Piper pulled it away. Piper silently groaned. She suspected Belle of attempting to match-make, something she wasn't buying into. Not that she didn't like men, she did. She hoped to resume a social life someday, but not just yet.

Belle introduced her to Jane Hill and her young lover, Melody, no last name, just Melody. Jane was one of those women who went out of her way to look unattractive, relying on money and professional status to get her young, starlet partners. Her gray, frizzy hair, streaked with yellow, was pulled into a sloppy chignon at the nape of her neck. Her deep red lipstick bled into the creases in her upper lip. White pet hairs stuck to her designer pantsuit.

The first chance she got, she followed Belle into the kitchen. From the large cage in the alcove of the bay window, she heard a deep, rakish chuckle. Dr. Jekyll lifted his claw, bobbed his head, and said, "Nice rack, babe."

Piper looked down at the low neckline of her blouse and laughed. "You made me look, you dirty bird."

"Pretty boy," he said.

"No, not a pretty boy. A dirty bird."

He chuckled.

Belle laughed and handed her a tray of lobster-stuffed mushroom caps. "He's just expressing the obvious. You look gorgeous. When I think of all those wasted years with that bloody scoundrel, I want to cry. You deserve so much better than him."

For years, Piper assumed the Vogt's had been the ones to distance themselves from her and Gordon. When Piper ran into Belle at an art gallery in Brentwood and told her that she was leaving her husband of five years, Belle had whooped and immediately offered Piper the guesthouse. She also put her in touch with an attorney friend.

"I know you mean well," Piper said, "but I'm not looking for a love connection. At least not until the bloody scoundrel is out of my life. I meet with the lawyer on Monday."

"Oh lighten up. I was simply trying for more balance, boys to girls. Four women to one man is a bit much, even for Mick. Anyway, Eric's not your type."

She wondered what her type was. Her first husband had exchanged his jockey shorts for lace panties, and her second husband his sheep clothing for a wolf hide. The two couldn't have been more unalike in every aspect. "Do I have a type?"

"Yes, you just haven't found him yet."

At the dinner table, the topic of the trembler earlier that afternoon opened the dinner conversation.

"I'm so used to the ground shaking, I merely assume I'm falling in love again," said Jane, the producer of women's documentaries. She slipped a hand under the glass tabletop to squeeze the bare thigh of her female companion.

"Is it earthquake season already?" Mick's crack got the expected laughs.

Eric Billing, a director of slasher movies, asked what Piper did. She answered quickly, eager to move the topic away from earthquakes.

"Film editing. Freelance, mostly."

"What projects have you worked on?"

His Nordic good looks reminded her of Gordon and left her cold until she noticed the tiny gap between his two front teeth. A flaw she found charming in this age of perfectly spaced, dazzling white teeth.

"Well, not much…lately. I've been out of the loop for awhile." These people had been discussing current and critically acclaimed projects. Her last noteworthy endeavor had been five years ago—a lifetime in this business.

"Like most film editors, Piper is being modest." Mick brushed at a black eyebrow. "Having to work in the shadow of egotistical producers, such as myself, they don't expect much recognition. Before her husband locked her away in the ivory tower, she was, and is, quite a gifted editor. She cut Cromnon's *The Last Clock*, and my *Devil's Due*. She can spot a dead frame—trimming time is her gift. In fact, Piper will start cutting my documentary as soon as we leave for Hong Kong."

"Going for another Oscar, Mick? Is this one at least full-length and not a short?" Eric asked.

"An Oscar's an Oscar."

"Hong Kong," Jane said, "So you'll finally be making *Jaded Paradise*. I thought you'd take that script to your grave."

"It's a go after ten years in development. That's one I'd love for Piper to cut, but Zimmerman is directing and has his own people, and you know Zimmerman."

"Mick, I'm honored that you asked me to cut your documentary," Piper said. "And knowing how much *Jaded Paradise* means to you, I'm beyond flattered that you'd even consider me on such a great project. Thank you."

Throughout dinner, the conversation remained on film, projects, and then actors. During dessert, Belle poised her spoon in the air and asked her guests, "Guess what famous star of the silver screen was spotted swimming in her pool in the buff today?"

"Not your neighbor—Silvia … Sybil—Sybil Whatsherface?" Melody asked.

"How soon they forget. She's only one of the top actresses of her time. Sybil Squire."

"I thought she was dead," Melody said. "She was old in *The Book of Love.*"

"Ancient at forty." Jane rolled her eyes then touched Melody on the tip of her nose. "Ah, my dear, you are adorable."

"Lady Squire is eighty-five and very much alive," Belle said. "Be careful what you say about her. Piper is a devoted fan."

"Is that so?" Eric's eyebrows lifted. "I don't remember much about her except she had some pretty hard knocks. What, six husbands all died tragically, plus her kids. Right? That's messed up. I heard she chugged Drano or battery acid after her baby boy drowned."

"A rumor," Jane said.

"She was institutionalized then," Eric added. "Shock treatments. Lobotomy. Lobotomies were the deal back then."

Piper moaned.

"No, sweet boy, you're confusing her with her daughter," Jane said.

"Maybe both," Melody said. "Like mother like daughter."

"Farmer," Mick slipped in. "Frances Farmer had the lobotomy."

Dr. J whistled, barked and then whistled again.

"Didn't they call her the Black Widow or the Night Widow?" Melody said.

"Platinum Widow. The white hair, y'know."

Piper gripped her coffee cup tightly in both hands. Rumors. They were only repeating what they'd read in the biographies and gossip columns written by writers famous for twisting and embellishing the truth. Jane was the only one not spewing gossip.

She looked at Jane and asked, "Did you know her?"

Jane nodded. "We were close once. Not intimate close. Just friends."

"Are you related to Edward Hill?" Edward Hill was the studio head for *Transworld Artists*, the studio that made Sybil famous.

"He was my father."

"Then you know all about her." Piper leaned forward and almost knocked over her water glass.

"We don't...communicate with each other. Haven't for many years. She cut me off when she cut herself off from the rest of the world. We'd become close when her daughter went abroad to school."

After dinner, Piper excused herself. She declined Eric's offer to walk her to her door and his request to call her. It had been a day of extremes, escaping Gordon, moving into her new safe haven, and not only hearing about her screen idol, but also seeing her.

Piper waited until the Vogt's guests had left before stepping out onto the deck. She couldn't sleep. The subtle breeze blew across her skin. Exhaustion more than gravity pulled her down into the mesh chair. She drew long and slow on the second of the two cigarettes she allowed herself each day. The city lights blinked below, though her attention was elsewhere. Through the gray-blue smoke, she stared at the house next door. The mausoleum-like structure looked formidable in the shadows of olive and pepper trees, no sounds of music or TV or singing canaries. A single light burned in an upstairs window.

Piper admired the woman's ability to remain sane in a prison of grief. The same trait she admired in her grandmother. Both women had suffered. Sybil's grief spanned many years. Nana's grief came all at once when she lost her husband and two of her three children in a house fire in Orange County.

Piper lifted the faded photograph and gazed at it. A child and two women sat on the side of a swimming pool, skirt hems hiked up above their knees, their bare feet dangling in the water. Piper turned it over. In ink on the back, it read: *Maggy, me and Sybil June '67.* Her mother Maggy, Nana Ruth, and Sybil Squire.

A pair of bats dove at the moths circling a porch lantern at the rear of the mansion. For nearly half a century, the actress's life remained a mystery. Piper wondered what she was doing at this very moment behind those arched windows and ochre-colored stucco walls.

A car with tinted windows eased to a stop across the street from the Vogt house, redirecting Piper's attention. She hadn't seen the headlights approach. From the dark shadows of her deck, she watched, waiting for someone to exit the car. A moment later, it pulled away. The dark sedan looked similar to the one Piper had spotted earlier that evening.

The next day, Piper drove to a Hollywood branch of the Bank of America. Although she did her banking online, she wanted to switch her account to the closest branch to her new home. When she told Gordon she wanted a divorce, he'd wasted no time clearing out the joint bank account and canceling the credit cards. So typical of him. Yet she was prepared, thanks to Lee, who advised her to open a separate bank account and sign up for her own credit card. "He'll screw you royally if given a chance," Lee had said. Lee was right. Without the funds in Piper's own account, she'd be financially strapped. Lee had a gift for judging people.

While waiting in line for a teller, Piper glanced around. A distinguished elderly woman stood at the teller window to her right. There was something familiar about her. The way she held herself. The shiny platinum hair.

The teller asked, "Will you need someone to escort you to the safe-deposit box this afternoon, Mrs. Squire?"

"No thank you, Teresa, not today."

The woman turned toward Piper. Her mature face, smooth around the tiny creases, was made up with care. She was still lovely. Their eyes met. Glistening blue eyes that had riveted thousands of moviegoers over many years now held Piper's. Sybil Squire's platinum hair had been her trademark feature, but to Piper it was her stunning pale blue eyes that she found so extraordinary. Yet now there was something else, a sad—haunted look. The same look she saw countless times in her grandmother's eyes. She sucked in a sharp breath, startled by the intensity of her feelings.

Sybil Squire was halfway across the bank, her dated yet classic Italian leather pumps soundless on the marble floor, when Piper snapped out of her trance. A security guard in the foyer held open the door for her, his face passive, blank. Did he have any idea who she was? Or that she had been *somebody* at one time? Mrs. Squire nodded at him as she passed through the door. She stopped at the curb and looked up and down the street.

Moments later, Piper pushed through the glass door without waiting for the guard to open it. "Mrs. Squire?" she said with a sense of breathlessness.

She turned. "Yes?"

"I saw you inside the bank and...well, I wanted to introduce myself. I'm Piper Lundberg, a neighbor of yours. I recently moved into the Vogt's guesthouse."

"The Vogts?"

"Theirs is the house above yours on Wilson Drive."

"Oh, yes. How do you do, Mrs. Lundberg." She extended a gloved hand. Her smile merely polite, her handshake a brief encounter. She glanced down the street. A light breeze lifted the collar of her blouse.

"I've been a fan of yours for years and years. When I saw you inside, I...well, I just wanted to tell you that." Piper could have said, 'You knew my Grandmother Ruth, you helped her and my mother through a terrible time in their life.' Yet she didn't. Bringing up past tragedies to a woman weighed down with them seemed wrong. Start fresh, she told herself.

"Thank you. You're very kind."

"I'm in the business, too. A film editor."

"I'm not in the business anymore."

"Maybe not, but you're an icon in today's film culture."

She allowed herself a soft chuckle. "I hardly think so."

"Oh, yes. In fact, my next project will be to cut Mick Vogt's documentary on film noir, the classics. One of your films is among the ten greatest."

Piper thought she would ask her which film, but her only reaction was to raise a perfectly arched eyebrow. A shiny black vintage Lincoln pulled up to the curb in front of Sybil. The driver, a redheaded woman, leaned over and opened the front passenger door. Mrs. Squire extended her hand again. "It was a pleasure to meet you, Mrs. Lundberg. Good luck with your project."

The bank guard stepped out onto the sidewalk, his gaze riveted to the retreating car, admiration burning in his eyes.

"Do you know who that is?" Piper asked him.

He shook his head. "Uh uh, know the car though. Sixty-four Continental with suicide doors. Mint condition. Quite the car. Yessiree, quite the car."

CHAPTER 2

Sybil Squire was born Dolores Annamaria Teresa Robles on June 10th 1926 in Baja, California, in a small village on the Mexican peninsula. Her father, Victor Robles, a fisherman with his own trawler, married her mother when the fifteen-year-old became heavy with child. Victor hoped for a son and was disappointed with a daughter. To make matters worse, when Dolores' hair grew in as white as the sails on the boats in the harbor (villagers referred to the child as "angel hair"), and her eyes lightened to a pale blue, Victor's disappointment shifted to distrust, then anger. A desperate Annamaria dyed the infant's wispy white hair brown; burning her tender scalp in the process...it did no good. Victor sent his wife and her daughter packing.

—*Excerpt from the biography of* Sybil Squire: The Platinum Widow *by Russell Cassevantes.*

TODAY WAS PIPER'S THIRTY-sixth birthday. By Hollywood standards, passing thirty-five was like falling off a cliff. According to Melody's standards, she was closing in on ancient. Piper could care less about Hollywood standards. Tonight she would celebrate with Lee, if the super agent to the stars could squeeze her into her outrageous schedule. What she'd missed most was not hearing from Nana this year. What family she had had died with her grandmother. There had never been a father figure in her life. Her mother, Maggy, pregnant as a teen and unmarried, relinquished the role of nurturer to Nana. Maggy was happy to assume the role of older sister.

Since moving into the guesthouse, she filled her days with editing workshops, reacquainting herself with the updated systems and learning the new software. Mick'd had the editing bay set up in the dining area of the guesthouse the day she moved in.

Standing at the deck railing, taking in her new surroundings, she thought again how much she loved the neighborhood in this section of the hills. The compelling view had a certain nostalgic charm, the mature landscaping that wove up, down and around the maze of twisted streets of 40s bungalows mixed in with renovated mid-century modern and Mediterranean villa-style estates. It was no longer the wealthiest neighborhood. Those were further west. This was old Hollywood, established and eclectic, saturated with culture and a hundred-year history of filmmaking. Not far away was the Hollywood strip, Schwab's (now a shopping complex and movie theater), the original Spago's, the Sunset Towers and Chateau Marmont. This community inspired her like no other. She felt alive, eager to rejoin this surreal world of make-believe.

Piper leaned on the railing and faced the two-story Squire mansion. The earthy hue of the red tile roof and ochre exterior appeared richer in the morning light. A pair of doves nested in an arc in the roof tiles. Living in that house was an icon of the old Hollywood, Sybil Squire. An icon who would unfortunately be remembered for her real life role as a tragic leading lady and not her many outstanding and versatile performances.

Since that day at the bank a week ago, there had been no further contact between them. Piper had made the first move. It was up to Sybil now. Although Sybil was considered a loner, she wasn't one to remain cloistered away, hidden behind window shades and heavy drapes. The drapes were opened every morning, left open throughout the day and sometimes late into the night. The afternoon breeze drifting through the hills carried the sweet songs of the canaries to Piper as she sat on the deck. At dusk, the birds fell silent. Of course, she didn't make it a practice to spy on Sybil, yet she couldn't help but notice when she swam in the pool, or rode off in the passenger seat of the Continental, or strolled around the grounds. Her redheaded housekeeper usually arrived at ten o'clock in an old Volkswagen bug. Piper heard her car long before it turned into the driveway, chugging to a stop at the back. They were close, the housekeeper and Mrs. Squire, apparent by the quality time they spent together. With the passing days a pattern emerged. Every afternoon at three o'clock, they played a card game in the shade of the back patio. At six, they both sat down to the meal the housekeeper had prepared, eating in the formal dining room, sharing a bottle of wine. From what she had observed, Sybil led a quiet, unassuming existence. Her life seemed tranquil-- at least during the daylight hours. If there were demons snapping at her heels, they came out at night when she was alone, at a time when demons do their best work.

Sybil appeared in the garden wearing a wide-brimmed straw hat, a long skirt and a short-sleeved tunic in pale blue. Piper felt a tingle at the back of her neck, as though she had somehow conjured her presence with thoughts of her. After leaning down to take in the fragrance of several red roses, Sybil pulled a weed from the base of the rose bush, pulled another, then tossed the weeds aside and moved away. She strolled to a padded wrought-iron bench, sat, opened a brown book, and began to write in it.

A journal or a memoir. It was an intimate moment, someone writing down their innermost thoughts. Piper stood up to leave, to allow Sybil her privacy. Just then the phone inside rang. Sybil looked up, searching for the source of the ringing. Their eyes met. Piper raised a hand in greeting, then looked away and retreated into the guesthouse.

Lee's office phone number lit up her Caller ID.

"There's been a change in plans," Lee said as soon as she answered. "Things at the office got screwed up. Incompetent idiots. Can you meet me here?"

"Sure."

"See you at seven. Happy birthday, Piper."

Not more than five minutes after talking to Lee, there was a knock at the door. Assuming it was Belle, she called out, "Come in." When the door didn't open, she looked up from her computer screen. Sybil Squire's housekeeper stood to one side of the glass door.

Piper crossed the room and opened the door. "Yes?"

"You Mrs. Lundberg?" the woman asked. She was a thin, wiry woman with teased, orangish-red hair, a shopworn face, and tight, flashy clothes too young for her sixty-plus years.

Piper nodded.

She handed her a folded piece of paper and grinned. "A note. Don't this seem Victorian and all? But she didn't know your phone number."

Piper unfolded the paper. Written on a sheet of notepaper printed with: *From the Desk of Sybil Squire,* she read:

Please join me for coffee, if convenient. S.

Piper looked up, trying to appear casual, and feeling anything but. "Now?"

"What?" the housekeeper said, leaning toward her. Piper saw she wore a hearing aid.

"Now? Does she mean now?"

"Only if it's convenient," the housekeeper said, pointing at the note.

"Yes. Yes, it is. Convenient," she said. She glanced down at her bare feet. "Could you give me a minute?"

The woman shrugged. "I guess you know where she lives." She started down the steps "She'll be by the pool. Use the driveway entrance."

"I'll be right there. Tell her I'll be right there."

Outside on the street, Piper caught a glimpse of the car with tinted windows cruising up the hill. That was the third time she'd seen it in the neighborhood. There was something ominous about a dark car with tinted windows. She hadn't heard a word from Gordon since she'd packed up and moved out. His words—*You'll regret this*—echoed in her head.

She shook her head. Sybil Squire had issued an invitation to tea--well, coffee actually, but close enough--and on her birthday. Nothing was going to spoil this day. She ran fingers through her hair, looking around the room for her sandals.

"Yes," she said laughing. "Yes. Yes."

Sybil was seated at a wrought-iron patio table when Piper let herself in through the gate along the south side of the property. A hummingbird hovered at the honeysuckle vines covering the fence. The red-tailed hawk was back, circling. Two cups and saucers and an old-fashioned carafe sat on the table. When she approached, Sybil motioned for her to sit. She sat with her back to the pool house, the morning sun bright in her face. To her right she heard the canaries singing, to her left the soft swish of a pool sweep.

"Thank you for inviting me."

"You're welcome. Sugar? Cream?"

"No thank you. Black is fine." She took cream, but there was none on the table.

While Sybil poured, Piper took in her surroundings. The yard was well kept. A lawn service came once a week. She supposed Sybil herself tended the rose garden. The rest of the foliage consisted of hardy ivy, ground cover, and silvery Russian Olive hedges.

Piper looked back at Sybil. She was watching her. She smiled.

Piper returned her smile. "I know you must hear this all the time, but I think you're even more stunning in person,"

"Thank you. You're wondering if the hair is natural or from a bottle."

"Oh, no, I know it's natural. Although it's extraordinary."

"It's been both a curse and a boon. My father cast me off because of it. I can't say I blame him. My parents were of Hispanic descent. Both dark. So what happened?"

"A flaw in the gene pool?"

She shrugged. "Maybe."

"But he came back into your life later."

"Oh yes. Whatever prejudices he harbored suddenly vanished when the ugly duckling became the white swan—or should I say, the golden goose?"

"He helped with your career," Piper added, wanting to hear more, to know all there was to know about this woman.

"Yes. Do I sound ungrateful or bitter?"

Piper shrugged. "You have reason to."

"You've been reading. Those biographers love conflict. What's that saying? Without conflict, there is no story. My life is one huge conflict."

"I don't believe everything I read in them, especially the unauthorized ones," Piper said.

"Russell's book is close enough, but that other one, the woman writer, a pack of lies. I think she was on LSD when she gathered her information. She had me confused with at least two other actresses. Now that columnist, Cricket Summers, she was just plain evil. In the end, she got what she deserved with that libel suit. But enough about me."

When Sybil pushed the coffee cup and saucer across the tabletop, Piper noticed a beautiful diamond ring on her left hand. Emerald cut stones set in platinum, two carats each.

"Your Mr. Vogt is an accomplished producer. The way he's going, he'll soon be too good for this neighborhood."

Piper dragged her gaze away from the ring to her face. "You're familiar with his work?"

She nodded. "I looked into it. *Upper Limits.* Are you the Piper listed in the credits?"

"Yes. They used my maiden name."

"Excellent film in every respect. Good editing. You managed to project or help the audience experience an essential subconscious emotion. You should be very proud."

Piper couldn't believe it. Sybil Squire had taken the time to look up something she'd had a hand in. She was complimenting her. "I am. Thank you."

"If it's not prying, may I ask why you're working on documentaries rather than feature film? Being affiliated with

23

an Oscar nominated project should have opened a door or two for you. Yes?"

"No. I mean, no it's not prying. Not at all. And yes, after that one, I worked on *Devil's Due* and *The Last Clock.*"

"Impressive. And?"

"I, well, I took a hiatus."

"Oh?"

"I got married."

"And moved away?"

"No, we lived in Santa Monica."

"Ahhh," she said. "I see." Yet it didn't look as if she saw at all. Her eyes flickered upward, toward the guesthouse.

Piper looked down. "We're separated."

"Was he abusive?"

"No, not really. He lied to me."

"Another woman?"

Piper nodded. "But that's not why I left him. He told me he wanted kids as much as I did. He said if I quit my job, we could start a family right away. What he didn't tell me was that after we were married, during a business trip to Geneva, he had a vasectomy. He didn't intend to have a family. Ever."

"How did you find out?"

"He was sleeping on and off with his receptionist. She told me. She was with him in Geneva."

Sybil's eyes held hers. Piper saw compassion there. Sympathy. She felt a strong tugging deep inside. Whatever she had felt for this woman in the past, the sense of closeness, the admiration, intensified in those few seconds of looking into her expressive, soulful eyes.

"You did the right thing. Family is everything. Love cannot thrive on deception and lies." Sybil took Piper's hand in both her hands and squeezed. "If I had been more like you, my life might have been entirely different."

Piper was about to ask her what she meant by that when Sybil's face softened and she said, "Are you related to Ruth Parrish?"

"She was my grandmother."

"There's a strong resemblance. And of course, your maiden name on the film credits. I was sorry to read about her passing early this year. She had a beautiful soul."

"She thought the world of you. You were there for her when she had no one to turn to. She never forgot that."

"She would've done the same for me. Ruth and I had a lot in common, much of it bad, but some good. We bonded right away. She mailed me a picture of you when you were just a toddler. The proud grandmother. I didn't respond. I have no excuse. Self-absorbed, I suppose. I regret that." She looked away. "How is your mother? I remember she loved the pool. Swam like a fish."

"She died in ninety-four. In the Northridge earthquake."

"I'm sorry. More heartache for Ruth. Well, at least your grandmother had you."

It was Piper's turn to change the subject. "I can hear your canaries singing when the wind's just right. It's nice. How many are there?"

Sybil brightened and said, "Five right now. All males. Only the males sing, you know. They seem to compete with each other. Mario is the leader, the others follow."

"Mrs. Vogt has a cockatoo. He tries to imitate your canaries' songs."

She laughed, a delightful laugh that made Piper smile.

"He also screeches. There were times, before I realized it was only a bird, when I wondered if someone in the neighborhood was being attacked," Sybil said. "I took up the care of canaries about fifteen years ago. They give me so much pleasure. Would you like to see them?"

"Yes, very much."

"How about a tour of the house? I know you must be curious."

"I'd love it." They started to rise. Piper had pushed back her chair, but before she could stand, the housekeeper, who had quietly come up on them, interrupted them.

"Sybil, there's someone at the front door asking to see you." The housekeeper turned to look down the driveway. A late-model car sat in the drive, partially obscured by the corner of the house and the bushes lining the wall.

The expression on Sybil Squire's face was one of bafflement. In fact, both women had the same expression. There seemed to be some unspoken communication between them because Sybil didn't ask any further questions. When she rose, Piper rose too.

"Dear, this shouldn't take long. Help yourself to more coffee. Then we'll tour the house."

Together the two women crossed the patio and entered the house through the sunroom door. Piper caught a few whispered words spoken by the housekeeper that sounded like: ". . . your estate...papers looked real enough."

Instead of sitting down, Piper strolled to the edge of the swimming pool. The water looked clean, yet she'd never noticed a pool service at the house. Probably the housekeeper's chore.

She glanced down the driveway at the parked car. The sun reflected off the windshield. The first visitor she'd seen since moving in next door. She squatted on her heels, ran her fingers through the water. It was cold. Bone-chilling cold. How could Sybil stand to swim in such frigid water? She returned to the patio table and sat. Minutes passed. She refilled her cup and drank the bitter brew, now lukewarm. It was strange to see Sybil's perspective of the neighborhood.

Her downward view of the hills was the same as Piper's. Yet her upward view was partially blocked by the Vogt's guesthouse and peaked roof of the two-story Tudor. She pretended to be Sybil, sitting in her yard looking up at the guesthouse to the deck where she, the new neighbor, sat in the morning and evening. Had Sybil observed her as she had observed Sybil?

The hair along Piper's arms rose, the skin tingled. Suddenly she had the feeling she was being watched. She turned her gaze from the guesthouse to the Squire mansion. The house sat quiet. No figures were present in any of the windows within her view. The dove that had been cooing all morning was silent. Everything around her seemed still. She rubbed at her arms. The skin at the back of her head tightened. Twisting around, she stared down the driveway at the car parked there. The windshield, bright with sunlight, obscured the interior. A hand reached out of the passenger window and curled around the upper door where it met the car's roof. Someone was in the car, watching her.

She stood and moved back until she was out of sight. She glanced at her watch. How long had Sybil been gone? It seemed ages. She considered leaving, but the thought of walking past the parked car with its silent observer creeped her out.

Hearing footsteps on the walk at the front of the house, she moved back to the table and caught a glimpse of a short Asian man coming around the car to the driver's side. He opened the door and climbed inside. In the split second before his head cleared the opening and the door slammed shut, he looked at her. Then the car started, backed out, and drove away.

It was another five minutes before Sybil returned, apologizing for taking so long. She lowered herself into the chair, her face devoid of expression. The blank, bewildered look of shock. As she sipped the cold coffee, her fingers trembled, splashing coffee into the saucer.

"Is something wrong?" Piper asked.

Sybil looked at her. "What?" Then she lowered her cup and dropped her hands to her lap. "No. Nothing. Some news. Unexpected news. I'm sorry." She reached out. "Where were we? You were saying you've taken a hiatus—no, you've just returned from a hiatus." She rubbed her forehead, squeezed her eyes shut.

The housekeeper stepped out of the backdoor, twisting a dishtowel.

Piper stood up. "Mrs. Squire, I think I should go. Another time, maybe?"

"Another time? Yes. Another time." She came to her feet, swaying.

The housekeeper hurried to her side.

"You can go that way." The housekeeper pointed to the corner at the back of the lot. "It's shorter."

Piper went behind the pool house to the corner of the stone wall where she slipped through a gap between the two walls, coming out at the Vogt's garage/guesthouse. She looked back at the Squire mansion. Another time, she told herself.

CHAPTER 3

A penniless Annamaria, discarded by her husband, took her child across the border into the U.S., where she found work as a housekeeper in the Dodson's San Diego home. The child was a constant reminder of Annamaria's rejection and forced exile.

"I can't tell you how appalled I was by that poor baby's appearance," said June Dodson. "We paid Annamaria a good salary, but the child looked like a street waif—starved, scrapes and bruises, nose running like a leaky faucet. What made her different from those pathetic urchins running around on the streets in Tijuana was her hair--like spun angel hair. And those blue eyes—haunting. We always sent food home for her."

—Excerpt from the biography of Sybil Squire: The Platinum Widow *By Russell Cassevantes.*

CAROL DAVIS LUCE

PIPER ARRIVED TEN MINUTES late. Lee Sikes crossed the expansive, pristine lobby of IAM, International Artists Management, with long, smooth strides. The soft material of her skirt billowed around her shapely legs as her incredibly high heels clicked on the polished floor, like the buildup of a drum roll. A row of suits seated on the leather sofa in the waiting area watched her advance. Even a nod from Lee Sikes would make them feel a rung higher on the LA entertainment food chain.

Lee came up to the reception desk, her arms open. "Happy *Your* Day, Piper. Late as usual." She hugged Piper and kissed her on the cheek. "I have time for a quicky celebration tonight and then I've got a screening I just can't get out of. Tomorrow I'm treating both of us to the works at Isadora's. I look like something the cat hacked up."

"Yeah, right. A chip in your nail polish? Or did an end split?"

Lee winked. Her almond-shaped hazel eyes were her most arresting feature. Lee had started out as Piper's high school sweetheart, Leroy Sikes, and they married while in college. With Leroy, she could talk, laugh, and cry. They had so much in common. High on the list of things in common was makeup, lingerie, and dress shoes.

Lee divorced Piper after realizing he was more than a closet cross-dresser. Brokenhearted, Piper thought he had found someone else. He had, but that *someone* was hiding inside his own body. He couldn't live the lie any longer. Piper knew nothing about his gender dysphoria or his desire to be a complete woman until months after their divorce. Once she learned of his plans, she offered her wholehearted support. Now, ten years later, Lee had made the full transition. No easy feat, and by no means the perfect Cinderella story. But lately the good days outweighed the bad.

30

"You look great, Piper. Leaving that self-serving, pompous turd was the best thing you've done since you got rid of me," Lee said, loud enough to turn heads in the lobby. In a softer voice, she added, "If you wanted a childless marriage, you could have stayed with me. At least I didn't lie to you. Damn, if I were a man, I'd knock the crap out of him. If I'd known about that macho shit he pulled on you when we were getting your stuff, I'd've planted a knee in the ol' family jewels. Seriously."

Piper laughed. That was why she hadn't mentioned it to Lee. The last thing she wanted to see was her ex-husband rolling in the dirt with her soon-to-be ex-husband.

"Can you leave now?" Piper was eager to take their conversation somewhere less public.

"I'm all yours—for an hour, anyway." Lee took Piper's arm and led her across the lobby to the main doors. "What's the birthday girl feel like eating?"

"Asian?"

"I know just the place."

Six blocks down on Wilshire at The Dragon, Lee ordered champagne as soon as they were seated. The food came out quickly. Piper ate. Lee nibbled.

Piper captured a shrimp with her chopsticks. "Mick and Belle surprised me with a DVD of Sybil Squire's last movie, *Judgment Day*, the last film of her career."

"He had to pull some stings to get an unreleased copy. I'm impressed." Lee poured champagne into their glasses. "Have you talked to Sybil since the bank encounter?"

"She invited me to coffee this morning."

"Cool. Did you tell her you're Nana's granddaughter?"

"She already knew. She was very nice, Lee. I think we're going to be good friends."

Lee stood, pulled a video camera from her bag and backed up to shoot Piper and the birthday cake that a throng of waiters was carrying to their table with candles blazing. "Happy Birthday, Piper!"

After the dishes had been cleared away, Lee paid the check and handed Piper a fortune cookie. "What's it say, Piper?"

Piper broke it in half, pulled out the strip of paper and read it to herself. *Beware of false icons.*

"Read it aloud," Lee said, posed behind the video camera directed at her.

"It says 'you will prosper and be happy.'" She crumbled the fortune and slipped it into the pocket of her blouse.

Piper turned off the brightly lit Sunset Boulevard and headed upward into the Hollywood hills. She was eager to get home and watch Sybil's last film.

The farther up the hill she went the more people she noticed on foot, going upward. Some milled around, alone or in small groups along the edge of the street and in the densely landscaped yards of the stately homes. Another block up she saw colored lights strobing over manicured hedges and shrubs with an eerie red-and-blue glow glistening on the shiny pavement. Why was the pavement wet? There wasn't a cloud in the sky. Reflections from the whirling dome lights jumped across houses and cars. Police cars sat at odd angles, blocking the road. Creeping forward, wondering what had happened to bring the local news people and emergency vehicles into these hills, she was stopped when she attempted to enter her street. Static bursts of conversation crackled from their radios.

A uniformed cop leaned down and asked, "What's your business, miss?"

"I live up the street."

"You'll have to park beyond these barriers and walk up."

"What's happened?" she asked.

"A house fire at the corner."

The Vogts lived on the corner.

She quickly locked the Honda and hurried up the hill. A fire engine loomed big in front of the Vogt's driveway. Was it their beautiful Tudor house or the guesthouse? Had she left a candle burning or something cooking on the stove? An image of Nana Ruth's house burning to the ground, taking all but one member of her family, sent a chill through her. She began to run. As she got closer, she saw a second fire truck parked around the corner on the street where Sybil Squire lived. Her instant relief quickly turned sour. The fire was not at the Vogts but at the Squire mansion.

Dirty water ran down the gutters and along the cracks in the asphalt under her feet, soaking into her shoes. The acrid smell of smoke hung in the air. A front window of the Mediterranean house was shattered, a partially charred wingback chair lay on its side several feet into the yard. Heavy drapes, what was left of them, lay in a sodden heap beside the chair. A green garden hose snaked over the windowsill and disappeared inside. No sign of fire or smoke. The fire had been extinguished.

An ambulance stood in the driveway, its back doors open. Milling police officers and firefighters blocked her view of the interior. She was certain Sybil was inside that ambulance. It was nine o'clock. Sybil would have been alone in the house. How badly was she injured? Was she dead?

The streetlight at the corner flickered, growing brighter as the night descended. Neighbors stood in knots, talking and gesturing. Firemen were busy rolling up the hoses and checking inside and out for any hot spots. Policemen took reports.

Belle called out to her from a small cluster standing in the middle of the street. Piper joined them.

"What happened?" Piper asked. "Is Sybil okay?"

"We're not sure. Dr. Oates, the man over there talking to the fire marshal, saw smoke and came to the rescue. He found Sybil unconscious on the living room floor. That's where the fire started, I'm told. The doctor carried her out of the house and kept the flames under control with the garden hose. They're working on her now."

The group around the ambulance moved away. Inside, two paramedics hovered over her, administering oxygen and an IV. Her hand lifted, a weak gesture, and dropped onto her chest. She was alive at least. Then the back doors closed. The ambulance started up and pulled out of the driveway. The group drifted to the other side of the street, moving out of its way. The dome lights flicked on and the siren followed. Then the ambulance screamed down the road and disappeared into the night.

Piper felt sick to her stomach. Tragedy still had a firm grip on Sybil Squire.

CHAPTER 4

When a San Clemente High School drama teacher took in the abused and neglected Dolores Robles, the teenager's life changed drastically. Abigail Lightfoot saw something more than extraordinary beauty in the white-haired sophomore. She saw sheer magnetism fueled by raw talent. "My mother sold me to Miss Lightfoot," Dolores Robles told an interviewer early in her career. "She hocked me for a hundred dollars, a broken down automobile, and a smelly fox stole."

Annamaria would try unsuccessfully to reclaim her daughter through the court a year later when Dolores, now Sybil Squire, had begun to make her mark in show business.

—Excerpt from the biography of Sybil Squire: The Platinum Widow *by Russell Cassevantes.*

ON THE MORNING AFTER the fire, Piper stood on her deck in her robe, sipping coffee. She watched a stream of vehicles next door come and go, a glazier truck, a janitorial van, the housekeeper's chartreuse VW bug, and wondered how Sybil was doing. Were her injuries serious? At her age, complications could prove fatal. Piper had no idea which hospital she had been taken to in a city with dozens of private clinics and several general hospitals. The housekeeper, she was sure, was the person to ask. Although she hurried with her shower, by the time she had dressed the green VW was gone.

At midmorning, she waited on the deck for Lee, who had their entire day planned. The first stop was Isadora's, her favorite salon in Century City. Since leaving Gordon, weekly professional salon care seemed extravagant and time consuming to Piper. As the wife of a successful attorney, she was expected to be well groomed, to look the part. Doing it for Gordon had made it a chore. Today, doing it for herself seemed different, special even. She looked forward to the massage and sauna. The tension in the past week had her muscles knotted and achy.

Activity next door had stopped and all was quiet once again. Everyone gone, or so she thought until minutes later when she spotted someone in a second floor room.

She hurried down the staircase and had just passed the Vogt's side door when Belle came out. "Piper, where're you off to in such a rush?"

"There's someone still inside the house," she said, slowing. "Someone that might know which hospital Sybil was taken to."

"Hold up, I'll walk with you."

A huge orange tomcat slipped out the bushes and joined them.

36

"Shoo, go away," Belle said, pushing the cat away with a slippered foot.

"He looks hungry."

"He's the neighborhood scrounger, a stray, going from house to house. Don't feed him. If you do, he'll hang around. He makes Doc crazy. Shoo, you cheeky littl' bugger." She duck-walked with the cat between her furry feet, herding him down the driveway.

Piper heard Dr. J squawking inside the kitchen.

"This neighborhood's filthy with cats. So many of them wild," Belle said. "They live off the rodents in the brush and the unsuspecting birds that use the bird feeders. Half the neighborhood has a cat. The other half has a bird feeder."

The cats preyed on the birds and rodents, the hawk in turn preyed on the cats. The coyotes preyed on them all. "Circle of life," Piper said.

"Not if I can help it."

At the mailbox, Belle collected the daily Variety then together they rounded the stone wall and walked up the path to the Squire house.

"I don't see any vehicles," Belle said.

"Well, somebody's there."

A sheet of bright new glass sparkled in the window frame. The janitorial service had cleaned up most of the yard, hauling away the burned chair and drapes. Smoke residue on the ochre stucco around the window, a thin layer of soot on everything nearby and puddles of brackish water, were all that remained to indicate the previous night's fire.

Piper knocked on the wooden door. "Hello. Is anyone here! Hello!"

They waited in the shade of the arched porch. Belle rang the doorbell, a loud bell that went on and on. There was no way anyone inside the house could miss it.

"That's odd. I saw someone in the upstairs rooms just a few minutes ago."

"Man or woman?"

"Couldn't tell. A person moving from room to room."

"Check the backyard. It's probably someone from the cleanup service."

"I don't know. Should we be wandering around? Someone might call the cops."

"We're concerned neighbors. Go. Look. I'll wait here." She rang the bell again.

Piper left Belle on the porch and walked along the driveway toward the back, the same route she'd taken yesterday. Something was different. Something was missing. *The canaries.* No sounds of singing. They sang every day as soon as the drapes opened. Canaries were delicate birds, easily traumatized. If last night's fire and smoke hadn't gotten to them, the commotion with the firefighters and trucks may have shocked them into silence. Or caused them to drop dead.

She rounded the back of the house to the sunroom. The drapes were closed. They wouldn't sing in a dark room. It didn't prove they were all right, but at least it explained their silence. She glanced around the rear yard. No sign of any workers. Turning, she headed back toward the front of the house.

Midway down the driveway, she looked up at the windows on the second story and stopped. The skin at the nape of her neck tightened. Returning was that creepy feeling from the day before, that same eerie sense of being watched. She held her breath and listened. A pair of doves cooed, calling out to one another. A dog barked in a yard beyond the Vogt's back wall. Normal, everyday sounds, yet the dark feeling pressed down on her. She glanced from window to window. So many windows. Was someone watching her from behind one of them? Her chest felt tight, as if a boa constrictor had wrapped itself around her torso and was squeezing the air out of her. She realized she was holding her breath.

A shadow slid over her from above.

She instinctively ducked, looking up at the same time.

The hawk circled overhead. She sucked in air, filling her lungs, trying to control her pounding heart.

Dammit, she was scaring herself, giving into her own silly fears. No sooner had the beating of her heart begun to slow, when from the front of the house Belle cried out, sending it into overdrive again. She ran to her.

Piper pulled up short when she saw Belle gingerly step over a puddle to peer into the front window. She held her furry slippers in one hand.

"What? What is it…are you okay?" Piper's voice cracked.

"I can't believe this. Those are genuine Letecs on that shelf. Q. Letecs." She motioned for Piper to come closer.

"My god, I thought you were being attacked."

"Don't be a ninny. You watch far too many cloak and dagger films. Letecs," she repeated. "Come look. I wanted to start a collection of his figurines, but they were much too pricey. Way out of my league, not to mention impossible to get these days unless you know a collector. She must have two dozen or more. Oh, I hate her."

Piper exhaled, relieved. Belle leaped back and pulled Piper toward the window. Piper held onto a branch of an evergreen tree, its sap sticky on her palm, the sharp scent of pine filling her head. She tried to step over the puddle and slid into it. Mud squished between the toes of her sandals. "Damn." she merely glanced at the figurines, which held little interest for her, and instead scanned the room. Her gaze stopped on the blackened patch of carpet on the other side of the room. "That must be where Dr. Oates found her." Piper pointed.

"Ummm. Probably. She's damn lucky he happened to be driving by and saw the smoke," Belle said. "With the park across the street and the way this house is situated on the corner behind all these trees, this front part is hidden from both neighboring houses. Even if you'd been home, Piper, I doubt you would have spotted the smoke in time."

"What's lucky is that a doctor pulled her out of the house."

"Well, he's not that kind of doctor. Oates is a plastic surgeon. He has a swank office in Brentwood. However, let me tell you, if I were looking to go under the knife, I'd look elsewhere. He cut the nerve in Paula Wintrie's eyelid and now it droops, which is criminal because Paula's eyes were her one and only good feature and—"

"Belle, we were talking about the doctor saving Sybil," Piper cut in.

"Oh. Right. She was unconscious, but breathing. I overheard Oates telling the paramedics he thought she passed out from excessive alcohol consumption, and not the smoke. He smelled it on her breath. In other words, the ol' gal was three sheets to the wind. Drinking and smoking, followed by loss of consciousness…quite a lethal combination, that. The firefighters lifted a cigarette butt from the smoldering chair."

She gave Piper a hand and pulled her from the puddle.

"You know, it's not the first time she's had too much to drink and suffered the consequences. Emily Crammer, her neighbor on the other side, said she fell down the stairs early this year. Sybil's housekeeper found her the next morning lying on the bottom step with a nasty bump on her head. Ambulance carted her off to hospital. She was fortunate to get only bumps and bruises. Drunks are resilient, you know? Like cats, nine lives and all that."

"A drinker." It was not a question. Sybil had kept the drapes open late into the night. For the past week she'd seen her roam the house every night, cigarette in one hand, glass in the other.

"Drinker? Ha! Your shining star is a stumbling calamity."

Before leaving the grounds, they called out and knocked several more times. No one answered.

While Sybil recovered in the hospital, the housekeeper came everyday to air out the house, collect the mail and, Piper assumed, to care for the canaries. Their sweet singing resumed the following day, though not as spirited as before. The housekeeper came early and left before Piper rolled out of bed, the sound of the VW waking her as she drove away. Piper learned from Dr. Oates that Sybil had been taken to a small private hospital in West Hollywood. When she called the nurse's station to inquire about her condition, she was told the patient was recovering well, but was not taking calls or visitors.

Late one balmy evening, unable to sleep, she went out onto the deck. From there she caught a glimpse of a flashlight beam moving around in the sunroom, the only room in the house next door where the drapes now remained open around the clock. She called the police and reported a possible break-in and burglary. A police cruiser responded within twenty minutes but found no sign of an intruder. If the person with the flashlight had returned in the subsequent days, he was careful to keep his nighttime roaming a secret from prying eyes.

CHAPTER 5

The Star Tattler—January 1942 [Archive]

Sources report the estranged mother of sixteen-year-old Sybil Squire was forcefully escorted off the RKO lot yesterday after causing a scene outside of the actress's dressing room. Annamaria Robles, drunk, cursing, and destroying props on Stage 54, threatened to kill herself if she couldn't talk to her daughter. "I don't have a mother," Miss Squire told our source.
—*Cricket Summers: Columnist to the Stars*

SUNLIGHT SPILLED ACROSS THE floor of the commissary at the Warner Brothers Studio and highlighted a tall purple floral arrangement nearby. The shiny black of the lacquered chairs contrasted sharply with the white tablecloths and the overall pale cream of the interior. Understated elegance. Piper felt more comfortable in the cafeteria commissary, the one for the not-so-famous, but this was part of her turf, her old stomping grounds when she'd edited films for WB. *Before* she married Gordon. Her turf again, at least for the next couple of weeks. Sandy Goodmore, an editor friend at the studio, agreed to let her assist on a horror film she was cutting. It was like an internship, wages at scale, yet it gave her a chance to jump back in, hands-on.

Lee had invited her to lunch. On the lot with paperwork, Lee had signed an A-List actress making the move up with an Academy win. Lee finessed her own win. She couldn't go two paces without being greeted. Everyone knew her, or knew *of* her. Despite her gender change, which had tongues wagging for two seasons back, she'd made her mark with killer instincts, sharp business tactics, and superb people skills. With all the schmoozing and constant bullshitting, she rarely got down more than three bites during a meal. Her cell phone never stopped ringing, beeping, or vibrating, linked to a half dozen neurotic and often hysterical clients.

Lee took a long drink from her iced tea. Piper watched her Adam's apple bob with each gulp. It was the one thing Lee couldn't do anything about, her prominent Adam's apple. Yet she didn't seem bothered by it. In fact, she displayed it like a badge of honor with open necklines and no scarves or jewelry. Was it a last testament to a previous life? To Leroy?

"He's such a dick," Lee said, referring to Gordon. "He was always a dick."

"Unlike you," Piper said, not unkindly.

"I was a dick when I had a dick. Now, according to my enemies, and some whiny producers, I'm a big C. And proud of it." She chewed a piece of ice. "I told you, I warned you, that Gordon was a control freak before you married him."

"And I'm supposed to listen to my ex-husband bash my future husband?"

"Why the hell not? We parted friends. You know what a good judge of character I am. I chose you, didn't I?"

"That only proves you have good taste."

She smiled. "Has the Gorgon tried to contact you in any way?"

"Nothing. I thought I'd hear from him after the papers were served, but not a word." Piper lowered her voice. "There's been a car cruising my neighborhood since I moved in there. Odd hours of the day and night. Tinted windows. Belle never saw it before I moved in. You think he's having me watched?"

"I wouldn't put anything past him. He's a sore loser and a grudge holder. Like I said, he's a dick."

A waiter in white set down their orders, two swordfish sandwiches. Lee asked for extra mayo.

The comedy sitcom star, Ted Truman, stopped to pay tribute to Lee. Although she rarely represented television actors, there was always the exception. If she consented to take on a TV personality, it was to launch him or her into major motion pictures. Her clientele list was small, but impressive. It included Oscar winners and a few Emmy winners. Lee wasted no time on small-scale actors and politely dismissed the comedian after assuring him he was bound to be nominated for an Emmy next time around. He returned to his table grinning like a delirious chimp beneath his bearded face.

"That one has potential," Lee said, looking after him. "But he's too high-maintenance. A babysitter for TV talent, I'm not."

Throughout their meal, they talked about the biz, the new crop of young executives, the wannabes infesting the industry, and those struggling to stay on top and those on the way out. Lee waved at George Clooney who sat at the table next to them. Lee and Piper briefly chatted with several studio execs, dinosaurs at Warner Brothers, who had stopped at their table on their way to a major meeting.

Gary Ott, the director who gave Piper her first big break, left his table to come to theirs. He held her hand, made a fuss over seeing her, and asked if she was back in the saddle. She took that to mean back to work in film editing. "I'm back." He told her he might have a project for her if she was interested. "I'm very interested," she said. He kissed her temple, a real kiss that made contact, not the airy kind, and then returned to his table and the young gum-chewing starlet who gazed at him with adoration and hope.

"Look out," Lee said. "'Back in the saddle' to that horndog can mean a number of things. All sexually related."

"I'm too old for him. He only likes to bang starlets. Young ones. Impressionable ones. Nothing impresses me these days. So how's *your* love life?"

Lee rolled her eyes. "Erica and I are going through a rough patch. We're far enough into the relationship to start screwing with each other's heads. She knows she's more than just a piece of ass, so she wants to mess with me, try to break my balls whenever she can."

"What balls?"

"The quasi balls. The ones up here." Lee touched a fingertip to her temple. "The ones she knows I'll always have because she has them too."

Erica was a transsexual Lee had met in group therapy six months earlier.

"You're perfect for each other, why can't you two get along?"

"Just because we're both male-to-female transsexuals doesn't mean we're perfect for each other. Erica is high risk," Lee said, tucking a strand of shiny hair behind her ear with a perfectly manicured nail. "She's bisexual, you know. Not that that bothers me—her sexuality—it's the damn relationships she gets herself into. Jesus, the last one was right out of *The Crying Game*. The guy didn't know she was TS until …

well…you know? She spent three days in the hospital after that gross error in judgment."

Speaking of hospitals, Sybil's still in that private clinic and she isn't taking phone calls or visitors. She doesn't seem to want company."

"Send her flowers."

"I tried. The florist said they were undeliverable."

"Wait till she's home." Lee raised a perfectly arched eyebrow and added, "I might be able to get her unlisted phone number."

"Could you? Would you?"

CHAPTER 6

The Star Tattler June 1943 [Archive]

Certain rumors have surfaced that one 'South of the Border' actress of mystery movie fame, before being legally adopted by her high school drama teacher, may have been a product of child prostitution and child abuse. An anonymous source reports photographs have surfaced in the child porn rings being investigated by the police

Looks like she made her theatrical debut long before the RKO studio screen test had them scrambling to sign her up.
—Cricket Summers: Columnist to the Stars.

LATE ONE UNSEASONABLY HOT autumn afternoon, Piper heard the soft whirring of the air-conditioning unit at the side of the Squire house. She saw lights upstairs in Sybil's bedroom and knew she was home again. The aging actress stayed seven days in the hospital. Two silhouettes behind the window shade of the bathroom told her she wasn't alone. Piper looked for the housekeeper's VW. Except for the Lincoln parked in the carport, there were no other cars on the property. The hospital or social services had probably sent along a nurse to care for her. *Good.* It eased her mind to know Sybil was not stumbling around alone in that huge house with her liquor and cigarettes, a calamity waiting to happen. Of course, what Sybil Squire did or didn't do was none of her business. Although she was eager to make a courtesy visit, she held off rushing right over. She'd give her a day or two to settle in.

Early the next morning, before leaving for the studio, she heard the housekeeper's VW pull into the driveway next door. Minutes later, she heard a vocal commotion at the back door of the mansion. She recognized the voice of the housekeeper, raised in anger. Strings of words drifted in the air, "…the hell you say…ain't leaving till…Just who do you think you are?!" Then she was shouting, "Sybil, honey, it's Vera! Can you hear me? I ain't leaving till you talk to me! Sybil-l-l!" Ten minutes later she heard a car door slam. The VW started up with a roar, backed erratically down the driveway, then tore off down the street.

All day at the studio, Piper thought about the episode outside the Squire mansion. What was that all about? A falling out between the housekeeper and her mistress? Over what? The two had seemed so close, so compatible.

Lee came through with Sybil's unlisted home number. Piper called that afternoon. A woman who identified herself as a registered nurse in charge of Mrs. Squire said her patient was not accepting calls or visitors. Piper called two days later and was told the same thing. When she tried to inquire about her health, the connection was broken. She decided to bide her time. If she saw Sybil in her yard, she would make a move to reach out again.

Her final week at the studio was hectic, but not so hectic that she didn't think about Sybil. Since she'd come home from the hospital there was little or no movement around the house, at least none that Piper could detect. The drapes were opened in the mornings and closed some time before dark each evening. The canaries continued to sing, but Sybil did not venture outdoors.

The housekeeper's green bug remained conspicuously absent, which surprised Piper. Whatever they had argued about had been more serious than she originally thought. The confrontation reminded her of something Nana had told her about Sybil. She'd suffered abuse at the hands of her mother. Years of neglect, malnutrition, beatings, and possibly sexual exploitation--men eager to pay for a short time in the company of the young girl with spun angel hair. "Mother hated me," Sybil had told Nana. "She hated me for everything bad that had ever happened to her. There was no good in her life, only bad. Someone had to pay. I guess that someone was me." A sympathetic drama teacher, a spinster, had thrown Sybil the lifeline that would pluck her from a life of unbelievable oppression and clear the way for happiness and her future success. The teacher became a legal guardian to fifteen-year-old Dolores Robles, and with her limited studio connections was able to get her ward a screen test with RKO. Sybil wowed them. Her first roles had been a deranged babysitter in the dark thriller, *Crybaby,* and an evil sorceress in *Moon Madness.* Two films that had recently captured a robust cult following.

Piper finished the WB job and found herself at home again. She needed to find work until the Vogt's left for Hong Kong at the end of the month. She dug out her old day/date books from her memento box. It had been five years since

CAROL DAVIS LUCE

her last editing job. This was the part of the job she dreaded, calling every contract she knew or didn't know to say "hi" and "I'm back. Need a good editor?" So many dead ends and brush-offs. The receptionists took her name and number only when she insisted. Gary Ott's assistant saying, "Mr. Ott's still on location, may I take a message?" Piper had seen him on the lot yesterday.

Between sending out resumes and cold calling, she thought about Sybil Squire.

Several days later at the bank, the same bank where she'd met Sybil Squire those many weeks ago, she again caught sight of her. The white hair, the light blue eyes--unmistakably Sybil Squire. She almost didn't recognize her. She seemed different. Not her physical appearance so much, but something in her demeanor. Something was definitely off-kilter. Sybil perched stiffly on a padded bench alongside the wall, her back straight, her feet flat on the floor, neatly aligned. Her hands were in her lap, pulled tight against her stomach. Medical gauze covered one hand completely. A large bandage covered the back of the other hand. A woman in her late fifties or early sixties, slightly disheveled, sat beside her. The contrast between the two women was startling. Sybil's knit suit and pumps were dated, yet classic. Her trademark platinum hair was neatly coiffed. Her face, now thinner, more mature with tiny creases, was expertly made up and as lovely as ever. The other woman wore baggy gray sweats, no make-up, her dark, gray-streaked hair hanging limp around her face.

A bank employee approached the two women and said, "Mrs. Squire, Mr. Oberson can see you now." The other woman rose to her feet. Sybil seemed not to have heard the employee and remained sitting. Sybil's companion took hold of her upper arm and lifted her. They walked to a desk several feet away, the desk of an associate bank manager.

Sybil seemed confused, and sat only after the dark haired woman pressed down on her shoulder. Who was this woman leading Sybil Squire around like a dog on a leash? Not a relative. If what she'd heard from Nana was true, Sybil had no living family after the brutal murder of her daughter four decades ago.

For once Piper didn't mind waiting in line, even allowing others to go ahead of her. When she could stall no longer and her transaction with the teller was completed, she stepped to the center counter and pretended to scan pamphlets on money market accounts while she continued to spy on the two women. The other woman did all the talking, with Sybil merely nodding, her gaze fixed straight ahead. Papers were passed from one to another and signed. The three stood, both women shook hands with the banker, though Sybil merely placed her fingers in the palm of the man's hand. Then they headed out the glass door, the stranger, with a hand cupping Sybil's elbow, guiding her.

Piper hurried to catch up. "Mrs. Squire," Piper said, stepping out onto the bright sunlit sidewalk. They stopped, turned. "It's good to see you again. I'm so sorry to hear about the fire and…your injuries."

Sybil Squire squinted against the sun. She looked at a point on Piper's forehead. She smiled tentatively.

"It's Piper. Piper Lundberg. I live in the guesthouse next door. We had coffee in your patio the day of the fire."

The smiled faded. Any emotion resembling the slightest bit of enthusiasm or interest disappeared, replaced by a blank stare.

The woman with Sybil spoke up. "That's nice that you're concerned, but Mrs. Squire isn't…well, isn't strong enough to be socializing yet. She'll give you a call when she's ready. Won't you, dear?" Without waiting for Sybil to respond, she took her arm again, turned and led her away.

Piper stood on the sidewalk staring at their retreating backs.

Something woke her. The luminous dial on the clock read 4:10. Without turning on the light, Piper put on her robe and went out onto the deck. The sweet scent of night blooming jasmine hung in the air. She breathed it in. A faint odor of chlorine co-mingled with the jasmine. The pool probably hadn't been vacant for long. Was Sybil swimming again? She shook out a cigarette from the pack, the third cigarette of the night, hoping it would relax her enough to let her go back to sleep.

A cat screamed, then another. Mating or fighting, she couldn't tell which. The screams settled into the high-pitched wails that sounded so much like the cries of a baby. Not fighting. *Mating.* That's probably what woke her.

The muted whop-whop from the rotors of a police helicopter flying high up in the hills oddly melded with the animals sounds. The beam of the copter's searchlight probed the thick foliage along Mulholland Drive. She looked away, lighting the cigarette.

The bulky square shape of the Squire house reared up cold and ugly in the moonlight, its windows dark except for several on the second floor. Piper's gaze was drawn to them. In a window straight across from her, Sybil's bedroom window, she saw something odd. Something she couldn't get her mind around for a moment or two. A figure stood at the arched window. There was no doubt in her mind it was Sybil Squire who stood pressed tight against the window. The heavy drapes were open, sheer transparent panels covered her back, allowing the filtered light from within to outline her pale, naked body. Her arms were stretched straight out above shoulder height, fingers splayed wide against the panes, head bowed. Her white hair, usually worn close to her head, fanned out in wild abandonment. The sheer oddness of her action sent a chill through Piper and made her shudder. Sybil was in pain. Piper could feel it through the void separating their houses.

A hand grabbed Sybil's arm and pulled her away from the window. The heavy drapes were flung together, shutting out the light from behind. The face of the companion appeared in the place Sybil had occupied. She looked straight at the guesthouse.

Piper cupped her cigarette to hide the glow, then stepped back, deeper into the shadows of the deck.

CHAPTER 7

The Star Tattler—May 1944 [Archive]

Sybil Squire, the star of Crybaby *and* A Pocket Full of Lies, *is rumored to have collapsed on the set of her latest project due to exhaustion. Or maybe drugs and booze? Daddy Dearest denies she fired him minutes before paramedics rushed her to the hospital. "Lies," he shouted to a group of concerned cast and crew members. "She'd be nothing without me. A two-bit actress playing whores and hussies."*

—Cricket Summers: Columnist to the Stars

PIPER STOOD IN THE cool, shaded archway of Sybil Squire's front entrance. In one hand, she clutched a potted African violet with purple blossoms. In the other, a plate of homemade date bars. Nana Ruth said that Sybil loved dates and would often drive to a little town outside of Palm Springs to buy them fresh. Dark residue on the stucco surrounding the front window was a reminder of the fire. Belle found the cleanup team's failure to remove it annoying. She had threatened to send her handyman over to fix it on her dime, or maybe work out some kind of deal on one of those Q. Letec figurines.

Belle had begged off going with her, using her frantic schedule as an excuse, but Piper knew better. Belle had no interest in meeting her reclusive neighbor. Having lived side by side for ten years, nothing had changed to make her want to be pals, not even the figurines she coveted. The fire merely added to the ongoing saga and confirmed Belle's suspicions that the lady lived under a dark cloud, and she wanted no part of it.

Piper pressed the doorbell and was immediately sorry. The chiming pealed throughout the house, going on and on. Too late, she remembered it from the day she and Belle had come over.

On the other side of the massive mahogany door, the grating sound of bolts scraped and clanked. The door jerked open, causing her to take a startled step backward. Instead of Sybil or the female companion from the bank, a short Asian man peered out. He was about her age, mid-thirties or younger. He wore round eyeglasses with lenses so thick they magnified his eyes to enormous proportions. His gaze moved from her face to the items in her hands and back to her face. The man's resemblance to the actor Peter Lorre was uncanny. A young, bespeckled Peter Lorre in the role of Mr. Moto, master of disguise. She loved Mr. Moto, loved the wily, charming character with his biting wit. Yet, within those initial seconds, something told her that there was nothing charming or witty about this man.

"What do you want?" he demanded.

"I'm Piper Lundberg from next door." She tipped her head in the direction of her guesthouse. "I'd like to see Ms. Squire."

He closed the door in her face.

She waited, thinking he would return or that someone else would come to the door, but after five minutes, she realized she had been dismissed.

This time she used the large, brass knocker, giving it three solid raps.

Twice more she rapped with the brass knocker. Louder. Time passed. She exhaled and turned away. The door opened again. The dark-haired woman from the bank stood stiff and unyielding in the opening.

"Hi, I'm from next door. We met outside the bank a while ago. Remember?" Piper asked. When the woman didn't respond, she continued. "Could you tell Mrs. Squire that Piper Lundberg would like to see her?"

"I thought I made it clear she wasn't seeing people."

"I think I'd like to hear her tell me that, if you don't mind."

"Look, Pepper—"

"Piper."

"Whatever. She isn't up to having company."

"Is she ill?"

"She's…well, let's just say she has a problem maintaining mental balance. She gets upset if things don't keep to a certain routine. You, Ms. Lundberg, are not a part of that routine. Now I'm sure you don't want to upset her, do you?"

What the hell did she mean by that? Maintaining mental balance? Was she implying that Sybil Squire was mentally incompetent?

"No, of course I don't want to upset—"

The door closed again. This time with a finality as the bolts slammed home.

****

"From what I observed in her stay with us, Mrs. Lundberg, I'd say Mrs. Squire's mental state seemed perfectly normal to me." Dr. Lowdell poured coffee into a mug, moved down the counter of the hospital cafeteria, and selected a bear claw from the tray of pastries. "As you know, this is a medical hospital, not a mental facility. We treated her for physical injuries."

Piper poured coffee, but passed on the pastries as she moved along with him to the cashier. He pointed to a table by the window. She had to rush to keep up with him. They pushed the littered contents of the last diner's food to the side and took seats opposite each other. Outside, a stiff breeze played with the row of towering palms along the entire block. They swayed gently, rhythmically, as though choreographed to the canned music in the cafeteria. She'd obtained the name of Sybil's doctor from Dr. Oates, the plastic surgeon who had pulled her from her burning house. Using Dr. Oates' name had gotten her a brief interview with him.

"We treated her for burns to her hands," he said. "During her week at the clinic, I found her to be quite lucid--charming, in fact. She was eager to be done with us here, and back in her own home. If she's exhibiting any mental deficiencies, they didn't surface while she was under my care. Tell me again, what is your connection to Mrs. Squire?"

"I'm her neighbor and a great admirer of hers. I'm concerned about her."

"Concerned in what way?"

"Concerned for her safety. There've been some strange things going on next door. Things I don't think Sybil would allow if she had a say in the matter."

The doctor frowned. "Such as?"

"Yesterday when I went to the house to…to see for myself that she was…well, okay, I was told by her nurse that she wasn't up to having visitors. She said Sybil had a problem maintaining mental balance and visitors would upset her."

Dr. Lowdell sipped his coffee, frowned again. "I agreed to talk with you because I thought you were a close friend. Not just a neighbor. I'm really not at liberty to discuss my patient with you, Mrs. Lundberg."

"I know that, Doctor. I don't consider myself *just* a neighbor. I know she has a drinking problem and that alcohol and a smoldering cigarette were what put her here. I'm more than concerned."

He looked into her eyes. She held his gaze. He leaned back. "Mrs. Squire was admitted to the hospital for treatment for first and second degree burns, her hands primarily. She came very close to burning her house down and dying in that fire. As you know, she lived alone. I think a domestic came in every other day to cook and clean, but Mrs. Squire was the only one in the house when it caught fire. It could happen again if I let her go back there alone. I tried to persuade her to move into an assisted living facility. She flatly refused. She said that her father tried to run her life when she was a young woman and that she preferred a life of loneliness to a life of tyranny," the doctor said. "You see, she's somewhat of a free spirit."

"Yes, I know. She swims laps in the nude."

He smiled. "She's a remarkable woman, but stubborn. She won't give up her scotch and cigarettes. She's eighty-five and it hasn't killed her yet. In all good conscience, I could not release her without someone there to prevent what happened before. She agreed to live-in help. I made the arrangements and it was approved by social services."

"And this live-in help…they're qualified?"

58

"Of course."

"Do you check on your patients once they've been released from the hospital?"

He lowered the bear claw without taking a bite. "You mean a house call?"

"Yes."

"As a rule, no."

"Could you make an exception?"

"I can notify social services."

"They wouldn't know what to look for."

"And what is it that I should look for, Ms. Lundberg?"

"The patient you treated here in the clinic, a lucid and charming woman."

"And if I find that woman?"

"Then you made a house call for nothing."

His pager went off. He checked it, rising to the feet. "Look, I'll see what I can do," he said. His long strides carried him out of the room.

CHAPTER 8

Victor Robles reclaimed his daughter and manufactured a star. Transworld Artists championed her in their dark crime and detective pictures. Her platinum hair and pale eyes--eyes as cool as icicles--mesmerized from the screen. Sybil Squire was the most sought-after gorgeous, predatory, double-crossing femme fatale of her day. At twenty-one she had fame and fortune. She had her father to thank for that. A man she hated with every fiber of her being.

—*Excerpt from the biography of* Sybil Squire: The Platinum Widow *by Russell Cassevantes.*

WITH A BOW AND an exaggerated flourish, Mick handed over the footage, storyboard and shot/clip list for his documentary to Piper on Saturday. The day before they left for Hong Kong. The moment the film was hers, Piper felt a tingle run up her spine. She couldn't wait to start on it. He trusted her to do the job on her own. She was more than qualified to piece it together. This was old-school. She was in her element. It had a great analog feel, shot over a period of years using top directors, producers, and actors. This documentary, *Greatest Classics: Film Noir* was a documentary any number of good editors could probably cut in their sleep. Yet she had an edge over the others. She knew the genre inside and out. Lived and breathed it. Embraced it.

Because of Nana Ruth's influence, she became addicted to the old thrillers in early childhood. She analyzed the classics, particularly the noir films, and studied the masters in the field. Directors like Hitchcock, Wilder, and the more modern Pankow. She yearned to get closer to film, the process, the magic. As a graduate student fresh out of UCLA, she took on low-level film jobs, assistant work to producers, directors, and studio execs, doing whatever came her way while searching for her niche. She found it in a Studio City cutting room editing a rock concert documentary, an exhilarating process. From there she went on to cut commercials, television movies, then her first major film. She was hooked. Editing held the secrets to the magic of the subjects she loved. Several years later, a director on a Mick Vogt film gave her her first big break, a chance to work directly with him as the film editor on *Upper Limits,* a 2003 Oscar nominee.

At ten o'clock that evening, she began to organize the new project. Being a nocturnal creature and a sun worshiper, she preferred to work after the sun set into the early a.m. when the gray morning fog hung over the hills of LA. Two hours into the digitizing process, thunder cracked and boomed beyond the thick stucco walls.

Rain pinged against the window, pelting it at times. This was the first rain of the season. She always looked forward to the first storm. This time a pulsing pain behind her eyes, now a full-blown headache, pounded in sync with the driving rain. She needed aspirin and to stretch.

In the dark, she stepped to the window and drew back the drapes. Sheets of water cascaded down the glass. She scanned the house and grounds next door for any movement, any sign of Sybil Squire, as she did every night since moving into the guesthouse. She even checked the pool, knowing no one in their right mind would swim in this kind of weather. The rain beat down on the surface of the pool, violently churning it up. It resembled a piranha feeding frenzy.

A flash of movement. Something white near the wall dividing the two houses. She pressed closer to the glass to see. That something was a person. *Sybil.* There was no mistaking that white hair. Wet and plastered to her head, it stood out in the darkness like a soft moon glow. She appeared to be wandering aimlessly. She fell, struggled upward only to fall again.

Piper pulled on her raincoat and dashed down the wet concrete steps, now slick with sodden leaves. Her bare feet slapped against the concrete driveway as she ran. The gate to the Squire property resisted when she pushed at it. She used her back and shoulder to buffet the gate. It sprung open, dropping her to the ground. She pulled herself up, pushed the wet hair from her eyes, and ran into the yard, heading toward the place where she had last seen Sybil. She called her name. No response. She caught a glimpse of the whitish glow of her hair and the pale outline of her nightgown. When she reached Sybil, she was on her hands and knees.

"Mrs. Squire, are you all right?" She shouted to be heard over the wind and rain. Piper dropped down in front of her and placed a hand on her shoulder.

Sybil came up on her knees, her back straight, her head bowed. She swiped a dirty hand through her hair, depositing a trail of debris through the wet strands. Lightning lit up the sky. Her knees were crusted with mud, leaves, and grass.

"Mrs. Squire, what can I do to help you? Please, let me help you."

Sybil grabbed Piper's forearm and squeezed. Raising her head, Sybil stared at Piper with glazed eyes, eyes devoid of expression. Eyes that in no way were close to resembling the expressive "movie" eyes she had once been so famous for.

"I'm going to call the police," Piper said, helping her to her feet. Sybil leaned into her. "I'm taking you to my place, right next door there, and I'm calling the police."

"No." Sybil jerked back. "No police."

Piper smelled alcohol on her breath.

"Okay, no police. But you're coming to my place."

"Sybil. Sybil, what am I going to do with you?" the nurse shouted to be heard. "You promised, didn't you? You promised, and then you went back on your word." A hand wrapped around Sybil's upper arm and yanked her away.

"She's coming with me," Piper said, blocking the way.

"This is none of your business," the woman said. "Everything is fine. I know how to handle it."

"Fine? She's soaking wet and shaking like a leaf. She was out here stumbling around in the rain, falling into the mud. What if she slipped into the pool and drowned? Is that how you handle it?"

"You're trespassing. Get off this property. Call the police and I'll report you for trespassing. Then we'll see who gets into trouble."

Piper turned to Sybil Squire. "Would you like to come home with me?"

"Sybil?" the woman said her tone sharp.

"No." Sybil pushed Piper's hand away from her arm. Then she allowed the nurse to put an arm around her waist and lead her away willingly, like a wayward lamb.

Piper watched them disappear into the heavy rain. She stood there in the rain, cold feet in the wet leaves.

Go home, the rational side of her brain said. *Go home. Don't get involved.*

Piper refused to listen to the voice of reason. Early the next morning she rounded the stone wall separating the Vogt's driveway and strode up the Squire driveway. This time she bore no gifts. She marched up the brick walkway into the arched porch and smacked the doorbell with the palm of her hand. All through the previous night, tossing and turning, unable to sleep, she had replayed the bizarre scene in the garden. What possessed Sybil to wander around in the rain so late at night? What possessed her to crawl around on her hands and knees in the dirt? Was she, as the nurse had implied, mentally incompetent? She was drunk or drugged, that was clear from the alcohol on her breath and the glazed look her in eyes. But had she lost her ability to reason? Dr. Lowdell said her mental state was intact when he treated her two weeks ago. Could a person's mental capacity deteriorate in so short a time?

The small, bespeckled Mr. Moto-look-a-like answered the door. An instant later the nurse appeared behind him.

"I want to see Mrs. Squire," Piper said, ignoring the man and talking directly to the woman. "Now. No excuses."

"She's not well."

"Really? Why am I not surprised? It might be a bit much for a frail, elderly woman to stumble around in her nightgown in the middle of the night in a freezing rainstorm. But then, you know how to handle that sort of thing, don't you?"

The woman clamped her mouth shut, a grim line in a stony mask of a face. Her black eyes bored into Piper's.

Piper took a step forward. The nurse barred the threshold.

"You have no right to stop me from seeing her. If she's okay, then let her tell me so."

"Leave us alone."

"I can't do that. Not until I've talked to Sybil."

The door began to close.

"Dammit, I'll sit here on the step until you let me see her."

"Suit yourself."

"Social services might appreciate a call. Dr. Lowdell too," Piper added.

The door continued to close, but before it shut completely, the woman said, "Seven o'clock. She'll see you then."

CHAPTER 9

THAT AFTERNOON MICK FLOODED Piper with last-minute instructions for the documentary. He wanted to walk through the entire storyboard and clip list. The list was so long the documentary would need to be a mini-series to include all of them. Her mind was at the house next door. At seven that evening she would finally sit down with Sybil and find out what the hell was going on. The hours dragged, despite Belle taking over when Mick finished. They went over her first week's schedule. As their house sitter, she would look after the place, feeding the cockatoo and watering the dozens of plants that seemed to overrun every room throughout the nine-room Tudor. Although the yard was maintained by a weekly lawn service, Piper insisted on tending the outdoor planters. That included watering, weeding, and cutting flowers for the two houses. This she did to indulge her compulsion for sunshine and fresh air when she wasn't shut away in a dark room working.

At three o'clock, the studio's white Lincoln Towncar arrived to take the Vogts to LAX. The bags were loaded into the trunk. Piper hugged her friends and watched them climb into the back seat of the car. Belle lowered the window. "You have our number and our email. Remember the time difference, okay?"

"Okay, I'll try not to call in the middle of the night."

The car drove down the driveway. Piper walked backwards, waving as she went. Just before the driver pulled away from the house, Belle called out the window. "Piper! Darling, if anything goes haywire in either of the houses, call our handyman, Luke. His number's on the fridge. He'll take care of any problems."

Piper nodded, waved as the car disappeared around the bend, and then started up the steps to the guesthouse. In the yard next door, footsteps crunched on leaves. She hurried up the steps to the deck and looked over the rail into the Squire property. Mr. Moto--her name for him now--stepped into the gardening shed beyond the wall. Moments later he came out with a rake and began clearing away the pepper leaves knocked to the ground from the previous night's downpour. The hair on the back of her neck rose. She rubbed at the goose bumps along her arms. The man gave her the creeps.

At seven o'clock Judith Avidon showed her into the Squire house. The nurse gave her name only after Piper asked her for it, along with an attitude. Piper followed her into the living room, the large room at the front. The room glowed with late afternoon sunlight. She looked away from the light into the dim expanse of the room.

The expensive fifties furnishings, though faded in places from years of afternoon sunlight, looked in good condition. The various paintings and sculptures, if not genuine, were impressive reproductions. A Jackson Pollock canvas hung on the wall behind the grand piano. From what Nana had told her about Sybil's taste, it leaned toward the eclectic. Bookshelves lined the walls on two sides. One bookcase, divided by a massive open hearth, held the dozens of figurines, the beautifully crafted replicas of European aristocrats by the nineteenth century French artist. She had looked up the Q. Letec collection and was surprised that work so fine and delicate would appeal to Sybil. Yet anyone who loved songbirds would appreciate fine beauty and grace.

Sybil sat in a black mohair wingback chair with ivory piping. Her posture was stiff, wooden, the same unnatural posture she'd displayed that day in the bank. A portable oxygen tank stood to one side of her chair, unused now. On the opposite side was a birdcage on a stand. The bright yellow canary was silent, preening himself.

"They're beautiful," Piper said of the figurines, hoping to open their visit with casual dialogue that would put them both at ease. Sybil remained as silent and as inanimate as the figurines lining the bookshelves. Piper cleared her throat, rubbed her hands together nervously, and moved into the room.

Sybil watched Piper approach. Sybil seemed thinner, frailer than that afternoon at the bank. Piper extended her hand. After an uncomfortable pause, Sybil raised a hand and gingerly touched Piper's palm before placing her hand back into her lap.

"Mrs. Squire, I've been worried about you. I hope you don't think I'm being too pushy. I wanted to see you. To tell you how sorry I am about the fire. I hope you're recovering okay from the burns."

"I am, thank you," Sybil said in a level tone.

Piper knew, without turning, that the nurse was still within earshot. Did she intend to monitor their entire conversation?

"Mick—that's Mick Vogt, the producer—gave me the footage today for the documentary. The one I was telling you about on film noir. The one I'll be editing. When I get it whipped into some sort of shape, I'd like you to come over and have a look at it…to give me your opinion, your input. Would you do that?"

Sybil reached over to a table beside her chair and picked up a photograph. A black and white glossy of herself. A publicity photo from the classic thriller, *A Pocketful of Lies.* "Would you like me to autograph this for you?"

Piper was confused and disappointed. Instead of answering her, she offered to autograph a publicity photo, something she had given to countless fans in the past. Did she think Piper was nothing more than an overzealous fan, looking for a celebrity keepsake? Although they'd had only the one meeting, in those few minutes she thought they had shared something more intimate than fan-to-idol chitchat. Sybil had seemed interested in her work, praising her achievements, inquiring about her personal life and encouraging her to be independent. *Where was that kind, caring woman now*, she wondered.

Without waiting for an answer, Sybil said, "Hand me that pen, dear, the one on the table."

Piper handed her the pen. The closest seat was the matching black couch, far away on the other side of the large oval coffee table. Piper bent down at her feet, squatting on her heels.

She signed the photograph with a shaky hand. Piper took it, thanking her.

"Do you have a smoke?" Sybil said under her breath.

Piper turned to see if the nurse was still in the room.

"She's gone."

Piper patted the breast pocket of her blouse. She reached inside and pulled out a slip of paper. It was the fortune from her birthday dinner. *Beware of false icons.* She dropped it back into her pocket. "I'm sorry, I left them at home. I'm really not a fulltime smoker. Maybe one or two in the evening, on the deck."

"Sometimes three."

That surprised her. Sybil had been watching her, as she watched Sybil.

"Do you have *Sins of the Family*?" Sybil asked.

"Sins of the Family? Well, no, but—"

Sybil cut in, "What's your favorite?"

"Of your films?"

She nodded.

"*Black Ribbon*," Piper said without hesitation. *Sins of the Family* was not one of Sybil's films. Why had she mentioned it? Maybe confusion or a ploy to test the validity of her admiration as a fan?

"May I offer you something to drink?"

Piper declined; afraid she would summon one of her aides.

Sybil lifted the rock glass at her elbow, put it to her lips, and threw back the amber liquid. Then she began to rise.

Piper stood and reached for her glass. "I'll get that for you."

Taking the glass, Piper stepped to the bar cart on the other side of the lamp table. It wasn't hard to figure out what she was drinking. The three bottles lined up were all scotch, the brand unfamiliar to her. She poured a shot, neat. Just the way Sybil had been drinking it. The canary twittered. Sybil twisted to the side and began rooting through a full ashtray on the end table. After snagging a butt, she carefully straightened it, lifted the crystal lighter and tried to light it. Piper took the heavy lighter from her trembling fingers, clicked it and held it out to her. Sybil leaned in, squinting one eye as the flame caught the end and flared. Ashes and sparks flew in the air, landing on her gauzy dress, singeing it in several places.

The bird began to sing. It had a strong, clear tone.

"He sings beautifully," Piper said.

"They don't sing as much since the fire. The smoke and soot, I guess."

Piper saw more evidence of the fire that had sent Sybil to the hospital. To the left of her chair a portion of the carpet had been cut away but not replaced. A space on the other side of the lamp table, where the burned matching chair had sat, looked oddly bare and unbalanced. The empty curtain rods held a fine film of soot.

"Belle has a handyman she highly recommends. I can give you his number when you're ready to renovate."

Mr. Moto came into the room. He sized her up and smiled a smile that was anything but friendly. He inspected the oxygen tank to make certain that it was turned off. Sybil did not acknowledge him. In fact, she seemed to avoid eye contact with him. Yet Piper swore she'd caught a spark of emotion in her eyes when he first entered the room: fear, anguish, hostility? Sybil sipped her scotch, picked absently at the tiny burn hole in her dress. Mr. Moto took his time, strolling around the room adjusting the blinds, an ashtray, and a magazine here and there. For one moment, she thought he might ask if Sybil wanted anything, but he didn't. Instead, he approached the birdcage, looked down at the publicity photo, and with the toe of his shoe flipped the picture over. The bird had stopped singing the moment he'd entered the room. Now it began to flap its wings. He reached for the cage. The bird flew around the cage wildly, crashing into the bars, dropping to the bottom of the cage. Moto slowly pulled his hand away, turned, and left the room.

Piper watched him go. When she no longer heard his footsteps in the hallway, she turned back to Sybil. Her eyes were closed. "Mrs. Squire?"

After lightly touching Sybil's hand and getting no response, she removed the smoldering butt from between her fingers. For the first time she noticed the angry scars from the deep burns on both of her hands. The exquisite diamond ring sparkled.

Piper sat on her heels staring into her face. She lightly stroked the back of one burned hand. Out of the corner of her eye, Piper spotted the nurse's dark silhouette at the end of the hall, arms folded across her chest, watching her. She rose to her feet, picked up the photo, and let herself out.

What have I accomplished? she asked herself. She still had no idea what was going on in that house, whether she was being properly cared for or not. By the amount of liquor Sybil had consumed, she was clearly not being deprived of any alcoholic fortification. She didn't seem to be in any great distress; no secret notes passed to her, no whispered pleas for help and no frantic eye movements. In fact, so unfazed was Sybil that she had dropped off to sleep. Yet something at the back of Piper's mind wriggled and squirmed uncomfortably. Mr. Moto's presence in the room was threatening to say to least. Had she feigned sleep? Why had she mentioned a movie that wasn't hers, and why give her a publicity photo without being asked for one?

Two things came to mind. Either Sybil was mentally unbalanced, as the nurse had said, or she was trying to tell Piper something

.

CHAPTER 10

The Star Tattler October 1945 [Archive]

*Nineteen-year-old actress Sybil Squire, touring with the
USO troupe, wowed our service boys on military bases
both at home and overseas. Look out movie America, this
platinum bombshell is on her way!*

—Cricket Summers:columnist to the stars

TWICE THAT WEEK THE Vogt's security alarm in the
main house went off in the middle of the night. Both times a
patrol car came to check it out, but found nothing. The three
main doors were motion activated. A good stiff breeze, or the
Vogt's cockatoo, loose from his cage, could have triggered the
alarm. After the second incident, she made certain Dr. J
stayed in his cage and that the cage door remained latched—
a form of punishment that pissed him off royally—and it
didn't happen again.

She fell into a daily routine of feeding the Vogt's bird, watering the plants throughout the two-story house, and going to the mailbox to fetch the newspapers and mail. Sorting through the mail, faxing or scanning items to Mick and Belle in Hong Kong, watering the never-ending plants— all were time-sucks when she had other priorities. Usually socializing with Dr J was a welcome break to stretch her legs and rest her eyes from the screens, both TV and monitors. Piper squeezed in her own networking phone calls to line up her next job. In this town, you had to get your next gig while the iron was hot, while you were still in demand, while you had a job.

The day flashed by like a blur, and by late afternoon, she was hard at work on the documentary. Sticking to her self-imposed schedule of seven hours on the documentary, she realized she needed to put in some additional research. She thought she knew the films, but the tiny details were illusive. She needed to watch them again with a fresh eye. Mick's notes and clip list sometimes lacked emotional specifics even though the time specifics made the clips easy to find. He'd write something like.... "that scene at the 22 minute mark where she looks screen right, use fifteen seconds then cut to..." Piper needed the time slots, but as the editor, she needed to understand the bigger picture of all of the films together, what emotional core linked them and made them the greatest of the film noirs.

Drawn to Sybil's classic movie, *Black Ribbon,* editing it was like a secret indulgence. She was being paid to do something she enjoyed. The Oscar-nominated thriller was the story of deep family ties. Of love, loss and sacrifice. A story that mimicked Sybil's own life.

No matter how many times Piper watched that final scene, tears filled her eyes and a lump rose in her throat.

****

A week after Piper's visit with Sybil, she saw Judith Avidon coming out of the bank. Preoccupied with counting a thick wad of cash, Avidon walked right by her on the sidewalk and into the drugstore. She was alone. Piper looked for and found the big black Lincoln parked in a lot across the street. Mr. Moto was nowhere around it. She waited a moment and then, like an amateur sleuth, followed the nurse into the drugstore. She lurked behind a display of sunglasses while the pharmacist filled four prescriptions, then rang up her other purchases of duct tape, a bottle of cheap Scotch, and a length of nylon clothesline.

Red flags went up. Piper considered notifying the authorities, someone connected with the fraud division or social services, but decided that a few sundry items bought at a drugstore was not enough to confront them with her suspicions. She would do some checking on her own first.

The next day, she witnessed another concerning situation. The huge orange tomcat, the neighborhood stray, sat on Sybil's patio. The blinds in the sunroom were open. Piper looked through the telescope that she had taken from the main house. Inside the room, she saw the birdcages, four of them. The birds were silent. Just then, the nurse stepped outside. She expected her to shoo the cat away. Instead, she bent over and placed a small bowl on the bricks. The cat practically dove at it, his back up, his face buried deep into the bowl. The nurse squatted on her heels and waited while the cat ate. When it had finished, she took the bowl and returned to the house. Minutes later Piper heard a woman's voice raised in anger. "Stupid pig!...stubborn, bullheaded idiot!" Then glass breaking.

That evening at twilight, Piper noticed the drapes in the master bedroom were partially open. Through the telescope lens, she saw Sybil sitting on the edge of her bed. She wore a dressing gown, one side draped off her swimmer's square, broad shoulder. Her hair uncombed, no makeup, Sybil sat staring straight ahead with her hands folded in her lap. Nurse Avidon came into view holding a bottle and a glass of water. She lifted Sybil's hand, turned it over and shook something into her palm. Pills. Sybil merely stared at her palm until the nurse pushed her hand toward her mouth. Sybil obediently took the pills into her mouth and drank from the glass. The nurse left the room.

Sybil rose from the bed unsteadily, crossed the room, spit the pills into her hand and dropped them out the open window.

Piper had to get those pills.

Piper waited until dark. Getting in and out unseen was one problem, finding the pills was another. She chose the back way, through the gap in the two property walls, the route pointed out by Sybil's housekeeper the day she joined Sybil for coffee. It was shorter to take the driveway route, a straight route from the street, but that way was in the open, with less trees and foliage for cover.

Lights burned in the back rooms of the mansion. Seeing Judith and Mr. Moto in the kitchen gave her the courage to make a dash from behind the pool house to the lemon tree across from Sybil's window. She paused for a moment to control her breathing, then stole across the driveway to the area under the window. There, she crouched on her haunches to the side of a lilac bush like a wary rabbit. She felt for the pill with her fingertips. She leaned down, wishing she had brought a penlight, and searched again. She heard voices from the house. The caregivers. As long as they remained inside the house, she felt safe. Where were those damn pills? Bright lights suddenly blazed beneath the pale green water of the swimming pool. The back door opened. Moto and Judith Avidon came through, speaking in hushed tones. They wore robes, and on their feet flip-flops that slapped on the concrete as they walked.

She held her breath. Her palms began to sweat. Moto's footsteps picked up speed, the slapping sound growing louder, coming nearer.

"You little bastard," he growled out. "I got you now!"

Piper flattened herself to the house, her heart pounding insanely in her chest.

She heard a screech. Something brushed past her ankle. A large cat raced past her and up into the branches of the lemon tree. It was the orange cat he was chasing after, and not her. Her relief was short-lived. Moto turned to follow the cat's path, a path that would lead straight to her and her hiding place.

"Let him go, Jack," the nurse called out. "I have plans for him."

Moto picked up a pebble and lobbed it at the cat crouched in the lower branches. The pebble hit the trunk with a solid thwack and dropped to the ground. He continued to come closer. It took all her will power not to bolt from her hiding place. He stopped three feet away. His feet in the flip-flops caught the light from the pool. At the tip of his big toe, she saw the pill. He turned. The flip-flops slapped their way back up the driveway.

Through the bush, she could see the pool. The nurse had removed the robe and was sitting on the steps, waist-deep in the water. Mr. Moto removed his eyeglasses and dove into the deep end. Piper reached out and snagged the pill. She made her escape then, moving briskly in the opposite direction, down the edge of the driveway to the street until she was out of their line of vision. Then she ran like hell.

Once inside the guesthouse, she opened her sweaty, trembling hand. The pill's engraved brand had dissolved away, but it still held its shape and color. She stashed it in the medicine cabinet for safekeeping until she could have it checked out.

CHAPTER 11

On the night she won an Oscar for her role in Shady Lady, Sybil eloped with western star, Chance Watson. Chance was the rough and tumble hero who had rescued Sybil from her taskmaster of a father. "He sent her daddy packing, but not before daddy had blown all of Sybil's money," said Sybil's friend, Mae Gilbert. "Chance and Sybil seemed happy enough until Chance got kicked in the head by that bucking horse. He wasn't right from then on. Turned mean and crazy. When that blood clot in his brain killed him, Sybil had to be…well, relieved." Sybil borrowed money from the studio to bury her husband. At twenty-five, she was a widow, three months pregnant and flat broke.

—Excerpt from the biography of Sybil Squire: The Platinum Widow *by Russell Cassevantes*

THE NEXT MORNING, PIPER sat with her coffee at the telescope, waiting. Sybil appeared outside the house sporting a black eye, a fist-sized shiner. Her translucent, pale skin made the shiner literally pulsate with color, giving her a haunting, ghoulish look. Her flyaway white hair only magnified the horror of this picture. She stood on the back steps wearing an ivory, full-length ermine coat. The heavy coat added to the oddity of the situation. The temperature that morning was in the eighties, and rising.

From behind the blackout curtains, Piper watched her tiptoe barefoot down the three brick steps and cross the patio to the swimming pool. She walked the length of the diving board to the end. From the pocket of her coat, she pulled out the black goggles, slipped them on her face. The coat slid from her thin naked body to drape across the board behind her, dangling down, the fur turning dark in the water. Her toes curled over the edge of the board, she lifted upward and executed a near-perfect swan dive into the deep water.

Sybil dove to the bottom of the pool and stayed there for what seemed a very long time. Piper felt her pulse accelerating, going into overdrive. Sybil seemed to be sitting on the bottom of the pool. Piper couldn't stand there and watch her die. She had to do something to help her.

She snatched up the phone and dialed 911 just as Sybil's two caregivers rushed outside. A moment later Sybil popped to the surface.

In a rush of words to the dispatcher Piper tried to explain what was happening next door. "I think she's in danger. Send someone…Please. Hurry."

She yanked the drapes aside and watched the two try to coax Sybil from the pool. She ignored them, continuing to swim from end to end in the long, rectangular pool. Mr. Moto waded into the water fully clothed and snatched at her the moment she came within reach. Their struggles took him underwater. He came up sputtering and cursing, calling Sybil a bitch." The nurse waded in to assist him. It would have been comical if it had involved anyone other than Sybil Squire.

She quickly looked up the number for the clinic, dialed and asked for Dr. Lowdell, the GP who had treated her burns. While she waited for him to come on the line, she watched them haul Sybil out of the pool and practically drag her toward the house. They didn't bother to retrieve the fur coat. As the three climbed the brick steps, Judith Avidon cast a sharp glance at Piper standing in the open window, the cordless phone to her ear. Let them see her. Let them know they're being watched.

"Dr. Lowdell speaking," the voice on the phone said in a deep authoritative tone.

"Doctor, this is Piper Lundberg. We spoke a while back regarding Sybil Squire?"

"Yes, Mrs. Lundberg, I remember you." His tone now had a guarded edge to it.

"I think now's the time to pay a house call to Mrs. Squire. I've already called the police and they're on their way. Do you want to call Social Services, or should I?"

Piper stood on the deck watching the house next door. Dr. Lowdell and a young black woman with an accordion gusset briefcase, who Piper assumed to be a case worker from Social Services, had arrived an hour ago in separate cars, but joined up to enter the premises together. The police left first. When the doctor and the woman finally reemerged and returned to their respective cars, Dr. Lowdell paused at the door of his Lexus. He glanced around at the neighboring houses until he spotted her on the deck. After depositing his case into the trunk of the car, he headed up the driveway toward her.

She invited him inside, away from the prying eyes of the people next door. Of course, they knew she was the busybody who'd contacted the authorities, and she didn't care. The black eye was the proof. Sybil did not give herself a shiner.

"I thought the police would want to talk with me," Piper said.

"I told them I'd take care of it." Translated: *don't bother, the neighbor is a kook.* "She fell climbing out of the pool yesterday and hit the side of her face on the edge."

"Is that what they said happened to her?"

"No, that's what Mrs. Squire said happened and I have no reason not to believe her."

"Well how about fear of reprisal or fear for her life? Are those valid enough reasons?"

"I took her aside and asked her point-blank. I assured her that if anything criminal, or remotely suspicious, was going on in her house under the supervision of her caregivers, she would receive immediate protection and the guilty parties dealt with here and now."

"And?"

"And she said she fell while swimming alone in the pool."

"Doctor, she wears water goggles. Would she get that kind of an injury wearing goggles?"

He paused a moment, twisting his mouth to first one side and then the other. "I can't say for sure. Of course, anything is possible. I told her that you were concerned for her. That you thought she might be a victim of abuse."

Finally. Thank you.

"She said, and this is verbatim: 'My neighbor watches too many bad thrillers. She should find something better to do with her time than to look for menace makers.'"

Sybil's words stung. They were harsh and unkind. And odd. *Menace Maker*s was one of her movies, a thriller. There was something there, but she couldn't put her finger on it just yet.

She sighed. "Doctor, don't you see she's gone downhill since you released her from the hospital, and rather drastically? She's much thinner. Almost skin and bones. She walks around like she's in a fog. She's being drugged, I know it. Oh, shit, wait--" Piper ran into the bathroom, grabbed the pill from the medicine cabinet, and returned to him.

"They're making her take these," she said, holding out the pill. "Among others."

"Making her?"

"Sybil threw this pill out of her window when she thought no one could see her. If they weren't making her take them, why would she throw it out the window?"

He studied it. "From the size and color, I'd say it's a Xanax, an anti-anxiety medication. She takes this and a light tranquilizer, both prescribed by me. She doesn't sleep well, hasn't for years. Yes, she's frail," he continued. "She's eighty-five years old and drinks heavily. What you might think is a drug-induced stupor is more likely a result of alcohol. She's been drinking today already. I smelled it on her. So sure, her responses, her reactions, are slower than usual. But I blame it on the alcohol. Until she agrees to give up scotch and brandy, there's not much any one can do about it. Not unless she's committed. Is that what you want, Mrs. Lundberg, for your neighbor to be committed?"

"Of course not," Piper said. *Let it go. Just let it go.* "They dragged her from the pool today. Literally dragged her."

He nodded. "Yes, she said her caregivers might have acted impulsively in the pool, but they were afraid she was trying to drown herself. Drastic actions call for drastic measures."

"You said this caregiver has excellent credentials?"

"I said that, yes."

"And you know her personally?" she pressed.

"She worked at the clinic. I don't know her well, but the head nurse recommended her. I trust Avidon. After reviewing her file and asking around at the hospital, we were all satisfied that she was competent. I'm fond of Mrs. Squire, that's why I came out this afternoon. Like you, I don't want anything bad to happen to her."

"Doctor, when I spoke with you at the clinic, you mentioned a housekeeper, Sybil's housekeeper. Do you know her name or where I might get in touch with her?"

She saw him staring past her head, his expression intent, grim. She turned, following his gaze across the room to the corner window where the telescope and a camcorder stood on separate tripods, their lens's pointed in the direction of the Squire mansion.

"I suggest you accept the situation and move on, Mrs. Lundberg. Maybe concentrate on your own business."

She showed him out the door. When the door shut behind him, she added under her breath, "Thanks for nothing."

The next day she received a scented note card in the mail. The initials S and S in an ornate scroll on the letterhead and the back of the envelope left no question regarding the sender.

> Dear Mrs. Lundberg,
>
> Thank you for your concern in the matters of my personal affairs, but rest assured I neither need nor want your unwelcome assistance.
>
> MYOB.
>
> Forever Yours,
> Sybil Squire

MYOB. *Mind your own business.* The note was meant to make her back off. Yet Piper wasn't buying into it. Strange for Sybil to use MYOB and not write it out. Sybil was in danger. She knew it as sure as she knew Sybil was being forced to take medication and that she did not give herself a black eye.

She reread the note, pausing at the salutation. Forever Yours.

Forever Yours? That was peculiar. In all her publicity photos, she signed off with "Sincerely yours." Forever Yours was her third movie, a film about insanity and murder. She compared the handwriting with that of the publicity photo she'd autographed two weeks ago. The handwriting looked the same, but even more strange was that she had autographed the publicity photo Forever Yours as well. Piper hadn't noticed that before.

What did it mean? Was Sybil trying to tell her something? Or, was Piper looking for threats where none existed?

CHAPTER 12

The Star Tattler—August 1952 [Archive]

> *Guess who was spotted at a Dude Ranch in Reno last week, awaiting the required six-week residency? Not the western-star-turned-rebel, CW, but his platinum-haired wife, who is rumored to be in a delicate condition. CW broke down the door of a mutual friend demanding to see his missing wife. The friend set her dogs on him.*
> *CW, darling, you need help.*

—*Cricket Summers: Columnist to the Stars*

SYBIL SQUIRE WAS THE distraction that kept Piper from dwelling on her pending divorce. The papers had been served on Gordon and the process was in motion. Gordon's only response had been to send her an unpaid dentist bill.

At Les Deux, over wine, the words came gushing out. Piper filled Lee in on the last several days, Sybil's shiner, and her call to Dr. Lowdell.

"There's obviously a connection between the visits to the bank and the Squire estate," Lee said. "Crimes against the elderly have become big business in America, especially fraud."

"If they're mistreating her and stealing from her, they're being very transparent about the whole thing. That's the part I don't understand."

"Then they'll get caught."

"Before or after Sybil is dead?"

"I doubt they'll go that far. I'm missing all the mystery and intrigue. I want to come over and play spy with you. I'll bring my own telescope." Lee blew a kiss at two rival agents from CAA who stood chatting near the gurgling water tank in the restaurant's patio. "What about that mystery car cruising your neighborhood?"

Piper realized she hadn't seen the dark car with the tinted windows in weeks.

"I think it belonged to them. Before worming their way in as her caregivers, they'd staked out the house and neighborhood."

"So it wasn't the Gorgon after all?"

"Gordon never bothered to contact me, let alone try to get me back. I was such a sucker. I could've continued to stay with the asshole until he traded me in on a younger, more impressionable sucker. Lee, how could I have married such a cold, manipulative man?"

"You have a good heart. You're kind and trusting. Everyone is exposed to someone like Gordon in his or her lifetime. It's a rite of passage. Move on."

Since the Vogt's departure, Piper kept a running correspondence with them via the internet. She collected their mail and sent them a copy of whatever she thought important, faxing or scanning it into the computer. One day after scanning several pieces of mail to the Vogt's, Belle e-mailed back:

The letter you sent in that last batch was from Sybil Squire's former housekeeper. Seems she's concerned about Lady Squire. Because of your preoccupation with our tragic leading lady, I trust you'll want to follow up on this. A bit of advice, Piper, the less contact with the neighbors and their affairs, the better. It's not your concern.

Belle

Piper nearly jumped out of her chair. The housekeeper was someone she very much wanted to connect with. If she were concerned about Sybil, that made two of them. She could be her biggest ally. Together, they had a better chance of finding out what was going on over there. Piper dug through the morning mail until she found the letter signed by Vera Wade.

She paused for a moment before calling. Belle's advice was equivalent to Sybil's "mind your own business." Belle wasn't here. She didn't see what Piper saw. She quickly dialed the phone number at the bottom of the letter before she could change her mind.

It rang and rang. On the tenth ring, someone picked up.

"My name is Piper Lundberg. I'm calling about Sybil Squire."

"What's that about Sybil Squire?" she said.

"I live next door…in the guesthouse."

"Yes. Yes. Hello? Hello, are you still there?" she said, her voice rising with excitement.

"I'm here."

"I can't tell you how happy I am to get your call. The worry's been making me just sick. Sybil, er, Mrs. Squire, how's she doing, do you know? Have you seen her or talked to her lately?"

"Yes. I'm worried too." Piper tried to tell her what had transpired in the last few weeks, but most of what Piper said was lost to the woman, garbled because of her hearing aid.

"Look, I'm coming over there," Vera said. "We gotta talk face-to-face."

Piper paced the small living room, waiting. Black clouds rolled in and the wind picked up, whining under the eaves, blowing gusts strong enough to rattle the windows. Another storm was on the way. She waited, training the telescope on the narrow streets that snaked throughout the neighborhood. She could see a stretch of Sunset Boulevard.

An hour later, as the last glimmer of daylight faded, the familiar battered green VW chugged up the hill. It shuddered to a noisy stop in front of the Squire house. Vera Wade climbed out, the teased red hair—faded to an orange hue-- blew around wildly in the wind. She wore purple tights and a long pink t-shirt with a picture of two big-eyed kittens on the front.

She walked up the driveway toward Piper's place, slowing to look at the Squire mansion. She stopped, took a piece of gum from her lime-green purse, unwrapped it, and stuck it into her mouth. The wind snatched the wrapper from her fingers. With the rubber sole of her orthopedic shoes--the only thing about her that appeared stodgy and sensible--she stomped down on it before it could blow away. After depositing the wrapper into her purse, she continued up the driveway.

Piper had liked Vera the moment they met, the day she came to her door with an invitation to coffee. Not exactly the sort she would have expected to be a loyal, long-time housekeeper to a famous, reclusive star. Then again, loyalty came in all shapes and sizes.

After greeting Vera on the deck, she ushered her inside. The strong wind at her back pressed her along amid a swirl of eucalyptus leaves.

She stood on the hardwood just inside the door, smoothing down her flyaway hair with both hands. "That's a pretty big computer," Vera said pointing at the editing bay in the dining area.

"It's what I use to edit film. It's my job."

Vera nodded. "I should have thought to call you myself. You seemed to care about Mrs. Squire. It showed that day when you came for coffee. With you living right next door, well, you'd know as good as anybody if something funny was going on over there."

"That's an understatement."

She accepted a Heineken, waved away the glass, and drank straight from the bottle. She sat on the edge of the couch, her body poised for action, like someone not used to sitting for long periods of time.

Piper pulled up the ottoman and sat in front of her. "What happened? Why did you stop working for her?"

She adjusted her hearing aid by twisting a finger inside one ear. "I was told I wasn't needed no more. I went to visit her every day in the hospital and she never, not once, said anything about canning me. No one was more surprised than yours truly when I showed up that morning and this woman, the one they sent home with her, says 'She don't need you no more.'"

"And you accepted that?"

"Hell no. I told that stuck-up nurse that I don't take orders from her or nobody but the mistress. I told her if Mrs. Squire wants to let me go, she's gotta be the one to say so."

"And did she?"

Vera nodded. "I had to wait awhile, but Sybil signed my paycheck and handed it to me personally. That gal made it out for her cause Sybil's hands were still bandaged from the burns, but I watched her sign it. You coulda' knocked me over with a canary feather. Twenty years I worked for her, all day, five days a week. Sometimes on the weekends if she needed me. The only reason I wasn't a live-in is 'cause of Nutmeg. Nutmeg's my cat. Cats and canaries don't mix. Those birds are her life, you know? They're what kept her going all these years—her birds and me. We was friends. Good friends. She don't have much to do with people." Vera paused. "'Cept you. She took to you."

"She did? She said that?"

"Yeah. She don't invite people over unless she likes them. She talked about you that day I picked her up at the bank. You reminded her of someone from her past."

Her grandmother. Vera's words warmed her.

Since meeting Sybil, she had reread both biographies and every article written about her. There were plenty of discrepancies, but one thing remained undisputed. Sybil's life had been fraught with selfish, abusive, and deceptive people. People she loved, people who should have loved and protected her, but instead had hurt her. First her mother, then her father, then her first husband.

Now it seemed to be happening again. Only this time the villains were preying on an elderly Sybil.

"Do you know anything about these people living in her house?" Piper asked.

"Nothing, not a danged thing. She said if she wanted to stay in her own house, she had to have live-in help, something about Social Services setting it up."

"And that was it? She cut you off?"

She made a sour face. "I call, and that one over there," she tossed her head in the direction of the Squire house, "tells me the mistress will call me back. She don't call back. Except . . ." Vera leaned forward and lowered her voice. "Except that one night. She called me out of the blue. It was real late. I was sleeping. By the time I got my hearing aid adjusted so's I could get what she was saying, she was gone. I called back, but the line was busy an' stayed busy all night. Ain't been able to reach her since."

"When was that? Do you remember what night?"

The woman closed her eyes, deep in thought. "It was the night one of her old movies came on the tube. I watched it, like I always do when she's on. Then, by golly, she calls. I thought she might've wanted to talk about the movie. We used to do that, y'know, watch them together when they came on AMC, the matinees mostly. If one came on in the evening, we hashed it over the next day. She liked to tell me all about the location, or about the funny things that happened, bloopers, stuff like that. It was getting so I knew most of the stories."

Two of her movies had aired in the past month, *Delta Queen* and *Shady Lady*. "Shady Lady?" Piper asked.

"Yeah, that's the one, Shady Lady. She liked that one. Liked any roles where she got to be a tough gal with a soft heart. That one sure had meat to it."

Piper pulled up a TV guide on the internet, looking for the night *Shady Lady* had aired. Saturday. Saturday night at eleven p.m.

The night Piper found her wandering the garden in the rain.

"She has a black eye," Piper told Vera. "A shiner to rival all shiners."

"A shiner, huh? *They* do that to her?"

"She told her doctor she fell in the pool. He believes her. I don't. Would she lie to him?"

"Oh, honey, you bet she would. If it served her, she'd lie to the Pope. Drinkers and junkies live on lies. She's both. I ain't telling stories out of school. It's common knowledge that she's got problems where booze and pills are concerned. One time this quack doctor told her she had an addictive brain. That tickled her pretty good. 'Addictive brain? So that's what it is, is it?' she said and laughed and laughed." Vera shook her head from side to side. "She told me in the hospital that she wasn't responsible for the fire that put her there. That's a lie. She didn't want to lose her independence. She was afraid they wouldn't let her go back home if they knew she'd passed out and started the fire herself."

Piper leaned forward eagerly. "What did she say about the fire?"

"She said she blacked out, but not from booze. Claimed she hadn't had enough to make her pass out. She says she came to in her chair, couldn't move a muscle, not even her head. She swore she saw someone, a man, moving around her, doing something. Then she smelled smoke and, well, she blacked out again."

"Dr. Oates found her on the floor, not in the chair," Piper said.

"Don't put too much store in what she sees or thinks she sees, especially after she's been into the cups for a couple of hours. She gets confused."

It never occurred to Piper that the fire might have been caused by anyone other than Sybil. Now, groping, she shot questions at Vera. "Have you ever seen either of the two caregivers before? Had they been to the house? Did Sybil ever mention a Judith Avidon? What do you know—?"

"Hold it." Vera held up a hand to stop her. "One at a time. I didn't hear half a what you said."

"The caregivers, had you seen them before she went to the hospital?"

She shook her head. "I only saw the one woman, the one with dark hair and eyes. But I never saw her before that day."

"There's a man. Asian, I think, in his mid thirties, resembles Mr. Moto."

"Mr. Moto, huh?" Vera stared into the beer bottle as if it might supply the answer. "You know, right before the fire there was a Jap-looking guy came out to the house. The day Sybil had you over for coffee. He came to the door alone, but someone else was waiting in the car. Couldn't tell if it was a man or a woman though."

"I take it she wasn't expecting him?"

"Oh no, the only reason she agreed to talk to him was 'cause he seemed to know certain things about her."

"Did you hear their conversation?"

"Uh-uh. She was being real secretive. They didn't talk long. She told him to move along and closed the door in his face."

Piper recalled Sybil's state of mind when she returned to pool side. Dazed. Bordering on shock.

"It really shook her up. She poured herself a drink right after, and it wasn't even noon. Sybil didn't usually start drinking till four cause once she got started she kept right on going till she couldn't lift the glass no more. Anyway, she has me take her to the bank. And from that bank to another bank. It was all real secret-like. Then the fire happened." Vera leaned forward, grabbing Piper's arm. "You think this Moto guy might have something to do with what's going on over there? Him and that snooty one?"

"Yes."

Vera bounded up from the couch and crossed the room to the telescope. She made a clumsy attempt to look into the eyepiece before giving up and just staring out the window, hands planted on hips. "I'm going over there."

"I doubt if they'll let you see her."

"They let you in, why wouldn't they let me in?"

"I threatened to call Social Services. I don't think threats will work now. The authorities came out and did nothing."

"Well, I ain't taking no for an answer." She marched across the room, pulled a key from her purse and held it up proudly. "I never handed it over like Miss High n' Mighty ordered me to. I said I'd give it to Sybil if that's what she wanted."

"Look," Piper said, her tone becoming stern, "if you get caught using that key to get inside, you could be in real danger, especially if they had something to do with that fire. I don't trust either one of them."

"I got this too." She dug deeper and pulled out a canister of pepper spray the size of a cigarette lighter.

Piper opened her mouth to protest, but Vera cut her off.

"Don't worry, I ain't about to stir up no hornet's nest over there. I ain't nobody's fool. I just want to get in long enough to talk to Sybil and make my offer."

"What offer?"

"My offer to move in with her. My little Nutmeg passed. Twenty years I had that sweet girl—in cat years that's over a hundred, y'know--but now she's gone." She blinked tears away. "So now there's no problem for the canaries. I can move in and take care of Sybil full-time. We'd be helping each other. I could sell my place. I got a little house not far from here. Or maybe we could find something else, something that suits the both of us."

Piper nodded, thinking that if her plan panned out it could be the perfect scenario. Then she remembered a similar plan in the black comedy *What Ever Happened to Baby Jane.* The housekeeper and her mistress plot to relocate and set up house without the evil sister. The housekeeper is ambushed in the upstairs hallway by a crazed Baby Jane, who bashes in her head with a hammer. Piper suddenly felt cold.

"Look, it isn't going to be that easy, Vera. Judith Avidon and her troll aren't giving up whatever hold it is that they might have over her. Not without a fight. If I'm right, we're talking about Sybil's estate. Control over her *and* her finances."

"We'll see. Those two don't know me. Ain't nobody gonna mess with my friend." She snapped the clasp on her purse and stood up.

Piper jumped up. "You're going over there *now*?"

"Yeah."

"I don't know, Vera. Let's think about this. Wait for—"

"Wait for what?" she cut in. "For them to blacken her other eye. Knock out some teeth, maybe. I shoulda come back a long time ago. Shoulda never left. I just up and walked away. I abandoned her to a couple of con artists. You don't even know her and you did more for her than me. I won't be able to live with myself if…if anything happens to her because of them two."

Piper couldn't argue with her.

She walked Vera to the door. Raindrops hit the windowpanes. Piper handed her the umbrella that hung on the hook by the door. "Here, take this. You can return it later."

Vera thanked her. "I'll stop in to give you a report before I head home. I figure you'll be more'n anxious to hear how it went."

"God, yes, I won't be able to sleep until I know." Piper touched her arm. "Vera, be careful, okay?"

She winked, opened the umbrella, and stepped out. The umbrella scraped along the side of the stucco wall as she made her way down the stairs to the bottom.

While Piper waited for Vera to return, she smoked a week's allotment of cigarettes, cursing when she ran out. She crumbled the empty pack and threw it at the door. Too much nicotine had made her queasy. She sat on the floor, her back propped against the side of the sofa, using her knees to support her head, and waited.

When she awoke, the night was dead silent. The rain and wind had stopped.

She rubbed her eyes, licked her dry lips. Her mouth tasted of stale smoke, acrid and bitter. She stretched the cricks from her neck where the muscles had bunched into tight knots. Outside, the driveway and street glistened from the rain. The VW was gone.

Piper scrambled to her knees, pressing her palms flat against the cold panes in the door. Her breath fogged the glass. She swiped at the condensation, straining to see what she knew was no longer there. When had Vera gotten into her car and left? How could she have not heard the sound of that noisy, sputtering engine?

She found the scrap of paper with Vera's number on it, grabbed the phone and stabbed at the numbers. After seven rings, she looked at the clock on the table. Midnight. If Vera was home in bed, she might not hear the phone ringing. Three more rings and she hung up.

Why didn't she come back here? Vera knew she'd be waiting. Knew she'd be worried. Piper told her she wouldn't be able to sleep until she checked back.

She made a fried egg sandwich, took one bite, and chewed. Her churning stomach needed something to settle it. It didn't help. She spit it into the sink and tossed the sandwich into the trash.

CHAPTER 13

AFTER ONLY A FEW hours sleep, Piper began the first of many calls to Vera Wade's house at six a.m. She called every hour until four that afternoon. The drapes in the Squire house remained closed all day, the canaries' silent. A gray haze settled over the hills.

She looked up Vera's address on the letter she'd sent to Belle and drove in heavy rush-hour traffic to a seedy neighborhood near downtown Los Angeles. The tiny wood frame house was at the end of the block on a narrow street with wide potholes and no sidewalks. The potholes were filled with water from the previous night's rain. She zigzagged down the street like a drunken driver trying to avoid them. Vera's house was one of the better-kept ones in the neighborhood. At least the crabgrass was green. Pink and yellow dahlias bloomed among the overgrown shrubs bordering the house. The sight of the old VW parked in the carport should have given her a sense of relief. Instead, she felt her stomach twist into a knot.

In the yard next door, a large black dog, one of those mixed killer breeds, barked and strained to jump the chain link fence when she walked up the gravel driveway to Vera's house. The fence shook and rattled with each thrust of the dog's heavy body. In the shade of the carport, she touched the back of the VW, over the engine compartment. The metal was cold.

The back door was three steps from the car. Red-and-white-checked cafe curtains hung from the kitchen window. By rising up on her tiptoes, she could see inside. No sign of life in the kitchen. A coffee maker sat empty and clean. The kitchen table and sink were free of dishes. An assortment of fruit filled a hand-painted bowl.

Piper knocked with the edge of her fist, hoping Vera could hear her. She called out and knocked several more times before trying the knob. The hinges creaked as she opened the door.

"Vera?" she called out, leaning over the threshold. "Vera, are you here? It's Piper. Piper Lundberg. Hel-lo?"

She stepped in, leaving the door open behind her. The last thing she wanted to do was frighten the woman in her own home, possibly getting a dose of pepper spray in the face. Living alone in a high-risk neighborhood, coupled with a hearing impairment, could make her even more jittery to unexpected sound or movement. As she inched her way through the house, she called out to Vera. The house was neat and clean, appearing to have had a sole occupant for many years. Surfaces worn thin or smooth from repeated cleaning. Cooking and animal odors long ago absorbed into the walls, woodwork, and fibers. A large print of The Last Supper hung above the couch. On a corner table was a shrine of sorts of Mary, Jesus, and angel figurines surrounded by candles and a large crucifix.

Piper walked down the warm, airless hallway and approached the last room in the house.

"Vera?" She pressed her cheek against the closed bedroom door and tapped lightly. "Vera, please answer if you're in there." She dialed Vera's number on her cell phone and listened to it ring in both the kitchen and the bedroom. The ringing increased her anxiety. Her skin tingled. It rang ten times before she hit the End button. She paused, wondering what to do next. To open the door to someone's bedroom, someone she'd met only twice, and waltz in uninvited seemed inappropriate and extremely risky. But she'd come this far. Something creaked, a door hinge or a floorboard. Twisting around, her heart pounding in her chest, she looked down the short hallway into the kitchen. The back door stood ajar, just as she had left it.

This is ridiculous, she told herself. *Dive or get off the frigging board.* A fly buzzed in her face. She waved it away.

Taking a deep breath, Piper turned the knob on Vera Wade's bedroom door and pushed it open. Her first thought was that the housekeeper's neatness stopped at the door of her bedroom. The bed was unmade, and the covers spilled off onto the floor into a rumbled heap. Several more flies buzzed in the heavy air. She took a step inside, still holding onto the knob. Above the bed hung a large framed print of a painting Piper remembered from her childhood. Guardian Angel and Children Crossing Bridge. Nana Ruth had hung a smaller version of the painting in Piper's bedroom. The angel was so beautiful. She'd stared at it for hours before falling asleep, secure in the knowledge that the angel would keep her safe.

On the floor a cat lay curled up asleep under the twisted covers, its orange fur partially exposed. No, not a cat. Vera's cat was dead.

Piper lifted a corner of the blanket. "Vera. . ." she whispered. "Vera?" she said again, louder. Unfortunately, Vera couldn't hear her. She would never hear anything again. Her lifeless eyes, half-open and glazed over, stared up at her.

She was dead. They had killed her. Vera and her plans to interfere had cost her her life.

She touched the woman's throat, her body, stiff and unyielding in death, was beyond resuscitation.

Piper backed away from the body. She glanced one last time at the print above the bed. *The guardian angel hadn't kept Vera safe.* Piper turned and ran out the door, down the hall and into the kitchen, wanting to get as far away from death as possible.

She grabbed the wall phone and looked at the receiver in her hand. It occurred to her this could be a crime scene, fingerprints, footprints, fibers and whatever else it took to reconstruct a crime. She swiveled in place. What had she touched? Had she contaminated anything? The phone was contaminated. She dialed 911.

"A woman is dead. She's Sybil Squire's housekeeper. I think...I think she's...been murdered."

CHAPTER 14

DETECTIVE BOWER WAS IN his late thirties or early forties, tall and lean with dark hair and eyes. Latin eyes that bored into Piper's and demanded her attention. In the past hour, she had told the detective what she knew about Vera Wade, her relationship to Sybil Squire, and her suspicions. The coroner was still in the bedroom examining the body. From what Piper gathered by their comments and the way no one appeared concerned about preserving the crime scene, both men had pretty much ruled out foul play. With the exception of the body being found on the floor, there was no sign of a forced entry, or a struggle, or any apparent trauma—blood, bruises, ligature marks on the deceased—components that cops looked for to determine the probability of a homicide.

"And you think this couple killed Ms. Wade?" the detective asked.

They sat at the kitchen table with its matching rooster and chicken theme. She lined up the salt and peppershakers. "It's a strong possibility they murdered her. She marches into what she considers to be a potentially dangerous situation and ends up—" Piper jabbed a finger toward the bedroom, "*dead*."

"Potentially dangerous," he said as if pondering the meaning. "And she was a threat to them—how?"

"I told you. She wanted to remove her friend, Sybil Squire, from the clutches of her caregivers, two people who don't seem to be giving their patient the best of care."

"I thought Ms. Wade was the ex-housekeeper?"

"Yes, that and more. Vera and Sybil were long-time friends. If anyone could have persuaded Sybil to fire the caregivers, it would have been Vera. That's why she went there last night, to offer her assistance, and suddenly she's dead. She still had a key to the mansion. She might have let herself in and . . ."

"And what?"

"And they ambushed and killed her."

"How?"

"I don't know. The woman is a nurse. She has medical training. She could have shot her up with some lethal drug. One that's...well, virtually undetectable."

"There, at the Squire residence? Are you suggesting they killed her and then brought her back here?"

She nodded. "Why not? They kill her and bring her body home so that it looks like she died of natural causes in her own bedroom. If that's what happened, then their plan seems to be working, now doesn't it?"

He rubbed his temple then made notes in a notebook cupped in his palm. "If you think they're ruthless murderers, why aren't you afraid of them?"

"I am now. We've already had a couple run-ins."

"Such as?"

Piper told him some of what had transpired since she moved in, repeating what she'd told Dr. Lowdell only days ago. "They know I'm on to them. So I have reason to be concerned. Especially now, if they're responsible for Vera's death."

"Well, don't worry, we won't let on that you pointed a finger in their direction."

She felt more apprehensive than ever. "You *are* going to check them out, aren't you, to see if they have criminal records? Talk to Mrs. Squire—*privately?*"

"Yeah, we'll look into it. I assure you, Ms. Lundberg, if there's any indication of foul play, we will check them out thoroughly."

If? Her apprehension became compounded by exasperation. Why didn't they just seal the area until they could do a proper autopsy? Then there would be little chance of contaminating what could be a potential crime scene. She told the detective as much.

"You're in the crime field, are you, Mrs. Lundberg?" he asked.

"No. But I read. I watch TV."

"Did you play a detective on TV?"

"Very funny."

He leaned back in his chair. "These days everybody's an expert."

Piper heard voices in the hallway, wheels rolling on hardwood. An attendant pushed the gurney that carried the shrouded remains of Vera Wade. The coroner came through ahead of the gurney.

"Looks pretty routine to me," he said to the detective after glancing at her. "She was under a physician's care for her heart. Nitro." He shook a prescription bottle. "But we'll open her up just to be sure."

She sat back in the chair, relief flooding through her. Finally someone was going to do something.

"The deceased has been dead for at least twelve hours, maybe as long as sixteen. Rigor is pretty much complete."

"You last saw her alive at what time, Mrs. Lundberg?" Detective Bower asked.

"At eight p.m. But it wasn't until around midnight when I noticed her car was gone."

"Can you be more specific?"

"When I fell asleep around ten it was there. It was gone at twelve."

"So she was still alive at ten."

"Unless, of course, she didn't drive herself home."

The detective turned to the doctor. "Doc, any indication the body was moved postmortem?"

"Lividity doesn't seem to have been compromised. But we'll know more at the post exam."

"They could've drugged her, drove her home, and killed her here."

The two men exchanged looks.

"Like I said, I'll know more when I do the post. No point speculating about it now." The coroner followed the gurney and attendant out the door to the waiting van.

Detective Bower tapped his notebook. "Sybil Squire was big in the fifties. I remember her. She played a gun moll in that gangster movie back when those kinds of movies were really hot. What was the name of that film?"

"*Shady Lady.*"

He rubbed his chin. "Yeah, maybe."

Trust me, she wanted to say, but didn't.

"Mrs. Lundberg, if you're so concerned about this actress's welfare, why don't you call Social Services again?"

"And say what? Mrs. Squire won't admit that she's being mistreated or that she's in any danger whatsoever."

"Then I'd say let it be. You can't help people who don't want to be helped."

"I can't believe you're saying that, Detective. I'm sure you've been involved in more than your share of domestic abuse cases. The battered spouse refusing to press charges."

"Laws have changed. Now we can arrest the abuser without the victim's say-so. But we have to be relatively certain a crime has been committed. Eyewitnesses, obvious signs of physical abuse, and so on. But in the end it's up to the abused party to make a clean break."

"What if there are no eye witnesses? What if she has no choice but to pretend to be okay? Detective Bower, you don't live next door to her. You don't see what I see. She's deteriorated considerably since I first laid eyes on her. I think she wants help, she's just scared." Piper sat forward. "Look, I am not one of those nosy, meddlesome neighbors. In fact, I pretty much keep to myself and try to mind my own business. Only this is different. There's something going on over there. I just can't ignore it, now can I?"

He stood, touched her elbow to bring her to her feet. "You go on home. We'll take it from here. We appreciate your involvement. If you hadn't found Mrs. Wade, she might've lain in there unnoticed for a long time. Do you know if she had family we can notify?"

Piper shook her head. "Sybil Squire was a close friend-- she'd know."

He blinked, then scratched out something in his notebook. "I'll pay her a visit."

The detective gave Piper his card, then walked her to the back door. He stayed behind to lock up the house. The killer dog next door jumped at the chain link fence when she stepped out of the kitchen door, making Piper jump. As she passed the VW, she looked inside, remembering the umbrella she'd lent her and wondering if it might be in the car. She didn't see the umbrella, but something else caught her eye.

Barely visible under the seat on the passenger's side was a lime green strap. Vera carried a lime green purse. She looked back at the house. The detective was nowhere to be seen. The last patrol car had just pulled away and the coroner's van was backing out onto the street. She opened the car door and pulled on the strap, hauling the purse out from under the seat. It flopped open. She rummaged through it, looking for the two things Vera had bragged about. The two things that had given her the courage to stick her neck out, and may have cost her her life. The house key and the metal canister of pepper spray. Both were gone.

"What've you got there?" Detective Bower said, coming up behind her. The dog barked louder.

Piper's hands shook, but she managed to respond in a normal voice. "Her purse. It's here in the car. Why leave it in the car? Women don't do that."

"Hmm." He lifted it out by the strap. "Thank you. I'll just put this inside the house for now."

Piper nodded toward the barking dog. "You might want to ask the neighbors if they saw or heard anything. That dog would've woke up the whole neighborhood."

"I'm on it."

She turned away then turned back. "Last night I lent Vera my umbrella. She took it with her to the Squire house and—"

He cut her off. "If I come across it I'll let you know. Mrs. Lundberg, LAPD doesn't need any amateur sleuths. Go home. Please."

She climbed into her car and sat, staring straight ahead, wondering how someone could be so alive one day and gone the next. Had Vera died because she got in the way? She was sure the nurse and her sidekick were responsible--directly or indirectly. They wouldn't get away with it. Not if she could help it.

She looked up to see the detective staring at her through the front window of the house, his head tipped to the side as though trying to figure out what she was up to. There was something about the man that told her they'd possibly butt heads. If he did his job, everything would be fine and dandy. *If* he did his job.

That night when Piper climbed into bed, she considered the possibilities. Perhaps Vera had left on her own volition, was followed home and killed there. Or, before she could talk to Sybil, she was overtaken and killed at the mansion. However, if they'd moved the body, it would've shown up through lividity—the blood settling in the lowest area of the body. Or she could have been rendered unconscious, driven home and killed in her own bedroom. Either way, It had been a surprise attack. What little she knew of Vera Wade, her spunky nature, her loyalty to her mistress, told her she wouldn't have gone down without a fight.

She awoke to what sounded like footsteps on the deck, stopping at the glass door. Her heart raced. She rolled off the Murphy bed in the pitch-black room and kneeled on the floor, her eyes darting to the windows and the door. She crawled to the door, to the light switch on the wall and flicked on the porch light. There was no sound of footsteps running away. Had she dreamed hearing the steps? She separated the vertical slats and peered out onto the deck. No one stood at her door. Feeling braver now, she hurried from window to window and peered out. The deck was empty.

She left the porch light burning. Knowing sleep would be impossible, she dragged the club chair across the room to the corner windows, the ones facing the Squire house. There she spent the rest of the long, long night.

By morning, despite the fog clinging to the basin, the mere presence of daylight lifted her spirits. Vera's death scene suppositions began to break down bit by bit, a Swiss cheese scenario filled with holes. After she finished her second cup of coffee, she called Lee. She had to tell someone or she'd burst.

"Okay, that's settles it, I'm coming over," Lee said. "Just have to clear my calendar."

"And do what? Have a nail biting contest? Look, I'll be fine. I think my imagination got the best of me. I even thought I heard someone on the deck last night." She opened the door and stepped out onto the deck.

"Then meet me for lunch," Lee said. "One-thirty at The Grill."

"I don't know. I'll try." At the threshold of the door, a large snail lay crushed on the wooden planks. The snails had overtaken the flowers in the planter box attached to the railing, so she was used to seeing them on the deck. "Gotta go, bye." The dead snail had not been there when she went to bed last night. She squatted down. Leading away from the snail, every few feet, was a circle of slime. Whoever had stepped on it had squished it good, carrying the slime on the bottom of his or her shoe. The trail led to the edge of the staircase and down several steps.

Piper pulled out the short stack of mail from the mailbox. The Squire's mailbox stood only a few feet from the Vogt's, separated by the property wall. Since moving in, she'd never run into any occupants of the mansion at the mailboxes. So when she heard footsteps on the pavement she retreated behind the wall. Her skin tightened at the base of her neck. If she were a cat, the hairs would be standing on end.

Mr. Moto bypassed the mailbox, walked to the edge of the street and bent over, inspecting something on the pavement. A wad of something pink. Gum? Vera's gum? With a dry raspy cough, he picked it up and pocketed it. Piper edged closer. A twig snapped under her foot. Moto jerked around. She stood frozen in place staring back into his face. His eyes behind the round glasses were inflamed and bloodshot. The skin red.

As calmly as possible, Piper turned and walked slowly up the driveway, sorting through the mail. She wasn't going to let him see she was scared. When she reached the safety of the guesthouse, she hurried inside, locked the door, and dropped down on the couch. She buried her face in her hands. Behind her closed lids, she saw his raw, bloodshot eyes. Eyes that looked ravaged by a strong chemical. What chemical? Chlorine from the pool? Not strong enough to do that kind of damage. Pepper spray. Had Vera managed to get off a shot? If so, where was the canister? If the police searched for and found the canister at the Squire house, it would prove that Vera had been there and that Mr. Moto had taken a hefty dose of it in the face. That would certainly suggest foul play. Her mind reeled.

She wasted no time calling the number Detective Bower had given her. He came on the line immediately. She told him about the pepper spray and how the male caregiver looked like someone who'd taken a direct hit.

"You never mentioned anything about pepper spray," the detective said.

"Well, it didn't seem important until I saw the guy next door wheezing and all teary-eyed and I remembered the pepper spray canister Vera showed me, which later was missing from her purse. It…well…all came together then."

"How do you know the spray was missing from her purse?"

"I looked. In her purse…in the car yesterday. When she was at my house, she showed me a house key and the pepper spray. The key was going to get her inside, and maybe it did. The pepper spray was going to protect her. Well, obviously it didn't."

"This man who you think just committed homicide, who took a shot of mace in the eyes, strolls out to pick up the mail?"

Moto holding the pink wad crossed her mind. "Wait—" she said to Bower. She took a moment to assimilate Moto's actions. He was not collecting the mail. He was picking something up off the street. What looked like a wad of gum. Only it wasn't gum. It was a hearing aid. *Vera's hearing aid.*

"Did anyone find Mrs. Wade's hearing aid?" she blurted out.

"What?"

"She wore a hearing aid. I think that's what the Asian man was picking up when I came up on him. That's where her car was parked. Was a hearing aid with her personal effects at the morgue or the house?"

"I don't know anything about a hearing aid."

"Ask. Will you please ask?"

"Okay, I'll check into it," the detective said. "Anything else?"

"No. Not that I can think of."

"Good—oh, and Mrs. Lundberg?"

"Yes?"

"Let me remind you that by digging around where you shouldn't be digging around, you could be tampering with vital evidence, making it of no use to us. If there is a crime, your meddling could set the guilty party free on something as simple as a technicality. You wouldn't want to do that, now would you?"

"Well…no."

"Leave it to us. I promise you there will be a full investigation."

She wanted to believe him, but somehow she wasn't convinced. Gordon would've insisted she back off. Nana would've encouraged her to follow her gut. "Have they done the autopsy?"

"I doubt it. They're pretty backlogged at county."

"Ask them to look for pepper spray on her hands."

"Goodbye, Mrs. Lundberg."

The days passed with nothing further from Detective Bower about Vera's death. Four-twenty a.m. and unable to sleep, Piper rose out of bed and went to the window. Gazing at the house next door had became a habit, as automatic as brushing her teeth or making the bed, though she didn't expect to see anything, not tonight, not so soon after Vera's death. So when she caught sight of someone below, it snapped her awake. A flashlight beam crawled over and under the bushes next door. The half moon in the cloudless sky illuminated the area enough for her to see that the bearer of the flashlight looked to be male. Mr. Moto? What was he looking for at four in the morning?

The light continued to play over the shrubs near the rear door. What was he looking for? The pepper spray canister? The umbrella?

She grabbed the camcorder and began filming. Without night vision apparatus, the chances of catching anything more than the beam of light was remote, but it was all she had. The man bent and retrieved something. He held it under the flashlight beam. Whatever it was, it fit between his thumb and forefinger. Small, the size of Vera's canister. Headlights approaching the intersection at the corner washed over the house, illuminating the man briefly. The light held long enough for her to make out the back of a bandana-wrapped head. She gasped. *How many people were involved?* The car headlights passed, the flashlight beam went out, and the man was gone. She knew for certain, along with him, a piece of vital evidence would also disappear.

CHAPTER 15

Sybil Squire Husband Dead: *The manner of producer Paul Winger's death was grisly, serving only to fuel the rumors. Why did Winger kill himself? Who was the mystery woman at the couple's Pacific Palisades home that evening? What did Sybil Squire's ten-year-old daughter witness that fateful night?... "Everyone wants to make something sensational out of this tragedy," said Transworld Artists studio executive Edward Hill to reporters at a news conference. "This is real life, folks, not a horror show."—Los Angeles Times.*

The callousness displayed by the media regarding the tragic death of her second husband only proved that the public did not accept that Sybil had a real life.

—Excerpt from the biography of Sybil Squire: The Platinum Widow *by Russell Cassevantes.*

ON THE THIRD FLOOR of the glass and steel building of the Parker Center in downtown Los Angeles, in the Robbery-Homicide Division squad room, a female patrol officer directed Piper to the desk of Detective second-grade Jason Bower. The squad room, with its old wooden filing cabinets, outdated venetian blinds, and bright overhead fluorescent tube lights, gave Piper the feeling she was on a 50s film noir movie set. The men in the room were all dressed conservatively in dark suits and white shirts. Detective Bower, leaning against his desk with a phone to his ear, wore a deep blue suit and matching tie. He looked over at Piper, a surprised look on his face. He pulled a metal chair around and indicated for her to take a seat. He finished his conversation, hung up the landline, and turned to her.

"Mrs. Lundberg?"

"Detective Bower, I was wondering if you'd heard anything from the coroner. It's been over a week."

"Coroner?"

"The Vera Wade case."

"I know what case you're referring to." He shuffled through some papers and files in an 'in' box and those on the desktop. "No. I haven't gotten the coroner's report yet."

"Did you mention in your report to the coroner to look for pepper spray on her hands?"

"You could've phoned, Mrs. Lundberg, you didn't have to come all this way to ask me what I'm doing on the case."

"I thought I did. My call didn't seem to be very effective."

"Any new problems over there? Anything suspicious?"

"Yes." She crossed her arms and told him about the bandana-headed man with the flashlight at the Squire house in the wee hours of the morning.

"Oh?"

"I videotaped it, but it was dark." Piper brightened. "Maybe you have equipment that can enhance the footage. I can email you a copy of the video."

"Why don't you do that?" He glanced at his watch, checked his cell phone, and clipped it to his belt. "Mrs. Lundberg, I have to be somewhere now."

Fine. He didn't know how persistent she could be.

She made her way through the squad room to the elevator. A moment later Detective Bower joined her. The elevator came and they rode down to the ground floor in silence. When they exited the building, Piper stopped on the steps and asked, "Have you spoken with Mrs. Squire yet?"

He shook his head. "I'm in homicide, Mrs. Lundberg. There's nothing I can do until the death is declared a homicide. If the coroner hasn't completed the autopsy, I'll push him to move it up. That's the best I can do for now."

Piper suddenly became lightheaded. The ground beneath her feet rolled and shifted. Fifty yards away on the sidewalk, a flower vendor's cart shook, one-by-one the potted plants and cellophane wrapped bouquets tumbled to the concrete. Cars in the parking lot moved independently, as if on a suspension bridge, swaying from side to side. Piper's vertigo increased, making her sick to her stomach.

"Quake," Detective Bower said under his breath.

She looked up in terror at the towering glass building. The sunlight shimmered on the moving panes. Piper froze. All that glass. All that steel. If it collapsed…Her heart pounded beneath her ribcage. She bit down on her lip as wild thoughts raced through her mind. She fell against the detective. Her knees buckled and she felt herself going down. A moment later, she was lifted by strong arms and propelled down the steps, away from the building and toward the open spaces of the parking lot. The ground calmed, but the shriek of car alarms, honking horns, and screams of frightened people waged on around her, sounding like a city under siege. Detective Bower held onto her. She smelled his aftershave and shampoo, and felt his warm breath on the side of her neck.

"Are you alright?" the detective asked, still holding tight to her.

Piper looked down at his arms, secure around her.

He dropped his arms and stepped back as if realizing the moment had passed and it had now entered into a different moment.

She nodded and leaned against a car. "I'm fine."

He touched the corner of her mouth. "You're bleeding."

Piper touched the inside of her lower lip. Blood covered her fingertips. "Bit it."

She reached into her purse for a tissue. "I have to get home. The bird will be going nuts."

"There's bound to be aftershocks. You should wait before going out on the freeway."

With trembling hands, she dabbed at the blood on her lip. The ground jerked under her feet. She grabbed the detective's arm.

"Aftershock. I'll wait here with you for a while."

She offered him a weak smile. "I'll take the side streets. I really have to get home."

He walked her to her car. From behind the wheel, she watched him walk away. He turned once to look back at her. She quickly started the engine and drove out of the lot, in the opposite direction.

The drive was slow. Uniformed police directed traffic at intersections where lights were malfunctioning or out completely. Utility trucks were everywhere. Helicopters patrolled overhead.

On a street corner, Piper passed a broken fire hydrant spurting water into the air while a group of kids ran through it. The children seemed unfazed by the earthquake, laughing and playing. Piper loved to watch kids play. Gordon would have complained about these kids in the street. He always had some observation about misbehaving children.

Gordon had wasted five of her prime years. She thought back to their honeymoon, at a restaurant in Costa Rica when a couple with their kids entered the dining room, the kids ranging in age from toddler to teen. Gordon stiffened and frowned, obviously upset by their presence. Piper should've realized then that he wasn't into kids or anything family oriented. The first friends of hers to be dropped from their social circle were the ones with kids. Then eventually he found fault with all her friends. It shouldn't have taken her so long to catch on. Looking back on it now, Piper was glad that he'd deceived her. For the past two years, while questioning the validity of their marriage and her love for him, she realized she did not want Gordon to be the father of her children.

Nearing home, the radio reported on the quake. Centered in a remote part of the valley, it was 5.8 on the Richter-scale. A dozen injuries, but no deaths. She wondered what she'd find at the Vogt's house. She did a mental inventory of the two residences. The editing systems alone were fragile and expensive. There were paintings, glassware and china, the usual. The high-strung cockatoo would be completely traumatized by an earthquake. Scared of his own shadow, he freaked out if someone so much as entered the room unexpectedly.

The neighborhood was quiet compared to the racket of car alarms that had immediately followed the quake in downtown Los Angeles. She passed the Squire house and wondered how Sybil had coped during the quake. Wondered how solid the mansion was and if there had been damage to the pricey collection of figurines. The figurines, she learned from a news source on the internet, had not been her collection after all, but that of her second husband, Alec McDaniel. Alec had been one of the leading stage actors of his time. While filming in New York for *Transworld Artists,* Sybil had gone to see him in the Broadway play, *Donnybrook Fair.* At the backstage party, it was love at first sight for the dramatic thespian, thirty years her senior. He proposed before the evening was over. Struggling to raise a one-year-old daughter, with creditors badgering her day and night, Sybil told a friend she could learn to love the rotund Irishman with the sad hound dog eyes. She never got the chance. He died on their wedding night.

The drapes were open in the front of the mansion, yet she saw no movement. She hadn't seen any movement inside since the night Vera had gone there. The place had been closed up tight, the canaries unnaturally silent.

She pulled into the Vogt's driveway, shut off the engine and stepped out of the car near the glass-paned doors. One of the double doors stood open a crack. If the alarm had gone off, it was silent now. It was possible the quake had shifted the foundation slightly and popped the lock. Just in case, she palmed her cell phone before pushing open the door and stepping inside. She listened for any sounds of an intruder. Stepping quietly, she made her way through the house. Debris covered the floor.

In the dining room, the contents of Belle's China cabinet resembled the inside of a kaleidoscope--colored glass in tiny pieces on every shelf. Prism-like, the shards cast an array of rainbow images on the walls. About a dozen items remained intact; a goblet here, several wine glasses and a decanter there, the rest reduced to rubble.

Dr. J was quiet for a change. She went in the opposite direction of where he perched in his cage. Once he spotted her, or even so much as heard her footsteps, he would squawk and screech, demanding her attention. There was plenty of time later to smooth his ruffled feathers.

From room to room, she surveyed the damage. Paintings and wall decorations hung askew on the walls. The books in the bookshelves had toppled into a heap on the hardwood planks. Plants and picture frames on the mantle and tabletops had tipped over or fallen to the floor. The disheveled condition of the rooms was to be expected after a quake of that magnitude. She saw nothing suspicious, nothing to indicate someone had broken in.

She had covered most of the main floor and was halfway up the stairway to the second floor when she heard the noise. It came from the vicinity of the kitchen, where Dr. J resided in the nook of the bay window. It was a manmade sound, a clanking of metal against metal. Not a sound a cockatoo would make. Her pulse accelerated. She backtracked, stepping over items lying on the floor in her path. She passed through the dining room into the kitchen. The refrigerator door stood open, food lay scattered on the floor. It wasn't the only door open. The one to the basement was also ajar. Another clank rumbled up out of the darkness beneath the house. Piper's body instantly primed itself for fight or flight. Adrenalin surged through her. The reasoning portion of her brain signaled her to back off, to run from the house and call the police.

She gripped her cell phone, backed up, thumbing the nine and the one. A shrill scream filled the kitchen, a scream so piercing she thought her eardrums would burst. She spun around in shock. From the floor tiles, a ghostly whiteness rushed at her, obscuring her vision and lashing against her face. More whiteness floated in the air around her head, surrounding her face, flapping wildly. Dr. J, his wings beating the air, struck out, sharp talons scratched her hand as she held it up in an attempt to protect herself. She stumbled backward, away from him, turning just as the basement door flew open and slammed against the wall with a bang. A man charged at her. Fast, furious. A man she'd never seen before. His hand, raised above his head, gripped a large wrench. She fell, landing hard on her tailbone on the unyielding floor. She ducked her head, her arms raised to protect her head and face from another attack.

Seconds passed. She waited for the blow, defenseless and terrified, too stunned to move. When nothing happened, no attack, no running footsteps, she lifted her head and looked up. The man stood with his legs stretched apart, the wrench raised, prepared for battle. Now she could see his face, and the expression on it was clearly one of alarm and confusion. The arm with the wrench dropped with a thump to his thigh.

"Holy shit, where'd you come from? You scared the hell out of me," he said, running fingers through his straight blond hair. He reached out to her. "I didn't know anyone was in the house. You okay?"

Piper grabbed onto a kitchen chair and pulled herself to her feet, keeping the chair between them. "Who are you? What are you doing in here?"

"Luke. Luke Monte. I'm the Vogt's handyman. Didn't they tell you about me?"

"How did you get in?"

He jiggled a key ring on his belt. "The key. I have my own. They travel a lot, so I look in on the place while they're gone. As soon as the ground settled today, I came right over to check for any damage. The security alarm was blaring away. I'm afraid I had to disconnect it. I think it shorted out."

She brushed at her backside and gingerly rotated her shoulder.

"Are you hurt?" he asked.

"Yes. No. I'll be all right," she said. "Can I see some ID, please?"

He pulled out his wallet and showed her his driver's license.

"I'm Piper Lundberg."

"Yeah, the Vogt's told me you were living in the apartment above the garage. I did some work up there before you moved in."

They stood face-to-face with nothing to say. Piper broke the silence first.

"How did the bird get out of his cage?" She looked toward the room where Dr. J was now back inside his cage, his safe haven, rocking back and forth.

"He was out when I came in. I tried to catch him, but he went psycho on me." He held up an arm crisscrossed with fresh scratches. "He's better than any guard dog."

"How long have you been here...in the house?"

"About thirty minutes. I didn't get any further than the basement. Broken water pipe. I got the leak stopped, but now I have to pump out the water down there. It's flooded." He sucked in his flat belly and slipped the wrench into the front of his tight fitting jeans. He bent, picked up a carton of orange juice, and put it in the refrigerator.

Piper returned the other food items to the refrigerator and closed the door. "I was on my way upstairs when I heard the clanging in the basement and came to investigate. I'll go ahead and check it now."

He nodded. "Look for large cracks and broken windows, that sort of thing."

Upstairs she found two cracked windows and a dozen fine, spider-like fissures in the plaster of two bedrooms. She returned downstairs to report what she'd found. Through the dining room window, she saw the handyman standing in the driveway with hands on his hips, staring up at something on the side of the house.

She joined him outside. "What is it?"

He pointed to the massive brick chimney. Halfway to the top of the tall chimney, on one of the double flues, a half dozen bricks had fallen away.

"That's gotta be repaired before the whole thing takes a notion to come down. And maybe with it that side of the house. Brick work is my specialty."

"I'll call the Vogts." She started for the guesthouse.

"Tell them I can get everything back into shape in no time. Tell them not to worry."

Piper forgot about the difference in time zones and woke up an intolerant and cranky Belle in the middle of the night in Hong Kong. After reporting on the earthquake and the damage to their Tudor home, Belle's annoyance turned to concern.

"Are you okay?"

"I'm fine."

"Dr. Jekyll? Did anything fall on his irascible head?"

"Your bird is fine and as nasty as ever. He scratched the handyman."

"Tell Luke to get a tetanus shot and add the bill to the repair invoice."

She told Belle about the interior damage, ending with the brick chimney and the handyman's concern about it crumbling.

"He knows what to do. Just take pictures of the damage and keep receipts."

"What about insurance? Should I file a claim?" Piper asked.

"We'll handle it," Belle said. "Have Luke ring us if you've any problems. He has our number. Oh, and Piper dear, remind him about the time difference, would you?"

"Sorry, I forgot. I'll let you get back to sleep."

"I'm wide awake now. Anything more on that poor dead woman, the widow's housekeeper?"

Piper had been keeping Belle informed through email. "No, nothing yet."

"Honey, be careful. Stay away from those neighbors. Leave it alone."

"Right." She paced the deck. The handyman pulled a pickup truck into the driveway, parking behind her car. She watched him carry a small pump into the house. Moments later, brackish water gushed out through a hose from the tiny basement window into the yard. "How's the shoot going?" she asked Belle.

"It could be better. The only thing that has cooperated is the weather. You didn't hear this from me, but we may be calling in a new director. A new director means . . ." she paused for emphasis ". . . a new film editor."

My pulse quickened. "Who's the new director?"

"Gary Ott."

Ott had approached Piper two weeks ago in the WB commissary. "You gotta be kidding. Belle—"

"It's still up in the air, so don't get too tickled yet. I'll keep you abreast of the situation."

"Thanks, Belle. You and Mick are the best."

"I know. Give Dr. J a big juicy kiss for me."

"And risk losing my nose. He'll have to settle for a slice of pineapple."

They said their goodbyes and Piper hung up. She leaned over the railing and watched as the water continued to gush from the hose, reminding her she had been neglecting her gardening. But for now, she told herself, she had damage control from the quake to keep her busy. Her place had taken a beating too. Books, glassware, and her collection of cassettes littered the floor. One of the windows facing the Squire house had cracked in half, from corner to corner. With nothing around it or hanging over it, the editing equipment had at least come away unscathed.

Piper emailed the video clip to Detective Bower and then started the cleanup in the guesthouse. With the Vogt's handyman at the main house ankle deep in water, tracking it through the kitchen and patio, she decided to wait until he had finished pumping out the basement before tackling the damage there. Since she had very few possessions, her place took no time at all. The most severe damage was to the window. The long crack looked like it would hold until the handyman could get to it. It had held up over a half dozen aftershocks. She patched it from the inside with a strip of duct tape.

With a full wastebasket, she went downstairs to the trash barrel. Luke Monte, taking the small water pump back to his pickup truck, called out, "I got the last of the water up," he said, tipping his head toward the basement. "If you want to get into the house, it's all yours."

She glanced at her watch. Five o'clock. "Are you done for the day?" she had told him that Belle had given him a green light on any repairs that needed doing.

"Not by a long shot, but I won't be in your way. If you need a hand with anything heavy or high up, give a holler."

"I will. Thanks."

"Oh, you're gonna need work gloves, there's broken glass everywhere."

She went upstairs and grabbed a pair of canvas gardening gloves. She turned to leave and ran smack into the handyman on her deck. One of his hands went around her waist to steady her, the other one gripped her upper arm.

She stepped away.

He thrust a pair of gloves toward her. "I found these in the basement."

She held up her pair.

He smiled and then looked past her to the inside. "That's not good, that cracked window. I'll get to it as soon as I can. Until I do, keep away from it."

An hour later, at the main house, she stood on the ladder in the library returning books to the top shelf of the floor-to-ceiling bookcase. Luke stood below, handing them to her, saving her the tedious chore of having to climb up and down the ladder for each volume. If the Vogts used any sort of cataloguing system for the placement of their books, they would have to rearrange them when they returned home.

Every so often, Luke became preoccupied by a book, reading from it while she waited with an outstretched hand. This time a volume of *Best Loved Plays by Shakespeare* had piqued his interest.

"Are you interested in Shakespeare or in play writing?" she asked.

"Screenwriting."

No surprise. Everyone in Hollywood and the greater LA area who could type Fade In, Fade Out, and Cut To was a screenwriter with a script. The reality of it was that only about one percent of these writers would ever have anything produced.

"Have you shown any of your scripts to Mick?"

"Naw. I like my job here. I don't want to blow it."

"Blow it how?"

"The first thing he said to me when he hired me was that if I was a writer or an actor, he didn't want to know about it."

That sounded like something Mick would say. With Mick, gruff was mostly bluff. Mick Vogt was Bambi reincarnated. She was a testament to his soft side.

"If you like, I'll read one of your scripts. If I think it's something Mick might be interested in, I'll put in a good word."

He grinned and looked away.

Later that afternoon while cleaning up in the kitchen, she tried to make amends with Dr. J for stepping on him earlier. She offered him his favorite fruit, but he ignored it. Instead, he watched her with a wary eye and kept his head down, his way of sulking.

"I said I was sorry." She reached through the bars and scratched his head. He leaned closer to her fingers, some of his defenses breaking down. "You're a pretty boy, Doc. Pretty pretty boy."

". . . oy," he said.

"Hey, you can do better than that. *Oy*, what's that? C'mon, talk to me. Tell me you forgive me. We're still buddies, right?"

He pulled back, rising up and wildly flapping his wings, then screeched. It took a second for her to discover what had riled him. Through the glass doors, she caught a glimpse of someone walking by in the direction of the guesthouse. It wasn't Luke. He was upstairs in the Vogt's bedroom, removing broken glass from the window frames. She dropped the pineapple slice into the cage and went outside.

She approached the man in the driveway. She recognized the detective from his thick, dark hair and tall, lean frame. He didn't look like a cop. He looked like an actor.

"Detective Bower, I was expecting a call, not a personal visit."

"Could we go somewhere and talk?" he asked.

He'd found something. Why come all this way in the aftermath of an earthquake unless he'd found something?

She took him upstairs to her place. He refused her offer of a drink. He seemed ill at ease, edgy.

"You're an editor?" He ran his hand over one of the monitors in the dining room.

"Yes." She stared at him. "You have something?"

"Mrs. Wade's body was released yesterday to Morningside Society for cremation."

"*What?*" The word *cremation* exploded in her head.

"The death was classified as natural causes. Her heart most likely, though it was not conclusive. The causes are not always conclusive. It's the coroner's call. Mrs. Wade's wishes were for her remains to be cremated. There was no reason not to comply with her last wishes once the body was released."

Piper was outraged. How could they be so cavalier about a possible murder case? "She was murdered. I know she was."

"The coroner makes that distinction, Mrs. Lundberg. He saw nothing to indicate foul play. I'm sorry."

"Even after what I told you?'

"There's not enough there to make a case. Even if they found something to indicate foul play, there still wasn't enough to put a criminal case together. I was hoping this would give you some closure."

"You mean some closure for you."

"Look, the woman wasn't brutally attacked and killed. You should feel better knowing that the people living next door to you are not vicious killers."

"That's your opinion."

"C'mon, Mrs. Lundberg, try to see--"

"The hearing aid—was it found?" she cut in brusquely.

"Not that I'm aware of."

"Did they check for pepper spray on her hands or body?"

He looked down at his entwined fingers. "This doesn't mean anything, so don't jump to conclusions--"

"What?"

"The coroner found traces of pepper spray on the deceased's hands. But she could have tested the canister to see if it was, well, full or functioning properly. It doesn't mean she used it in self-defense against an attacker."

"It doesn't mean she didn't."

"I'm sorry, Mrs. Lundberg. It's done. The body was cremated. There's nothing further we can do in that regard."

"Did you review the video I emailed to you? Didn't it look to you like the person in the video picked up a something resembling a mace canister?"

He shrugged. "It wasn't that clear. I think you saw what you wanted to see. The man could have picked up anything."

"In the bushes, in the dark, at four in the morning?"

"Mrs. Lundberg. You have a good eye, a keen sense of crime savvy, and a suspicious nature. I wish that's all it took to make a case against those we consider to be the bad guy. But you're a bright woman, you know as well as I do that that isn't how it works." He paused. "You see, the only reason Homicide Special became involved in this case is because we assumed there was a celebrity involved. When you called nine-one-one, you reported that Sybil Squire's housekeeper had been murdered. As far as we're concerned, Mrs. Squire is not involved, directly."

"So you came all this way to tell me that you're going to do nothing?"

"Well, no, not exactly. Actually before I came over here, I paid a visit to the Squire house. More out of curiosity than police work. Mrs. Squire and I had a nice chat."

"You talked to Sybil?"

"Yes. I said I would and I did."

"But not before the case was closed."

"It would've made little difference. What your neighbor had to say merely confirmed what the coroner had already determined."

"What did she say?" Piper sank down on the sofa. "Were you alone with her?"

The detective leaned against the dining room table. "An Asian man opened the door to me and, after I identified myself and asked to speak to Ms. Squire, he showed me into the front room. Ten or fifteen minutes later Mrs. Squire entered the room with the man. I asked to speak with her alone and the man . . ." he consulted his notepad, "a Mr. Jack Ling...left the room. For the next ten minutes we discussed Vera Wade, their association, and her death. She was deeply saddened by the sudden loss of her friend, but she knew it was only a matter of time."

"Only a matter of time?" Piper asked, confused.

"Because of her heart condition."

"Did she say she and Vera spoke with each other that night?"

"Oh, yes, I asked her that. They had a *lovely* visit—her words. Mrs. Wade wanted to move into the house and care for Mrs. Squire, but Mrs. Squire, who loved her friend, felt that Mrs. Wade was incapable of dispensing the kind of care that she, Mrs. Squire, required. Especially after the fire. With Mrs. Wade's failing health, Mrs. Squire was afraid the roles would be reversed—with the patient caring for the caregiver."

Piper sat quietly, taking it all in. "The fire. Sybil told Vera she was certain someone, a man, was in her house minutes before the fire. Detective Bower, I was there earlier that day and two people, one of them Asian, came to the house. Whatever they said to Sybil, it upset her very much."

"Mrs. Lundberg, what do you want me to say? Even if what you tell me is true, it doesn't prove a thing. What Vera Wade said to you is hearsay. What Sybil Squire said happened that night is not terribly reliable because she had been drinking, and drinking heavily. You said so yourself."

Piper signed and leaned back against the sofa cushions. "Did Mrs. Squire seem withdrawn? Was she nervous or distressed?"

He shook his head. "No, nothing like that. Actually she seemed in high spirits, laughing and—" he chuckled, "—flirting even. She flirted with me. She's what? Eighty-five?"

"She was in good spirits? Are you sure?" The disappointment she felt made her question her own sensibilities. Wasn't that what she wanted, to see that Sybil was all right, that she wasn't being abused or slowly killed off for her money? Yet she didn't believe it for one moment.

"She smoked. Poured herself a drink," he said. "In no way did she act like someone who is being exploited or abused. I don't think you have anything to worry about regarding your neighbor. If she's the unwilling victim, as you say she is, she's quite the actress."

"Yes, she is quite the actress. I doubt that's changed."

"Probably not," Detective Bower said. "She gave me an autograph."

He had her full attention again. "May I see it?"

He straightened, pulled a scrap of paper from his jacket pocket. That's when she noticed the lipstick on his shirt collar. Her lipstick. An image of his arms around her in the parking lot, the ground shaking under their feet, flashed across her mind. He handed the paper to her. Their hands touched, sending a tingle through her fingertips.

She turned away.

The autograph was on a notepad page with the heading: *From the desk of Sybil Squire.* The same notepaper she'd written the invitation to coffee. In that flamboyant penmanship that she recognized as Sybil's, it read: *To Jason, Sincerely Yours, Sybil Squire.* She had signed it the way she signed all her autographs. Piper's mind flashed back to the salutation she'd penned on the publicity photo and the thank you note she'd sent the day after she visited her. Not *Sincerely Yours,* but *Forever Yours.* She had forgotten about that. She made a mental note to watch that particular movie again. Sybil was trying to tell her something. But what?

"I also spoke with her doctor," he said. "He assured me he saw nothing out of order in the Squire household on his last visit."

Piper figured the doctor had told him about the telescope trained on the house next door. The telescope Detective Bower had been glancing at throughout his entire visit. She wasn't surprised when he said, "Mrs. Lundberg, neighborhood watch is a positive program, and if it wasn't for conscientious people like you who are vigilant, looking out for others, a lot of crimes would go unreported and unsolved."

"But . . .?"

"Homicide is a serious accusation."

"It's a serious crime."

He closed his eyes, pinched the bridge of his nose. "I'm not asking you to stop being observant. I'm asking you to let the law do its job. Back off."

"When the law does its job, I'll be happy to back off."

He exhaled, nodded. Still holding the paper with the autograph, turning it in his fingers, he added, "Mrs. Wade had listed Sybil Squire as the contact person in case of an emergency. Or death, should that happen. It was Mrs. Squire who paid for the cremation, the urn and the deceased's final resting place."

"What's your point?"

"Why are you making this your battle? You said yourself you haven't known her very long."

Piper's anger intensified. Gordon had played his hand well for five years. The man she married, a master of deception and manipulation, had duped her. She'd been too trusting, assuming he was looking out for her. Now, because of him, her trust in others was compromised. She could count on the fingers of one hand the people she trusted completely.

"Because when I'm all alone I hope someone will look out for me. There are too many people in this world who lie and cheat and...and—" she stopped abruptly, covering her hand over her mouth.

He looked into her eyes and something passed between them. An unspoken understanding. He nodded and looked away.

"Goodbye, Detective."

He started down the stairway and paused. Something across the driveway had caught his eye. She followed his gaze to the Vogt's second floor where Luke Monte was bent over the window frame. When Luke saw them looking his way, he paused, then stood up slowly.

"The quake broke the window. That's the Vogt's handyman," she said.

Bower frowned. "Uh oh, trouble."

"What?" Piper's eyes locked on Luke.

"Those multi-pane windows, they're a real pain to replace. Expensive too." Bower raised a hand in greeting to Luke before continuing down the stairs.

CHAPTER 16

THE NEXT DAY LUKE Monte replaced the windows, spackled the cracks in the two bedroom walls, and helped Piper with the cleanup. The weather was beautiful. She supposed it was Mother Nature's way of making up for her fit of anger, for wreaking havoc on their quiet community.

From the glass door of her place, she had a clear view of Luke high atop the ladder that stood braced against the house. Bare from the waist up, the muscles in his tanned back and shoulders rippled as he pounded away at the bricks, knocking them to the lawn below. There was no denying Luke was attractive. His blond hair, trimmed close at the sides and neckline, was long on top, falling whichever way it took a fancy. His eyes were his best feature. Light blue irises made more striking by a ring of midnight blue. Cool blue eyes that, when lingering on her for longer than a few seconds, sent tingles up and down her spine.

She caught herself staring at his broad, bare shoulders, lean hips, and firm backside and quickly looked away. "Piper, don't go there," she whispered under her breath. "No men. No romance. Don't even look. Rebound's a bummer. Although the divorce was underway, she was still legally married to the jerk. Not that being married had any influence on Gordon's social behavior. Lee had spotted him with a Victoria Secret model at a Hollywood premiere.

She pretended not to notice the long glances Luke cast her way. The last thing she needed now, she told herself, was a nanny man. It was time to get her life back. Time to regain her independence. A man would only complicate things.

Piper watched Luke climb down the ladder, jumping backward the last four feet to the lawn. His chest glistened with a fine film of sweat. He looked up, saw her watching him, and smiled.

She resumed her spying at the back window. She was becoming quite the voyeur. Caught between two points of interest. Across the way, in the Squire's bird room, she saw Sybil's platinum hair as she sat near the window, her back to her. At least two birds were singing, a sweet chorus, one canary clearly the leader. She leaned against the side of the window and listened, wishing she had a canary. Gordon refused to have a pet, claiming allergies. Another lie.

The birds stopped singing. It was so abrupt it jarred her. Her eyes flew open. The nurse had entered the sunroom from the patio, holding a cat. The big orange tom, the one she'd seen the nurse feeding a few days ago. The cat squirmed in her arms. Its tail twitched and jerked back and forth. The nurse strolled up to one of the canary cages and held the cat up against the bars. The cat lashed out, its paw hitting the bars and rocking the cage on its metal hanger. The bird flew about wildly in the confined space, its frail body striking the sides of the cage. The nurse turned to Sybil and said something. Then, as quickly as she had entered the room, she backtracked, opened the door to the patio, and tossed the cat outside. The cat landed on his side, bounced to his feet and shook his head.

A cat allowed inside the Squire house, near her precious song birds, seemed irrational. Yet, from what she could see,

Sybil had not moved a muscle when the cat struck out at the frightened bird.

That afternoon, returning to her place with the mail, she saw the orange tomcat leap over the stone wall from the Squire property into the Vogt's yard. He darted under the thick foliage to the side of the glass doors. Inside, the cockatoo squawked and shrieked in alarm. Piper stepped closer, bent down, and caught sight of the cat hunched over in the deep shadows under a hedge, his large paws crossed in front of him. He glared up at her with eyes the color of saffron.

"What have you got there?" she said, remembering the food she saw the nurse handing out to him, not once, but many times since that first day. It seemed he'd grown attached to their yard, staying close, waiting for a handout. The cat looked away from her. "Don't worry, I don't want your priz—" the word froze in her mouth. She heard a squeak. The cat suddenly chomped down on whatever it had captured, as though afraid she might try to steal it away. He completed the kill, burying his fangs into his prey. The bright yellow canary stopped struggling.

She recalled Sybil's words to Dr. Lowdell: "'She should find something better to do with her time than to look for menace makers.'"

Was that what she was doing? Looking for menace? Yes. Yes, she was. She thought that was exactly what Sybil wanted her to do. She had *Menace Maker* and *Forever Yours* in her private collection. There was another film, one that wasn't one of Sybil's, yet she'd mentioned it during their last visit. What was that damn title? Something about sin. Yes. *Sins of the Family*. Piper found the movie online and loaded it onto her iPad. It was a stretch, of course, to think she might find an answer in these movies. But from what she knew of Sybil Squire, mystery and intrigue was in her blood.

CHAPTER 17

THE FOLLOWING MORNING, WET and chilly, Luke came to her door with a roll of clear plastic sheeting and a staple gun. The rain that day would keep him from working outdoors.

"Thought I'd take advantage of the bad weather and get your window fixed," he said. "A strong gust could cave it in on you."

Piper stepped aside to let him enter. She had been working on the documentary. The room was dim, the only light coming from the twin monitors.

He stopped and looked at her workspace. "So this is what a film editing system looks like? For some reason I thought there'd be more to it."

"This is all I need for what I'm working on now." She leaned over to pull open the drapes at the window nearest her worktable.

"Can I see how it works?" he asked.

"Sure." She let the drape fall back. She explained what she was working on and then gave him a brief demo of Film Editing 101, including viewing footage and cutting a segment.

"Editing seems to be a lot like putting together a jigsaw puzzle, except there's no picture on the box cover to guide you."

"It's better than a jigsaw puzzle. If the piece won't fit, I simply cut it to make it fit."

When she finished, she pulled open the drapes, letting the light into the room.

"How can you stand to be cooped up all day in a dark room?" Luke asked. "Don't you go stir crazy?"

"Not really. The weather dictates my schedule. During the day, I only edit when the weather's bad, like today. Usually I work at night."

"Is it lonely?'

"It can be. Unless I'm so pumped about a project that I forget about everything but the piece I'm cutting. That happens a lot. You should know. A writer's life isn't much different. You shut yourself away with only your characters for company."

He smiled.

"So when do I get to see one of your screenplays?" she asked, leaning back in her chair and rocking slightly.

"You were serious? I thought you were just shining me on."

"I wouldn't do that. I said I'd have a look. I can't guarantee anything except that I'll read it and let you know what I think."

"Yeah. Sure. That'd be cool."

His tone was casual, matter-of-fact, which she thought rather odd. It was her experience that whenever anyone close to a studio exec or a producer offered to read your work, that called for a celebration. At the very least, some measure of enthusiasm. Luke seemed almost put-off by her offer to help.

He removed the broken pane, taking down the entire frame. He stapled the plastic over the opening.

"Will you be home this evening?" he asked. "I'll go get the new pane and set it in tonight. That work for you?"

"I'll be here."

****

Piper spent the afternoon viewing all three movies, looking for anything that could shed light on Sybil and her life, past and present. By the second viewing, Piper's concentration dissolved. At five o'clock, frustrated, she gave up and soaked in the tub. What was Sybil trying to tell her? As a big fan, she should get it.

She dressed in a pair of faded jeans and a V-neck cotton top. At seven o'clock the headlights of Luke's truck swept across her front windows.

When she heard his steps on the stairs, she ran her fingers through her hair and answered the door in her bare feet.

"Come in," she said, moving aside for him to get by with the windowpane.

He wore clean jeans and a button-down faux-suede shirt in a deep blue that brought out the blue of his eyes. He leaned the windowpane against the wall. A quick trip to his pickup for tools and within minutes he was back upstairs and hard at work.

Not sure what to do with herself, she turned on the radio, a swing music station, and went into the kitchenette. "Care for something to drink?" she asked.

"Love something. Whatever you're drinking is fine."

"Wine?"

"Wine's great."

"Red. Or do you prefer beer?"

"Red's cool." He began to pull out the staples holding the plastic sheeting to the wall. A breeze caused the clear plastic to flap against the front of his jeans.

She took a glass to him.

He stopped in the middle of prying out a staple, took the glass and tapped it lightly against hers. "Here's to…whatever makes you happy."

141

"To whatever does." She drank.

"What would make you happy?" he asked.

"I'm happy."

He smiled and set his glass down. "Mind holding an end?"

She helped him position it into the empty frame.

While he reset the window, they talked about old movies and their mutual penchant for Hitchcock.

"What's your favorite?" she asked.

"Psycho."

"Why?"

"The obvious. The shower scene. What's yours?"

"Rear Window."

He glanced toward the Squire house. "You have your own rear window thing going on here, don't you? I couldn't help noticing the telescope pointed at the house next door. What's with that?"

She felt her face grow warm. Why hadn't she moved the damn telescope? "Busted," she said with a grin. "I'm a big fan of Sybil Squire." The expression on his face told her he wasn't sure what to make of that statement. She pointed at the bookshelf to her collection of Squire movies. "I'm not a groupie or a stalker. I just have an interest in her."

"An interest."

"Well, lately it's more than an interest. I'm concerned about her, actually."

"Yeah, how so?" he asked, tipping his head.

"Before I answer, let me ask you this," she said, detouring somewhat. "You've been around here for awhile, what do you know about her?"

"Not much. I know she was big in the movies at one time, old, and that she swims naked. Not appealing, if you know what I mean."

"Do you know anything about the people who take care of her?"

He shook his head. "Naw. I've seen the woman and the man coming and going, but I've never had reason to talk to them. The guy reminds me of that bug-eyed Chinese actor, what's his name?"

"Peter Lorre playing Mr. Moto."

"Exactly." He laughed, slapping the wall.

"Actually, Peter Lorre was not Chinese, or Asian even. He was Austrian or Hungarian."

"No kidding. I guess in those days they had white actors play all the foreign parts, made them up to look the part. Wonder why they did that? There was a shortage of foreign actors, or what?"

"I don't know."

"So does your neighbor still skinny-dip?"

"She hasn't in a while, at least not that I'm aware of."

"You'd be surprised how many of those old babes like to run around in the buff. No inhibitions. It's creepy. I've been on jobs where I have to move fast or risk being cornered and groped. I'm nobody's boy toy, that's for damn sure."

Piper smiled. She had no doubt he was telling the truth. "Have you ever done any jobs for her?"

He shook his head again. "An old relic like that—the house, not the lady—needs more than this handyman could handle. I'm not that ambitious. I'm into writing and music."

"Music? You're a musician?"

"Drummer."

"A band?" she said, refilling their glasses.

"What's left of it. The lead guitarist put the lead singer in the hospital when he caught him poking his ol' lady, and now he's serving two to five in Soledad. Second guitarist is in and out of rehab—in more than out, lately. Our manager stopped returning calls. Guess you could say I'm in search of a new group."

She nodded.

He hovered near the telescope. "Why are you so concerned about the naked swimmer?"

She told him about the fire and her week in the hospital. "They released her in the care of this nurse and that man. She doesn't seem the same anymore."

"They're hurting her?"

"I don't know. She had a black eye last week."

"No shit." He drank deeply. "That's extreme."

"Sybil's housekeeper died after going over there. I found the woman's body and now I'm involved."

He turned to Piper. "You think these two people did her in? What do the cops think?"

"They don't believe me. They closed the case."

"Hey, look, if these assholes threaten you in any way, I want to know. You let me know. Okay? *Okay?*"

She suddenly felt uneasy. Not sure where this conversation was going and sorry she had brought it up.

"Yeah. Okay." Even as she said that, she knew Luke would be the last person she'd go to if she were threatened. Something about the look in his eyes when he said those words disturbed her. She thought of Robert Mitchum in *Night of the Hunter*—a flash of evil behind a benevolent mask.

She went into the kitchenette and busied herself unloading the dishwasher while he wadded up the clear plastic sheeting. He used jerky, agitated movements, as if trying to punch the plastic into submission.

"Goddammit!" he hissed under his breath, shattering the uncomfortable silence. He stuck his finger into his mouth.

"Are you okay?" she asked.

"Staple. Burns like a sonofabitch." He snapped his hand in the air, then squeezed the wound until blood welled up and began to run down the padded flesh of his palm. "Gotta make it bleed. Gets rid of the poison."

She tore off some paper towels and brought them to him. He twisted the towels around his thumb, but not before blood had dripped onto the wooden floor and the fringed edge of the area rug.

"I'll get some antiseptic," she said.

"Don't bother. I'll live," he said. Then he smiled, his eyes suddenly bright and crinkly at the corners. "Hungry? How 'bout we go out for a bite? There's that Thai joint on Fairfax. Or are you into sushi?"

Although she was starving, going out with Luke, even on a casual basis, was not going to happen.

"No, I'm sorry, I...I can't. I—well, I don't date." She turned away.

"Who said anything about a date? You gotta eat. I'll run over and pick some up, bring it back here."

"Really, no. Thanks, but--" All of a sudden she was eager to say goodbye and have him gone.

"Okay." He sank down on the sofa, crossed his leg at the knee and leaned back, sipping his wine.

"I really should get back to work," she said, nodding toward the monitors.

He stared down into his glass, rolling the contents around. Just when she was about to repeat what she'd said, he downed the rest of his wine in one gulp. He stood, handing her the empty glass. While he gathered up his tools, she rinsed the wine glasses in the sink and dried them.

He walked to the door. Only after he opened the door did she cross the room to see him out.

145

Instead of stepping out onto the deck, Luke pulled her into his arms and lowered his head for a kiss. She pushed at him, turning her head. His mouth brushed across her temple.

"No," she said.

Luke's large hand cupped her jaw, turned her head toward him.

"Goodnight, Luke."

He dropped his arm, nodding. Without saying goodbye, he went down the stairs, taking them two at a time.

She spent the rest of the evening staring at Sybil Squire on the screen, yet she couldn't stop thinking about Luke. She saw his blue eyes become hard and dark. She saw the muscle in his jaw contracting with tension. His hand holding her face, squeezing. In an instant, something had made him change.

That night Piper woke with a scream echoing in her head. A woman's scream, bloodcurdling and shrill.

She leaped from the Murphy bed and stumbled to the window, stubbing her foot on the leg of a chair in her path. Her toes throbbed, making her curse. The house next door was dark and without movement inside or out. Then a light blinked on in Sybil's bedroom, a soft light from a bedside lamp. She focused the telescope at the window.

Sybil came into view. Wearing a long, shiny robe and carrying a rock glass filled with an amber liquid, she crossed to the window, staggering slightly. Behind the transparent sheers, she stood silhouetted in the dim light, gossamer and otherworldly, before she yanked the drapes closed. There was something familiar about her actions. A scene from one of her movies. Piper shook her head. She was beginning to jumble real life with make-believe.

Piper sank to the floor and rubbed her throbbing toes. She thought about what she'd seen and heard. The scream puzzled her. Had it come from Sybil? She looked fine. Probably the cats again.

She climbed back into bed and pulled the covers tightly around her. When she closed her eyes, she heard the scream, high-pitched and chilling. The perfect *movie* scream. Had there actually been a scream, or was it merely a figment of an overactive imagination?

CHAPTER 18

THE NEXT MORNING SHE called Detective Bower and told him about the scream in the night and Sybil Squire's strange appearance at the window. "Until last night, I haven't seen much of her at all. Before these people moved in, she was very visible. She swam every day, walked the grounds, and though she didn't go out much, she wasn't a total recluse, like now. Something's wrong, Detective Bower. I don't know who I can talk to about it. I'm freaking here. Can't you do something...*anything*?"

"Mrs. Lundberg, the Wade death is no longer an open case. If there's suspicious activity at the Squire house, you should be talking to the Hollywood PD."

She pulled the drapes aside and gazed out at the mansion. When she heard splashing, she looked down and saw a nude Sybil Squire doing the sidestroke in a swimming pool littered with leaves and pink rose petals. She wore the goggles and something new, a tight fitting swimming cap. She looked healthier and more robust than when she last saw her in the pool weeks ago, in an ermine coat and a swollen black eye.

"She's in the pool," she said without realizing she had spoken aloud.

"What?"

"She's swimming in the pool. I'm looking at her right now. She looks like her old self."

"Well there you go. See, things have a way of working themselves out." The line was silent. "Mrs. Lundberg, take my advice and give it a rest. If something does come up— something that you feel requires the attention of the police, the Hollywood precinct can handle any—"

"Goodbye, Detective." She disconnected and tossed the phone on the bed. What was going on? With the telescope leveled through a crack in the drapes, Piper spied on her until she exited the pool five minutes later. Leaves adhered to her thin body. She draped the robe over her shoulders, not bothering to dry herself first. Moments later, she was gone.

Sybil was swimming again. A robust and healthy Sybil, looking like she did the day Piper first saw her in the pool, before the fire, before the new caregivers.

What the hell?

With the sunshine and good weather, Luke resumed working on the chimney. Any apprehension she'd felt about him the night before gradually dissipated as the morning wore on and she watched him busy at work. His movements were smooth and swift. He was a gifted handyman.

At noon, when she crossed the driveway to the main house, he smiled and waved but made no move to talk to her or to climb down from the ladder. Relieved, she watered the plants, cleaned Dr. Jekyll's cage and gave him his fresh fruit and seed.

The bird demanded more and more of her time each day. He missed the Vogts, particularly Belle, and hated being alone.

He loved to cuddle and be the center of attention. Since the quake, she'd been visiting him twice a day, letting him out of the cage to exercise and explore. She quickly became his surrogate mother. He called out "'Lo, Mommy" whenever he saw her or heard her voice. She considered moving him in with her, but realized his screeching and rooster crowing would be too distracting while she worked. For company, she had put the portable TV next to his cage and kept it on a cartoon channel every day until the sun went down.

After an hour with the bird, she locked up and returned to the guesthouse, her footsteps climbing the staircase in sync with the tapping of Luke's trowel handle against brick. On her doormat lay a bound screenplay. The copy looked as if it had been carried around extensively, shopworn. The limp pages curled inward, smudged with dirty fingerprints and flicks of god-knows-what. She imagined it rolled and unrolled many times. She turned to see Luke on the ladder watching her. Holding up the script, she waved it in the air and retreated inside.

Piper had asked for it and he had delivered. Now that it was in her hands, she knew he would be eager to hear her thoughts on it. She silently prayed it wouldn't be as bad as the majority of scripts submitted by the thousands to Hollywood agencies and production companies. She brewed a cup of coffee and sat down to read *Searchlight*, a screenplay by Luke Monte. At the conclusion of the first act, she was hooked. It was a damn good piece of work; the story of a man in search of his identity and self-worth after kicking a life-long heroin addiction. When she reached the midpoint, she was interrupted by one of Mick's assistants calling on her cell phone from nearby Sunset Boulevard. Leslie needed help to root through Mick's projects for a copy of a pre-production script that had been misplaced or lost. There were handwritten notes on the script that he had to have. She pulled into the driveway minutes later.

Leslie looked so much like Connie Chung that Piper unconsciously called her Connie twice before she was sharply corrected. Piper led the way up the stairs and into Mick's relocated office and pointed to a waist-high stack of scripts on the floor against the wall. "You take those and I'll take these." Already hunkering down to tackle a pile in the corner. Mick saved everything. "That's what assistants are for," he said when he couldn't find anything in the clutter of his two offices.

Calls from Mick every twenty minutes asking for a progress report didn't help expedite the operation. To make matters worse, Belle got on the extension and wanted a word with Dr. Jekyll. Leaving Leslie on her knees in the corner, Piper enabled the speaker on the cordless phone, trotted down the stairs to the kitchen and held the instrument up to the cockatoo's cage. He flapped his white wings and fanned his top crest, but refused to talk. "Take him out of his cage," Belle said. "You know how bullheaded he can be when he feels like a caged bird. Have you been letting him out to spread his wings?"

"Every day, sometimes twice a day."

"Do you talk with him?" she asked. "If he doesn't have anyone to talk to, he forgets words."

"Yes, I know. We chat on a regular basis. He does most of the talking, so you don't have to worry." He had even picked up a few words from *Scooby Doo* but Belle didn't need to know that her precious was being babysat by cartoon characters.

"You're a sweetheart. I'm so glad we have you to watch over things. We usually get a house sitter when we go off on these long shoots. Thank you, Piper, for being there."

"Don't thank me. I'm the one who's in your debt." She opened the door of Dr. J's cage. She didn't have to coax him out. He loved his freedom. He hopped onto her arm, then to his T-bar. He strutted up and down, bobbing his head, feathers fluffed. He began to mutter "Scooby Doo".

"What's he saying?" Belle asked.

"He says the economy and the national debt are in horrendous state. He's pondering a position in politics, but fears the repercussions of campaign reform."

Belle laughed. "Say 'Mommy loves you'."

"Mommy loves you."

"Not to me. Say it to Dr. J, and with feeling."

"Here, you say it. You're on speaker." The bird cocked his head and blinked when he heard Belle's voice. The head crest rose to its full height. "…oy, cookie," he said. "Love ya. Love ya."

The two carried on a twisted and disjointed conversation, with Dr. J barking, then throwing in a wolf whistle, cat meow, and kissing sounds. Piper doubled up with laughter, tears streaming down her face until Mick came back on the line and reminded them there was work to be done. Dr. J was the best medicine. Like a happy child, his glee became contagious, cheering her instantly.

By the time they found the script and Leslie had faxed the specific pages to Hong Kong, it was late afternoon.

Back in the guesthouse, Piper picked up Luke's script and continued reading. The second half was even better than the first half. At the closing lines, tears filled her eyes as she hugged the script to her chest. Her perception of Luke changed once again. She saw the handyman in an entirely different light now. Sensitive. Insightful. Enigmatic. A gifted screenwriter. He had written a script that, in her opinion, was a star vehicle. She pictured Matt Damon in the lead role.

She reread the last act, reaching the end at six o'clock, just as Lee made an entrance in a Mercedes Sedan. Dabbing at her eyes with a tissue, Piper stepped out onto the deck. The driver opened the back door. Lee exited the car, waved at her, then detoured to where Luke worked on the ladder. She asked him something. He came down, spread mortar on a brick, shrugged and nodded toward the guesthouse before climbing the ladder again. The driver helped her with several shopping bags, clothes carriers, and Lee's familiar makeup kit, carrying them upstairs and depositing them in the living room.

Lee thanked him and instructed him to return at eight.

"Are you moving in?" Piper asked her when the driver left.

"We, you and I, are going to a fabulous wrap party this evening. I took the liberty of bringing clothes for you because I know you'll say you have nothing to wear."

"I'm not going to a wrap party, or any party. I have work to do."

"I have work to do, too. My job's to see that you have fun for one evening, even if I have to drag you there kicking and screaming. You're a free woman now—almost. Let's celebrate."

"I have work."

"This is not your ordinary wrap party, girlfriend. It's on a yacht in Marina del Rey."

"I get seasick."

"Liar. They're wrapping Tommy's film. *Blue Haven Highway.*"

"Thomas VanRaven?"

"The buzz is that *Highway* is a winner. Blockbuster, perhaps. But hell, that's not surprising. VanRaven could shoot a dripping faucet and get rave reviews. He has a slew of new films lined up like airplanes in a holding pattern. Meaning . . ."

"You don't have to tell me what working on a VanRaven vehicle could mean for me or my career." Tommy once told her she had a clear sense of a film's purpose, *his* films in particular. His brilliant unconventional storylines were a challenge and just the thing to help her to break back into the trade.

"Have I sold you yet?" Lee said.

"You had me at yacht."

Lee laughed. "Good." She reached for a hanging carrier and stopped in mid-motion. "Piper, who is that man?"

Piper didn't have to look to know she was talking about Luke. He'd taken off his shirt just before Lee had arrived.

"The Vogt's handyman."

"Does he have free run of their house? He just went inside and came out with a beer. He appears to be helping himself to his employer's stash."

Piper thought that odd, but maybe they did have some sort of agreement. She didn't know. She told Lee about the earthquake damage and his part in repairing the Vogt's house.

"So what's your part?"

"What do you mean?"

"Are you Lady Chatterly to the hot groundskeeper?"

"Wouldn't you like to know? But before you go off and do something incredibly outlandish—like ask him—no, I am not boffing the handyman."

"Good. Guys like that are trouble. They ooze sex. Sex and neuroses. They take, take, take. If they give anything in return it's a bun in the oven or a social disease. My judgment in human character, as you well know, is exceptional. That man has the look of deception about him. He's not what he appears to be."

"Not what he appears to be?" Piper's smile was wry. "He's a handyman, for crissakes. So what else might he be? A heart surgeon…a rocket scientist…posing as a handyman? You exchange half a dozen words with him for a couple of seconds and you know his deepest, darkest secrets. Miss Lee, you chose the wrong vocation. I hear the psychic hotline needs a few good mediums."

"Laugh. Go ahead and laugh. I had years of first-hand personal experience in deception and role-playing. I'm rarely wrong."

Piper looked out the window at him. "Maybe you're right," she said pensively. "He's written a wonderful screenplay." She picked it up and fanned the pages.

Lee took it from her and without even glancing at it, unzipped one of her clothes carriers, and stuffed it inside. "I'll read it. Maybe I'll want to represent him if it's as wonderful as you say. But enough talk about business and the sexy groundskeeper. We have more important things to hash over. Like tonight's attire."

"Okay, let's see what you have."

"Since when have wrap parties gone red carpet?" Piper asked. The wrap parties she'd been to were casual. Generally, they were a way for the cast and crew and their families to celebrate the project completion and say goodbye. Lee's major client played the female lead.

"They haven't. But Tommy's all about press and putting himself out there. He likes fireworks." Lee opened the dress carrier. "Nothing over-the-top. I brought us a couple of hot little black numbers to wear."

Lee stripped down and strutted around in front of the windows, uninhibited in skimpy sheer undergarments, unconcerned about who might see her from outside. No matter how many times Lee changed clothes in front of her, she would never get used to seeing her childhood sweetheart in a woman's body. Lee seemed so comfortable in her skin, so self-satisfied. Piper wasn't in the same place in her life.

VanRaven was renowned for his party extravaganzas. This elaborately catered excursion epitomized power and prestige and offered up the best publicity for him and his film. Open bars and live music at each end of the upper deck catered to an impressive guest list of studio heads and top actors. *Blue Haven Highway*, like all of VanRaven's pictures, had a cast of mega-stars. Usually thrown in was a cameo appearance by the greatest of the greats.

Lee dragged her from one end of the ship to the other, schmoozing and networking and courting the talent who in the past had grumbled, no matter how slight, about his or her current agent.

A heavyset woman in a black Chanel pants suit shrieked when she saw Lee, placed both hands on the sides of Lee's head, and kissed her soundly on the ear. The woman raved about Lee's dress and shoes.

"The bitch," Lee said moments later when the woman was out of earshot. "That's Constance, Johnny's agent. She never fails to dig her fat fingers into my hair when she does that kissy-kiss thing of hers. That's no accident. Even the most Neanderthal man knows you don't mess with the hair. She's an evil bitch and I'm going to do everything in my power to steal Johnny away from her."

They filled their plates from buffet tables serving an array of delicacies consisting of mounds of beluga caviar, whole Australian lobsters, imported cheeses, and desserts. Rich food. Fine wine. Piper skipped her usual martini and stuck with champagne instead. Good champagne was hard to turn down. She had learned long ago to not mix her poison.

No longer was she the drinker she used to be. Waking up in the morning with a relatively clear head had its undeniable advantages.

Throughout the evening, she kept an eye on VanRaven, hoping for a chance to catch him alone or at least without the usual mob surrounding him. There was no point in kidding herself. She was no different than any of the other wannabe deal makers hanging around him, paying tribute to the man and his latest brilliant film. Piper wanted him to know she had reentered the business. That she thought all his films were beyond brilliant. That working with him again was her dream of dreams.

The speeches, the presentation of the cast and crew jackets and gifts came and went. By midnight, the party neared its peak. She knew from past wrap parties that it would soon be a drunken revelry. In the ship's theater, on a continuous loop, ran a goody reel—outtakes and hysterical bloopers caught on film—shown in the hopes of dissolving any lingering hostility among the cast and crew.

A few minutes into the goody reel, she spotted VanRaven seated in the front row talking with a man who looked enough like Detective Bower to be a twin. VanRaven left his seat and approached her, a huge grin spreading across his face. "Piper, it's so good to see you again. I'd hoped we'd have a chance to chat, but I'm afraid I have to leave. Welcome back. I think I might have something for you. I'll call next week."

"That's great, Tommy. Thank you," she gushed and watched him exit the theater.

When she looked back at the man who'd been sitting with VanRaven, the seat was empty.

CHAPTER 19

LUKE'S TRUCK RATTLED TO a stop in the driveway, waking her. She groaned, rolled out of bed, and dressed while the coffee brewed. A knock on the glass of the door made her jump. She peeped through the blinds. Luke stood on the deck, a broad smile on his face.

"So what did you think?" he asked when she opened the door.

She stared at him, her mind a blank.

"The screenplay."

"The screenplay? Oh, the *screenplay. Your* screenplay. Of course. Luke, I loved it. I think it's good enough to be optioned."

"I'm not ready to go that route yet. I only showed it to you because you asked to see it." He looked behind her, glancing around inside her place. "Where is it?"

Her stomach tightened. "I don't have it. I gave it to Lee Sikes to read. She was here yesterday. She spoke to you in the yard."

The smile disappeared. "Why would you give it to her?"

"She's a talent agent. A very good one."

"You gave my screenplay to someone in the business?"

"Yes. Isn't that what you wanted? It's what every screenwriter wants."

"No. Goddammit, no!" He slammed the side of his fist against the stucco wall. His face grew a deep shade of red. "I'm not every screenwriter. You...you shouldn't have done that. God, I can't believe this."

"I'm sorry. Lee came in just as I finished it. It was so good, I had to tell her about it. I didn't realize—Luke, I'm sorry."

"Get it back." He closed his eyes, inhaled deeply. "Can you... can you get it back?"

"Sure. I'll call her right now and tell her not to read it. That you're not ready."

Luke's face relaxed, the redness vanished. He smiled. "Thanks." He touched her arm. His fingers felt heavy, damp. "So you liked it?"

She nodded. She no longer wanted to discuss it with him. His ugly reaction to her giving it to Lee had been unexpected and troubling. As was his instant change in mood. She had never known a writer to get angry about someone going out on a limb to champion them. Then again, writers were a curious breed and anything was possible.

The phone rang. She excused herself, hoping Luke would allow her some privacy and leave. He moved away from the door, but remained on the deck, pacing.

Belle's voice, tinny and strained started right in with, "Piper, I'm so glad I caught you in."

"What time is it there?" Piper asked.

"It's late. But I couldn't sleep until I got some answers."

"Answers to what?"

"Is Luke still working on the house?"

"Yes, in fact, he's here right now, on the deck. Do you want to talk with him?"

"He's there now? Can he hear you?"

Piper saw him leaning on the rail, looking out over the hillside. The door was still open. She moved to the far side of the house, out of voice range but not out of sight. Her stomach began to burn, and it wasn't from last night's rich food or champagne. "What's wrong?"

"I was curious when no invoices for the house repairs were going to our accountant. That's not like Luke to work from his own funds. So I rang him. The landlady at the boarding house where he lives says he took off the day of the earthquake and hasn't come back. Today she received a check in the mail for two months rent and a postcard from Florida, saying he was taking a long holiday. My question is, if Luke's in Florida, who the hell's working on the house?"

Piper glanced out the door. Luke was pacing again. "Belle, what does your handyman look like?"

"Short, thin, hairy all over expect for his head. Is that your fella?"

She felt her knees go weak and had to brace herself against the bookshelf. "No."

"Put him on. I want to talk to this bloke. I want to know what the hell he's doing at my house. Why he's impersonating our handyman."

Luke, or whoever he was, crossed the deck and started down the stairs.

"He went downstairs. Look, I don't know who he is or what he wants, but I don't think we should let him know we're on to him just yet."

"You're right. Call the police. Now."

This man knew his stuff. Knew his way around a construction project, knew how to turn a screwdriver and pound a nail. If what Belle said was true, he was working for nothing. Why would he do that?

Belle said, "Call the police."

"I will."

"I want a full report, Piper. I don't like this."

"Neither do I." Piper hung up and crossed the room to the door to close and lock it.

Luke popped his head in before she reached the door. She jumped, startled because she hadn't heard his footsteps on the stairs.

"Hey, pretty lady, can you give me a hand for a sec?" he asked, grabbing the door and pushing it open.

She nodded, quickly moving out onto the deck. She prayed he couldn't see her heart pounding beneath her cotton top. She felt safer outside in the bright sunlight. Having him inside the guesthouse with only the one door for escape unnerved her. She hurried down the steps with Luke behind her. At the bottom, she turned to him and blurted out, "Who are you?"

He was picking dried mortar from his fingers.

"Who the hell are you?" she repeated.

He looked directly into her eyes. Calmly, as if he knew he would be saying these words sooner than later, he said, "I'm a cop. My name is Arnold Copeland." He reached into his back pocket and pulled out a wallet. He flipped it open, revealing a gold shield and ID.

"A cop?" she said. "I don't understand."

"Undercover. I wanted to tell you from the start, but my superiors thought it best for all concerned if we kept the operation a covert one."

"What operation?"

"I'm with the L.A. Financial Crimes Division, Fraud section. We're investigating elder estate abuse."

"Sybil Squire?"

"Let's move away from the property. Never know who might be listening." He guided her to the shade of the Vogt's back door. She sat in a padded chair, still damp with morning dew. Luke, or Arnold, took another chair, turning it to face her and sat down. "Yes, your neighbor, Sybil Squire. Fraud and extortion for starters."

"My god, are you working with Detective Bower on the housekeeper's murder?"

"Bower? Never heard of him."

"He was here the day you were replacing the Vogt's window." She pointed upward. "He waved at you."

"Don't know him. I'm not with homicide. FCD is a different division."

"But you're investigating the caregivers next door?"

He nodded. "We received a call from the bank advising us of some unusual transactions regarding Mrs. Squire's account. That's the first thing we look out for."

"And have you found any criminal activity?"

"I'm not at liberty to discuss it with you. Sorry, Piper. That's why I had to keep you in the dark."

"How did you—christ, Luke, why the handyman impersonation?"

"A stakeout was our best bet and with the Vogts in the Orient, it occurred to us that their handyman was the most likely candidate to impersonate. The earthquake couldn't have come at a better time. It worked in our favor. We had to act fast."

"But—" she had dozens of questions. Luke cut her off.

"We hope to have it wrapped up in a day or two. In the meantime, I'm going to have to ask you to let us handle this without your intervention. We don't want them getting wise and doing something rash, if you get my meaning?"

By rash, he meant hurting Sybil, maybe killing her. The thought sickened her. But what he was telling her gave her a sense of relief. At last, someone else who believed Sybil was a victim. She sat up straight, pressing her palms down on the top of her knees and exhaled.

"Your friend, the one who was here yesterday, what does she know about the people next door?" he asked.

"She hasn't met them."

"Good, let's keep it that way."

After the former handyman, now undercover cop, went back to repairing the chimney, she looked up the telephone number for the Los Angeles Police Department and dialed. She asked to speak to Officer Arnold Copeland and was transferred to the Elder Abuse Unit. "Detective Copeland is in the field," a female voice said. "Would you care to leave a message on his voicemail?" Piper declined and hung up.

That night she called Belle and Mick and filled them in.

The next day life looked good again. Fog and rain had brought out the sharp, medicinal fragrance of a camphor tree. Piper breathed it in, remembering sick days as a kid, her grandmother slathering Vick's on her chest to break up the tightness. Closing her eyes, she inhaled the mentholated vapors, feeling the healing coolness seep deep into her lungs.

She missed Nana so much. Tomorrow was her birthday. She would've been seventy-five. Two things always reminded her of Nana. Camphor and clover. She thought back to that afternoon in the park with Nana long ago. A ten-year-old Piper had asked about the fire that killed her family. *"I had taken your mother to the dentist that day. We returned home to find it in flames. I tried to go inside, but people held me back, telling me it was too late…that they were…gone," Nana said as they lay on their bellies in the grass, their faces inches from the ground, probing meticulously through a patch of sweet-smelling clover. "Then, from the smoke and cinders, I saw your granddad and...and our two little ones, clinging to him. I saw them float like angels up from the roof of the house...up to heaven. Everyone said I was hallucinating, but I know what I saw, Piper. I saw them. I did."*

"Were they angels, Nana?"

"Yes, honey, they were angels. My guardian angels. Ah ha!" Nana rolled onto her side holding up a four-leaf clover. "Make a wish, Pipsqueak."

Piper had wished for Nana's angels to be happy in heaven.

The crank and whine of the city trash truck working its way up the hill brought her back to the present. It was their pickup day. The trash bin overflowed with the cleanup from the quake. She rolled the large plastic bin down the driveway to the street and placed it alongside the Squire's receptacle that, like every trash container on the block, was filled to the brim. She paused and stared at the receptacle.

She glanced around. Except for the waste employees going about their work two doors down, there was no one else within sight. She lifted the lid and peeked inside. In among the many crumbled cigarette packs, butts, and empty scotch bottles, she saw what looked like a bloody rag and tissues. There were also patches of orange fur, strands floated up and around her, sticking to her clothes and in her hair.

Who was bleeding? Sybil? The cat? That scream in the night flashed into her head.

The sound of the Lincoln starting up made her drop the lid with a guilty start. She wiped her hands on her jeans. Someone from the house was leaving. If Mr. Moto and the nurse were together, then Sybil would be alone in the house. Although she had promised Luke, aka Arnold Copeland, to stay out of it, she knew she couldn't keep that promise. Not after seeing bloody things in their trashcan. She had to see for herself that Sybil was okay.

The trash truck pulled up just as the shiny black car reached the end of the driveway. Mr. Moto sat behind the wheel. He looked straight ahead, his brow furrowed with annoyance at the truck blocking the access to the street. In the backseat sat Sybil Squire. She wore a two-piece linen suit in a soft gray. Gloves covered the scars on her hands. Her stunning blue eyes were hidden behind dark glasses. Piper had not been this close to her since the day in her living room when she'd fallen asleep--or pretended to fall asleep. She was certain now that Sybil had wanted her out of the house, away from her caregivers, for Piper's safety as well as her own.

She stepped up to the passenger side of the car, bent down, and through the closed window, over the loud whining of the truck, called out, "Mrs. Squire, do you have a minute?"

The trash truck pulled forward. Sybil turned away, a glum expression on her face. Mr. Moto cranked around in the driver's seat to consult with her. She said something Piper couldn't hear, but the movement of her hand, waving him on, was clear enough. The big car glided past, turned onto the street, and drove away.

Piper stared after it, hands balled into fists, her fingernails digging into her palms. Sybil looked all right, strong and healthy, but things weren't always as they seemed. Deep in her gut she knew something was still very wrong.

In no mood to go back to the guesthouse alone, she crossed to the Vogts. Dr. J's company was preferable to none. He called out when she entered. She released him from his cage. Doc was the best medicine for her when she was upset. It was her turn to do all the talking. For the next ten minutes she ranted and raved, using Doc as her sounding board. He ducked and bobbed his head as though in complete agreement with her complaints, and paced the length of his bar weaving in frustration, wholly sympathetic to her problems. When he'd had enough of her ranting, he climbed back into his cage and began to squawk.

She left him to his fresh nuts and berries and went to water the indoor plants. From a second story bedroom in the main house, she saw a different view of the Squire house, the back portion. That portion of the house appeared to be closed off or used for storage, the horizontal blinds shut at all times, the windows dark. As she misted a potted African violet, she glanced at the house. A tightly closed blind at an upstairs window flittered. She stopped misting and moved closer. It flittered again. Someone was trying to open the blinds. With Mr. Moto and Sybil still gone, the nurse was the only one in the house. What was she up to?

Piper dashed into the front office, grabbed a pair of binoculars and rushed back with them. It took a few seconds for her to find and focus on the window in question. Suddenly fingers clutched at four or five slats and yanked them down. She saw only the fingers and the back of the hand, the knuckles pressed against the pane. The fingers trembled, causing the blinds to shake. The fingernails were broken. The skin on the hand looked twisted, shriveled and discolored. Like burned skin.

Piper continued to watch, her heart beating like a wild thing in her chest, until the hand released its grip on the slats. The blinds quivered and then were still.

She covered her hand over her mouth.

Sybil.

It suddenly occurred to her why she had felt something was wrong, out of kilter. That was *not* Sybil in the car. It looked like her. Enough like her to fool even Piper, someone who thought she knew every feature of her face so well. But if it wasn't Sybil, who was it? Who was swimming in the pool and who was moving around in the house in plain sight, chatting with the police? Detective Bower had said "…flirting even".

She recalled the night of the scream. The night Sybil staggered drunkenly to her bedroom window. Sybil or an imposter? *Imposter*. Of course. That's how they're able to steal her identity and systematically strip her of her estate.

She quickly locked up the house and returned to the guesthouse. She considered calling Luke at the Fraud Division, but talking to him didn't feel right. This could be far more serious than fraud and extortion. Sybil was a celebrity, that's what Homicide Special dealt with, and that meant Bower. If she told the detective that Sybil was being held prisoner in her own home, he would have to act upon it, wouldn't he? It was all tied in to Vera's death, even though he denied there was any foul play involved. It could turn into another homicide. The problem was, if he did believe her, how fast could he act? A search warrant would take time. Enough time for the caregivers to return and do something with Sybil. Kill her even. There was no choice. She had to do it, and do it now.

Her phone rang just as she reached for it. Caller ID identified Lee. She quickly answered. "Lee, I can't talk now. Let—"

"Your friend plagiarized that screenplay. It was this year's winner in the state's annual screenwriter's competition. The author is a woman."

Piper's stomach dropped. Shit. No wonder he freaked when she told him she gave it to Lee.

"Did he really think he could get away with stealing a prize-winning script? One that Mick optioned. He helped himself to more than Mick's beer. Didn't I tell you your handyman was not who he seems to be? Didn't I?"

"There's more to it than that. He's not a handyman either."

"What is he? *Who* is he?"

Piper rubbed her forehead. "I don't know. I really don't know." That was true. If he'd lied about being a handyman, and lied about writing the script, was he also lying about being an undercover cop? "I'll call you back."

She dialed, asked for Detective Bower and was told he was in a meeting. She left her name and number.

Time was running out. She had to go next door herself. Had to find Sybil and get her out fast.

Piper got as far as her deck when she saw the black Lincoln climbing up the hill to the house. She watched helplessly as it pulled into the driveway. Her throat tightened and tears welled up. She sank down on the top step, pulled the hem of her t-shirt up, buried her face in the cloth, and cried.

For the next two hours, she picked up and put down the phone more than a dozen times. Bower had not called back. She dialed the number for the Hollywood police station, but hung up before it rang. What would she say? *I saw a hand in the upstairs window through my binoculars while I was spying on the house next door. The hand looked scarred, like the hand of Sybil Squire, only she was supposed to be out of the house at the time. Someone is impersonating her, I'm sure of it.* Would they believe her? Even if they did, would she be placing Sybil in more danger if the police found nothing. She couldn't do it. She needed proof—solid proof.

She picked up Detective Bower's card again, running her finger over the embossed seal. Why was he the first one she thought about to contact whenever she had a problem? It wasn't because of the Wade case. He'd made it clear the case was closed and therefore out of his hands. Yet Piper continued to look to him for help.

She called him, this time using the cell phone number on his card. When he came on the line, he was courteous.

"I have only one question to ask you," she said. "That day when you spoke with Mrs. Squire in her home, did you at any time see the female caregiver? Please think carefully."

The line was quiet for so long she thought he had hung up on her. "No. I can't say that I did. I asked about her and Mrs. Squire said she was running errands."

"Was the Lincoln there?"

"Yes. Yes, it was parked in the carport."

"Then she was there. No one walks anywhere in LA. Did you notice any burn scars on Sybil's hands?"

"That's three questions. But I want to help clear up whatever it is that's troubling you at this time, so I'll answer your questions. Scars? No, she wore gloves. The Asian man, Mr. Ling, let me in and he let me out. Was there anything else?"

"No, Detective Bower. You've been very helpful." She thanked him and hung up.

Luke returned that afternoon. When his truck pulled into the driveway, she went downstairs to meet him. She didn't want to be alone with him in the guesthouse. He had come to fill her in on the Squire case.

"Well, we're coming to a close in the investigation. Good news. What we suspected might be extortion and financial elder abuse turns out to be completely legit. Mrs. Squire is merely liquidating her assets here in California. She's moving to the east coast. There's nothing to keep her here, she says, and the last earthquake was all it took to get her moving."

"You spoke to her?"

"Yes."

"In person?"

"She came to the Crime Division to straighten everything out. She had papers and documents. Everything was in order."

"Where on the east coast?"

"I don't know. She has relatives in Miami, I think."

That was a lie. Sybil had no known relatives. The death of her daughter forty years ago wiped out the last of the thin family line.

"What about the caregivers?"

He shrugged. "What about them?"

"Will they be going along with her to...wherever?"

"I don't know. I do know that Jack Ming and Judith Avidon are clean. No priors to indicate they might be fleecing this patient, or any other patients. I can assure you your movie star idol is in no danger. Not from her caregivers, anyway."

He reached out and caressed her bare arm. She stepped away. He dropped his hand to his side, his brow furrowed. "Look, I have to go. There're still some things I have to iron out before I can close this case. I'll drop by later and explain everything in more detail."

Piper nodded. She just wanted him gone. She had questions, lots of them. If he had answers, she was pretty sure they weren't ones she was looking for. At that moment, her mind was like a nest of squirming snakes emerging from hibernation.

He walked across the patch of lawn to his tools and began picking them up and putting them into the bed of the truck. She was halfway up the staircase, when he called out to her. "Oh, about that screenplay. Tell your friend to toss it.

I didn't write it. It was part of my undercover strategy to protect my anonymity. Sorry I wasted your time and that I deceived you like that, Piper. Hope you won't hold it against me. Sometimes I have to do things I don't want to do."

Now there was something Piper had to do.

Inside the guesthouse, she took her digital camera with the zoom lens and snapped off a dozen shots of Arnold Copeland, alias Luke, as he cleaned up the mortar in the mortar box and deposited it and the last of the tools into his pickup. She imported the photos to her computer and printed them. After tucking the photos into an envelope, she drove to the Financial Crimes Division on North Los Angeles Street where she asked to speak to someone in charge of the elder abuse unit. A short time later, sitting opposite Acting Commanding Officer Lieutenant William Stroller, she told him everything she knew about the Squire investigation and Officer Arnold Copeland.

"Mrs. Lundberg, we would not put a man on a stakeout without the explicit permission of the homeowner, meaning, your friends the Vogts. Or at the very least, the person residing on the premises, which is you."

"Then there is no undercover investigation?"

"No, ma'am, not from this division."

She pulled out a picture of Luke from the photo envelope. "Is this Officer Copeland?"

He looked at several photos silently. "No," he said, putting the photos to one side. He reached for a pen. "What's your address, and the address of your neighbor? We'll send an officer to Mrs. Squire's to talk to her. In the meantime, stay away from her premises. If the man impersonating Officer Copeland returns to your house, call us immediately. Do not open your door to him or engage him in conversation."

"You'd be wasting your time by talking to Mrs. Squire."

"Why is that?"

"I think someone's impersonating her as well. Her nurse."

His eyebrows lifted.

Piper told him about Vera Wade and suggested he contact Detective Jason Bower at the Homicide-Robbery-Division.

"Have you contacted the Hollywood division of LAPD about your suspicions?"

"No. That's all they are—suspicions. Detective Bower has been my only police contact."

He jotted down the detective's name and came to his feet. "Thank you, Mrs. Lundberg, for bringing this matter to our attention. We'll be in touch."

CHAPTER 20

The Star Tattler—1965 [Archive]

Another drunken debacle and wild cabana party had the police out for the third time in two weeks to guess who's stately mansion in the Hollywood Hills? Last week two male guests pummeled each other in the street, damaging several cars in the process. This week a young starlet nearly drowned when she passed out and fell into the deep end of the pool.
When is Hollywood's platinum femme fatale going to crank it back a notch?

—Cricket Summers: Columnist to the Stars

THE NEXT DAY WHEN Lee called for an update on the latest developments at the Squire house, Piper invited herself to dinner at Lee's place. "I have to get away from here for awhile," she told Lee. "I need to decompress."

Lee promised a gourmet meal in exchange for all the juicy details.

At eight o'clock, she drove to Brentwood. Lee lived in a pseudo-adobe house, a stone's throw from where O.J.'s infamous house used to be on Rockingham before the bulldozers knocked it to the ground.

"Where's Erica?" They stood in the kitchen amid the aroma of fresh garlic cooking. Lee poured two glasses of chilled Chardonnay.

"Erica? Hmmm, that's a good question. To be honest, I don't know where she is. Even Erica doesn't know where she is. She's in a place where I can't go, which happens to be the major source of our screwed up relationship."

"Meaning?"

"She walked when I refused to agree to a *ménage à trois*."

"The other party being?"

"Her personal trainer. This big bruiser of a jock. God, I've never been so turned off by anyone in my life. A pinhead attached to a mountain of muscle and no neck. Disgusting."

"I'm sorry. I know how much you cared for her."

She waved it off and shrugged. "I knew it was mistake...our meeting in therapy. We're two transsexuals with similar hang-ups. Instead of pulling together, we only hurt and cripple each other. It's ironic though, the thing that broke us up was something we didn't have in common—a taste for semen."

Lee served salmon with asparagus on the wicker table in her courtyard. Water cascaded over the rocks of the stone waterfall, tinkling and gurgling. They ate by the glow of a burning citronella candle. Crickets serenaded them from the corner of the yard. It was a lovely night, the moon—a Dreamworks silver slice—and a handful of stars managed to shine through the haze.

Lee poured pinot noir for Piper and more Chardonnay for herself.

"You have circles under your eyes. You aren't sleeping well," Lee said.

"You wouldn't be sleeping well either, if you lived where I live, seen what I've seen." She speared a piece of asparagus and held it on the end of her fork. "Did you know asparagus makes your urine smell really funky?"

"What did you find out about the man, the one who steals screenplays?"

"I don't know who he is. Only that he's not who he said he was. Not a handyman. Not an undercover cop. So what do you think?"

"Did he threaten you in any way?"

Piper shook her head. "But there's definitely something threatening about him."

"You've never seen him at the house next door?"

"No."

"All right, let's try to think this through. You start butting into your neighbor's business and suddenly this guy shows up, pretending to be someone he's not in order to gain access into your life?"

"Yes, something like that," Piper said. "Though he couldn't possibly think he could get away with it. Not for long, anyway. He was operating with his own funds. That's why Belle got suspicious. Their handyman never paid for anything out of his own pocket, not so much as a nut or bolt. Luke—or whatever his name is—bought windows, spackle, bricks and mortar. Why would he do that?"

"If they're fleecing the old gal, they have the cash to do it. Her cash. But it takes time. It would be worth the expense to keep a close eye on you, to make sure you don't screw up the cash-cow flow before they've gotten everything there is to get out of it."

"If they killed Sybil's housekeeper, why haven't they tried to kill me?" she asked. "Luke's had more than one opportunity."

"One reason is that no one believes you. The police, social services, even her personal doctor thinks you're delusional. Even so, to go after you now would be too risky for them. You're probably safe until they've gotten everything they're after."

"And then?"

She grabbed Piper's hands and squeezed. "Look, stay here. For a couple of nights, at least. Get some good sound sleep. With Erica gone, I'm rattling around in this big place by myself. The guest room is made up. The fridge is full. Stay. We'll have that slumber party. I'll pop in some of those old movies you're so crazy about. I have everything you need like clothes, makeup, whatever. Lord knows I wore your stuff for years. You just didn't know it."

Piper laughed. Lee didn't have to press too hard. Going back to the Vogt's tonight held little appeal for her.

Lee opened another bottle of red wine. They tossed their shoes in a corner and drank wine while lying on throw pillows on the floor of the den and watching films from the fifties. She felt giddy. The pressures of the last week or two trickled away like the water in the courtyard fountain. She and Lee acted like two schoolgirls, rolling around on the carpet, giggling at the stiff dialogue and the corny special effects. She cracked up when Lee mimicked the melodramatic lines of the lead actress, exaggerating their already over-the-top dialogue. Tears streamed down her face. "Stop, I'm going to pee my pants," she said. They laughed harder, clutching at each other. Lee pressed on her belly, saying, "Gotta go, huh? Gotta pee?" Then suddenly everything changed. Lee's arms were around her, holding her in a different way, her hands on her buttocks, pulling her closer. Her mouth came down on Piper's, her tongue probing. *No. Don't ruin it, Lee. Please don't.*

She pulled back. Lee moved in again. Before Lee could kiss her again she pushed her away. Piper scrabbled backwards on the floor, shaking her head. "Dammit," was all she could say.

Lee reached for her. "Piper, I've never stopped loving you. You know that. I'm still the same person who loved you all those years ago. Inside . . ." she laid her palm flat against her chest, over her heart. "Inside here, you're my first love."

"No, Lee. No. It's not the same. It changed. When you changed, it changed—*that way*. I'm sorry."

Piper rose slowly to her feet, straightening her skirt and blouse. She quickly crossed the room, retrieved her shoes, and slipped them on, balancing with her hand against the wall. "I'm going to go home now."

"Ah, crap. Don't be mad. Don't go. It won't happen again. It was the wine. It was the breakup with Erica. It was— ah, shit, Piper, it won't happen again. I promise."

"I know. But I'm going to go home now."

Lee didn't walk her to the door. She knew Piper well enough to give her some space. Piper drove home through the clear night, the sliver of a moon following above, grinning like a madman.

Since her change, Lee had never let on that she wanted Piper in that way. Their relationship had grown strong because Piper believed they could be friends. Her feelings for Lee could never be passionate again. Confused and disturbed, she wondered if they could ever make it okay again, ever get back the close, platonic relationship which had taken years to develop after their divorce and throughout Lee's transition.

Brushing tears from her face, she wondered if Lee, too, had shed tears tonight. Why had this happened now? Was it something she had said or done to encourage her? Maybe it was nothing more than her leaving Gordon, which had brought them closer together again. Just how spontaneous were Lee's actions tonight? Piper thought about the romantic setting in the courtyard, the wine and the invitation to spend the night. Damn, she didn't see it coming, so wrapped up was she in her own affairs. Spontaneous or planned, it hurt to think she might have lost Lee. She needed Lee more now than ever. She was the only one to share her morbid interest in what was going on at the house next door. She was the only one to *believe* her.

Before pulling into the Vogt's driveway, she drove to the end of the street looking for Luke's truck. When she didn't see it, she pulled in and parked at the side of the main house. She wanted to check on Dr. Jekyll before going up to her place.

Dr. J seemed more agitated than usual. He squawked out a stream of nonsense words, refusing to say any of his learned words and refusing to cuddle, kiss or make his cooing sounds. Piper was in no mood tonight to put up with his pissy temper. It was too late to let him out to stretch his wings. Unless he had at least thirty minutes to strut and put on a show, he balked about returning to his cage. She didn't have thirty minutes. Not thirty minutes she wanted to spend with an irritable, screeching bird.

While still in the main house, she went upstairs to check out the back of the Squire estate. No lights burned in the window where she'd seen the hand. She checked through all the windows on the second floor. The house was dark.

She went up to her place, guided by a light from the lamppost near the garage. Standing on the threshold, she flipped the switch just inside the door, but the light did not go on. The closest light was straight ahead in the kitchenette. She paused. She had no intention of crossing the room in the dark. A definite rustle to her right. The hair on the back of her neck rose along with the goose bumps on her arms. She wanted to run but her feet were locked in place. Someone was in her living room. She couldn't see him but she knew he was there. A dark figure passed in front of the window. She caught a glimpse of a tall, well-built man an instant before he slammed into her. She screamed as she was knocked to the floor. She screamed again as a gloved hand clamped over her mouth. Kicking and twisting, she flailed out and raked her nails at the face above her. Over the roaring in her ears, she heard footsteps on the deck. The hand over her mouth eased off. It was too dark to see anything, except that there were two of them. Two tall men scrambling around on the deck. A thud, scuffling, and groans followed. One of them vaulted over the railing, hitting the ground below with an exaggerated grunt.

This wasn't happening. Her fears had been realized, she was now a target. There were two of them. One was still out there on the deck, his back to her, leaning over the railing holding a gun. Fighting the panic paralyzing her, she struggled to her feet and groped around inside the front door searching for something hard or sharp. Her fingers wrapped around the cast-iron doorstop. She sprang into action. The man spun around. She swung the heavy metal, catching him a glancing blow just above his eye, but the blow didn't drop him. She raised the doorstop again. He grabbed her, pinning both her arms to her body and pushed her against the front of the guesthouse, pressing his body into hers, hard. "Take it easy, Piper. It's me. It's Jason Bower."

Jason Bower?

"Detective Bower."

"Detective?" The doorstop slipped from her fingers when, in the light of the lamp below, she saw him in profile. A stream of blood coursed down the side of his face. "Oh my god."

"Inside," he said shielding her body with his as he propelled her through the doorway. "We're targets standing out here."

CHAPTER 21

". . . a dream come true. I'm married to the most marvelous man in the world," Sybil told Hollywood columnist Hedda Hopper. "We have a beautiful son. Our daughter Norma has returned to us from England and Sam has initiated steps to adopt her. With my loving family, the Oscar nomination for Black Ribbon, *and my upcoming film,* Judgment Day, *I couldn't be happier." Six months after that interview her baby boy was dead and her teen daughter committed to a sanatorium. A month later, her husband's private plane crashed into the side of a mountain range in rural Nevada. Shattered dreams.*

—Excerpt from the biography of Sybil Squire: The Platinum Widow *by Russell Cassevantes.*

INSIDE THE GUESTHOUSE, IN the dark, Piper felt her way around the editing bay to the kitchen and turned on the light.

Glass from the broken ceiling light fixture glittered on the editing equipment.

Piper looked back at the detective. He was dabbing at the cut on his head with the side of his thumb.

"Oh God, I'm sorry! Your head. I did that. I thought you were one of them. I have to get you to the emergency room."

"It's okay, it's not as bad as it looks. Head wounds always look worse than they are." He peeled off a paper towel from the holder on the bar counter then sat on a nearby stool holding the towel to his head. "How about you, are you hurt?"

"No. No, I don't think so. Really shook up, though." Piper hurried into the bathroom for something to dress the cut until he could get it properly tended to. He was on his cell phone when she came out. She heard him give out her address before disconnecting.

"The police are on their way."

With a wet washcloth, she cleaned away the blood on his cut brow.

"Did you see who it was?" he asked.

"No, but I'm pretty sure it was the man who's been posing as the handyman."

"The one I saw fixing the windows of the main house?"

"Yes." For the first time, he was wearing casual clothes. Off-duty? "Why are you here?" she asked.

"I got a call from the Fraud Section of the Financial Crime Division, a Lieutenant Stroller. Why didn't you inform me about that particular development?"

"Why? It had nothing to do with the now closed Wade case."

"I—okay—I guess I deserve that."

She put a dab of antiseptic on a Band-Aid and pressed it to his head a little harder than necessary. He winced.

"That doesn't answer my question. Why are you here. . . tonight?"

"I believe you," he said. "I checked out a few things. What I found turned things around. For instance, the nurse, Judith Avidon, has a son. It's possible that son is the phony handyman and the man that attacked you tonight."

Avidon had a son. That shocked her.

"If that's true, then we have them."

"When was the last time you saw Sybil Squire?" he asked.

"The real Sybil?"

"Real or otherwise."

"Yesterday. In an upstairs room that isn't her bedroom. Just before that, I tried to talk to the Sybil imposter before her accomplice drove her away in the Lincoln."

"Imposter?"

Piper told him about her theory. "That's how they've managed to fool everyone for so long. With this woman posing as Sybil to the authorities and denying that there's anything wrong, time is on their side. If we wait too long, they may kill Sybil."

"If they feel threatened they might kill her now and run. I suspect there's something they want from her that she's not giving them."

Yes. That made sense. And it had something to do with the bank. "Vera told me that the same day the stranger came to the Squire house, Sybil made Vera take her to the bank. She had a large valise, which she took with her to a second bank. It's my guess she cleaned out her account and safe-deposit box and transferred the contents to another one."

He nodded. "They want the safe-deposit key and she's not cooperating."

"When you were struggling with the man on the deck, did you see his face?"

He shook his head. "It all happened so fast. He wore a bandana on his head—like the man in the video clip you sent me."

"I have pictures of Luke." She glanced at the end of the counter where she'd left the envelope. It was gone. "He took them. But I've got the digital shots on the PC."

Piper uploaded the picture album on the computer. She scanned through it twice. "They're gone. He deleted them."

He stood and looked around. "Anything else missing?"

She crossed the room to the camcorder. It was empty. "The shots I've taken from the past weeks of the house next door. Gone." She sank down on the ottoman.

He went to the kitchen sink and dampened a paper towel. He picked up the antiseptic and Band-Aids, crossed the room and kneeled in front of her. When he touched her leg at the hemline of her skirt, she looked up at him.

"It's your turn."

Her right knee was skinned from where she'd been knocked to the deck. He gently dabbed at the scraped skin, then applied antiseptic to the Band-Aid and covered the abrasion. He was gentle but efficient, as if he'd done this many times before.

He smelled good. A knock on the door startled her.

"That's LAPD," Detective Bower said rising. "Let me handle this, okay?"

"Gladly."

Detective Bower let the two uniform police officers inside and explained the situation to them. He described the break-in and the assault to her, and his scuffle with the intruder. After thoroughly canvassing the grounds of the

Vogt estate, the two officers returned to the guesthouse and took a statement from her and the detective.

Detective Bower said, "Mrs. Lundberg and I have reason to believe the residents next door may be harboring a fugitive—the man that attacked her tonight. The owner of the house is a friend of Mrs. Lundberg and an innocent party to any of this. I know that legally you can't do anything without a warrant, but the owner of the home may let us in to interview her and her caregivers."

Officer Lovett knocked on the front door of the Squire residence. The door cracked open. Mr. Moto's face peered out, his expression one of bafflement when he saw the two officers, Piper and Jason.

The officer informed Mr. Moto that there had been a crime committed at the Vogt residence. "Would it be possible to speak with the lady of the house, Mrs. Squire?"

Piper looked directly into his eyes through his round glasses, and though his expression was grave, smug amusement shone in his eyes like happy on a clown. He bowed his head and stepped back, allowing them to enter. He showed them to the living room and left the room.

Piper held her breath. It seemed too damn smooth, too easy.

The first thing she noticed was the bare shelves where the dozens of Q. Letec figurines had once stood.

Minutes passed, minutes that felt like an eternity. Piper shifted from one foot to another. No one spoke.

A soft voice broke the silence. "Is there a problem?"

Piper whirled around to see a platinum-haired woman coming into the room. Her steps slow but sure as she walked to the wingback chair, with Mr. Moto at her side, she lowered herself into the chair. The woman's hair was perfectly coiffed. She wore an expensive dressing gown. On her feet were ballet-type slippers. Lacy gloves covered her hands and reached to well above her wrists. It was remarkable how much she resembled Sybil, especially the hair and eyes. In this town, she could be wearing a wig and contact lenses, even a latex mask, designed by a special effects film artist.

The birdcage next to the chair was empty.

"Excuse my informal attire," the woman said to no one in particular, looking around the room. "I was in bed." She turned to Piper. "Mrs. Lundberg, why are you doing this to me?"

"You're not Sybil Squire." Piper turned to the two officers. "She's not Sybil Squire."

"How well do you know Mrs. Squire?" Officer Lovett asked Piper.

"Well enough."

"I've had her to the house one time. The visit was short."

"Twice. I've been here twice. Sybil would know that."

"I didn't invite you the second time," she said.

"If she's not Mrs. Squire, who is she?" the other policeman asked her.

"I don't know. That man," Piper said, pointing to Mr. Moto, "is Sybil's caregiver. He and a nurse named Judith Avidon moved in about a month ago. There are more of them. At least one other man. I strongly believe they're financially exploiting their patient. Not to mention physical abuse."

"What proof do you have?"

"Well, for starters, ask her what happened to the figurines that used to be on these shelves, figurines worth hundreds of thousands of dollars."

"I sold them. I never liked them. They belonged to one of my late husbands. After the last earthquake, several were

186

damaged, so I decided to sell them to someone who loved them as much as Alec loved them. Officers, I'm liquidating my assets and moving east and possibly abroad." She turned to Piper again. "Is that all right with you, dear? Or do I need your permission?"

"What happened to the canaries?"

"I'm afraid they're gone." Tears sprang to her eyes. "One became sick and then all were sick. They died. That's the main reason I'm leaving. There's nothing to hold me here now."

"Where is Judith Avidon?" Piper asked.

"On the east coast. She's setting up things for me there. Preparing us for the move."

"She's lying. If you fingerprinted this woman and compared the prints to Sybil's, you'd see she's not who she says she is."

"Fingerprints to compare with what, Mrs. Lundberg? I've never been fingerprinted."

Piper refused to look at the imposter, directing her questions to the taller cop, Lovett, the one who seemed to be running the show. "What about DNA? Find something of Sybil's and run a DNA test."

"If it will make you happy, then take whatever is needed. My toothbrush, hairbrush, I have nothing to hide."

"If you have nothing to hide, let these policemen search through the house."

"Looking for what?"

"For the man who attacked me tonight and the real Sybil Squire."

She smiled. "If I allowed that then I'd be encouraging your paranoia, Mrs. Lundberg. The answer is no."

Piper realized then that they had thought of everything. All that belonged to Sybil, anything personal, would have been right here in this house. In the past forty years, Sybil had rarely left her home. Anything that might contain her DNA had long ago been substituted with that of the imposter. No wait, there was the autograph she gave Piper the last time she visited her. It would have her fingerprints on it. Or skin cells for DNA analysis.

"I have something of Sybil's. An autographed photo."

"Would you like a handwriting sample?" the woman said.

"She's wearing a wig and contact lenses."

With her gloved fingers, the woman tugged at her hair above her forehead. "It's mine. All mine," she said. "See for yourself."

Both officers leaned in and nodded.

The woman turned to Officer Lovett. "Mrs. Lundberg, sadly, is stalking me. I hoped it wouldn't come to this, but I may be forced to press charges against her. A restraining order, at the very least."

Piper's stomach dropped. She was turning everything around on her. Piper was the guilty party now. "I can prove this is not Sybil Squire. Sybil has scars on the backs of her hands. Ask this woman to remove her gloves."

"Now you're being ridiculous," the imposter said.

"Please," Piper said, pleading with the two police officers. "She can't make scars go away."

"Mrs. Squire?" Detective Bower spoke up for the first time since entering the house.

The woman looked from the detective, to Piper, to Mr. Moto and back to Piper again. Her brow furrowed and her cheeks seemed to redden. They had her now. She can't get away with this. Scars are forever.

"Do you need help?" Piper said, stepping forward. The short cop put an arm out to block her.

"Mrs. Squire, it's a reasonable request," Detective Bower spoke again. "If you will, please."

The woman looked down at her hands folded neatly in her lap. She sighed deeply, then began by tugging at the fingertips, inching the material down slowly. Piper wanted to grab her hand and yank them off, exposing her for the imposter she was. With her palm facing upward, the glove slid down and fell into her lap. She turned her hand over. The scars were red and angry. The other glove came off more quickly. The scars on that hand were not as severe, but without a doubt, they too were burn scars. Even her fingertips were scarred. Glittering on the ring finger of the left hand was the beautiful diamond ring belonging to the real Sybil Squire.

Piper felt numb inside. To what lengths would these people go to pull this off? How much money could there possibly be? Millions?

It was all slipping away. Piper's chance to save Sybil, gone. Unless Detective Bower believed her and was willing to help, there was nothing more she could do.

They returned to the guesthouse. Before driving off in the squad car, Officer Lovett had reminded her that the stalker laws in California were taken very seriously, especially where a celebrity was involved.

Piper sat on a tall stool at the kitchen counter. "So it must be the contents of the safe-deposit box and the missing key that's keeping them around this long."

"Keeping Sybil alive, you mean."

"Is she still alive?" she asked.

"As far as Lieutenant Stroller at the FCD is concerned, Sybil Squire is picking up roots and moving east. I'd say by now they've managed to clean out her bank account and sell off most of her assets. Instead of trying to sell the house, which would take too long, they could simply mortgage it to the hilt. My first assumption was that one of the caregivers had gotten a power of attorney, but now I realize they don't need one, not if they can become Sybil." He paced the room. "I wonder if, after tonight, they'll think the contents of the safe-deposit box still worth risking their necks for."

"Risking their necks?" Piper's laugh was dry and humorless. "Oh, the last thing they're worried about is their necks. They have no fear. You saw them tonight. Mr. Moto looking so frigging innocent and cooperative. And the phony lady Squire, she...she's so damn good at convincing not only the Hollywood police, and the FCD, but even Sybil's doctor. She burned her own hands." When Piper saw the burns on that imposter's hands, she actually doubted herself. "If we could just find Sybil," she said. "We have to find her. Only she can expose them."

"If Mrs. Squire turns up alive, she'd have to prove she's the real McCoy. Can she? You said it yourself, these people are determined, they've thought of everything. As of right now, they have the upper hand, and they know it."

"Maybe...for now." Then it hit her. "Blood," she said, her voice rising. "The private hospital where she went for her burns must have a sample of her blood. There's our DNA."

"It's a possibility, but only if they slipped up. Don't forget that the nurse took care of her in that hospital too. She had access to all the files and what went into them. She could have easily substituted blood samples, X-rays, tests, whatever, or even destroyed them."

Piper slumped down on the stool. "How will Sybil get her life back? That she might have to prove who she is never occurred to me. They've covered all the bases. Rescuing Sybil may not be enough, especially if she's given up and no longer wants to live."

"Mrs. Lundberg—"

"Could you call me Piper? I never did like that name."

He nodded. "Piper it is. I'll see if I can get the Wade case reopened. At least that'll open some doors for us, investigation-wise."

"Thank you, Detective Bower."

"Jason."

She looked up at him.

"Less formal. I may be working this case off the clock, Piper. With the backlog of homicides in all of L.A. County, I won't be able to devote a lot of time to it on the clock, unless I get more evidence. Something substantial."

"I understand." She paused. "Jason, I can't tell you how much it means to have someone believe me."

"Sorry it took me so long. I promised you I'd do a thorough investigation and I dropped the ball." Jason stepped to the door. He opened and closed it several times. "This door was jimmied. Is there a security alarm?"

She shook her head.

"Do you have somewhere else you can stay tonight? The main house?"

"Luke has the keys."

"You can't stay here until the place is secure."

Where could she go? Gordon had alienated most of her friends during their marriage. Lee was the only person she would dare to impose on this late at night. Despite what happened there earlier, Lee would welcome her with open arms. Piper wished now she had stayed and worked it out.

She called Lee on both lines. No answer. Not even voicemail. Lee had gone into shutdown mode. That was her way of handling a crisis.

Piper hung up and shook her head.

Emotionally exhausted after her adrenaline high, she felt completely drained. The thought of checking into in a motel room appealed to her even less than staying where she was, alone.

"I don't think he'll come back tonight. The door has a safety bolt in the floor. I'll be okay here."

"How'd I know you'd say that?" Jason Bower said. "All right, sit tight, I'll be right back. Bolt it as soon as I go out."

He left the house. Piper engaged the bolt.

In under three minutes he was back, winded from the run. He handed her a black gadget. "It's a 2-way radio. I'll be in my car around the corner. If you hear something or just get jumpy, press this button and start yelling. I'll be right here."

He placed a canister of mace on the counter and left.

She slid the safety bolt into place and then watched him walking down the driveway. He kept close to the wall, away from any prying eyes from the house next door. When he was out of sight the radio in her hand crackled. His voice came through loud and clear, "Are you there? Come in."

She pressed the button. "I'm here."

"Sleep tight. Over and out."

CHAPTER 22

On January 12th, 1968, Norma Watson Knoller was murdered in her private room at The Triple Oaks Sanatorium by fellow inmate, Wanda Berganstoff. No reason or motive for the crime was given. The press flocked to the Hollywood hills house for comments regarding the murder of Sybil Squire's daughter. They were turned away by the housekeeper with the words. "No comment. Not now, not ever."

—*Excerpt from the biography of* Sybil Squire: The Platinum Widow *by Russell Cassevantes*

PIPER DID NOT SLEEP. The radio Jason Bower left with her beeped and blinked. She stuffed it under a pillow at the side of the Murphy bed, but still she couldn't sleep. Her mind ran on and on, playing the events of the past weeks in a continuous loop.

These people were not typical in-and-out amateur scam artists. They were hard players prepared to go all the way, no matter how long it took or what extremes were necessary. She sensed the break-in was a warning to scare her, to get her to back off. How far would they go?

At six that morning, Jason called on the radio to check on her. He told he was going home to change and then to the precinct. They arranged to get together later in the day at the main house. Piper suggested he use the front entrance, which faced away from the Squire property.

The locksmith had changed the locks at the guesthouse and the main house and left by the time Jason arrived. He wore a charcoal-gray suit over a button-down shirt and a black tie. A butterfly bandage covered the cut above his eye. They sat in the living room.

"I ran a check on the two caregivers. Before nurse Avidon went to work at the clinic where Squire was treated for her burns, she was a registered nurse for an elderly man in Hancock Park. When he died, guess who was named beneficiary?"

"Avidon. Was there anything suspicious about his death?"

"No more suspicious than the housekeeper's death. Her son has a rap sheet--assault and battery, drunk and disorderly--but has managed to stay out of prison. Arrests, but no convictions. He has at least half a dozen aliases. I suspect one or both of them are pretty savvy about computers, and good at forgery and falsifying whatever papers or certificates that they need. Shields too."

"What about the other man? Ling? Where does he fit in?"

"Nothing on him."

Jason paced. "I want to pay a visit to the clinic where Ms. Squire and Avidon were introduced. Avidon doesn't have a criminal past—but she may have had problems on the job."

He headed for the front door, paused, then turned. "Are you coming?"

At noon, in West Hollywood, they climbed the concrete steps of the main entrance of the hospital. At the nurse's station, Jason showed his credentials to the doctor's head nurse and asked about Judith Avidon. The nurse was reluctant to discuss Avidon's records until she learned that someone she had recommended might soon be up on criminal charges. She motioned for them to join her at the end of the counter.

In a hushed tone, she said, "Nurse Avidon was only here a couple months before she went to work for Mrs. Squire. She was efficient, reliable, with a good bedside manner. When she heard that Dr. Lowdell was asking about a live-in nurse for the actress, she stepped right up. The doctor asked for recommendations and I gave him Judy's name. Like I said, she was a stellar nurse. The patients seemed to like her."

"Did she work in a clinic or hospital prior to coming here?" Jason asked.

The nurse excused herself and crossed the hall to an office. Minutes later she was back with a manila file folder. She opened it on the counter top. "Let's see, her last two positions were in private practice. Patients now both deceased."

"May we have their names?"

"I'm sorry. Because they were private positions, I'm afraid I can't give you that information without a court order. I can only tell you she worked at County General and another private clinic." She started to close the file.

"What other clinic?" Jason said.

She flipped the file open again. "It's probably irrelevant. It was forty-odd years ago."

Both Jason and Piper leaned in to get a better look.

"Triple Oaks. It was a sanitarium in Los Feliz," the nurse said.

"She was a nurse there?" Piper asked, hardly able to get the words out. Her chest felt constricted.

"I believe so."

They thanked her and left. When they reached the parking lot, Piper grabbed Jason's arm and blurted out, "Triple Oaks is the sanitarium where Sybil Squire's daughter was murdered. She's left a trail that we can follow."

"Let's go," Jason said.

On the way to Los Feliz and the Triple Oaks Clinic, no longer called a Sanitarium, they went over details of the case. Within the last five years, Judith Avidon had cared for two separate patients on a live-in basis. Both had died in her care. Were estates involved in both? It wasn't a coincidence that Avidon and her cohorts had found Sybil Squire at a very vulnerable time in her life.

"I don't think this nurse just happened to be working at the very hospital where they took Sybil Squire after the fire," she said.

"What are you getting at?"

"I bet Avidon knew beforehand which hospital Sybil would be taken to, the one where her doctor practiced. Even if the paramedics had taken Sybil to another hospital, she more than likely would have transferred to the private clinic. That fire was no accident."

"How do you know that?"

"While Sybil was in the hospital she told her housekeeper that someone had been in her house the night of the fire, a man. The morning of the fire she had visitors. I was there having coffee with her by the pool. I saw them come and go. Sybil was really shook up. That same day she went from bank to bank."

"You saw the visitor?"

"I saw the car and someone was sitting in the passenger seat. I couldn't see his or her face. There were two of them."

"Interesting."

"Also interesting is that this particular nurse was employed at two separate hospitals, where first the daughter, then the mother, happened to be patients."

"You'd make a good investigator," Jason said.

"It's all those mystery stories. Who says you can't learn from movies and TV?"

They pulled up to the rusty gates of Triple Oaks Clinic at 2:00 p.m. Although she'd never been here, Piper suspected it hadn't changed much in the past forty years. A mission-style structure sitting on acres of rolling hills. She spotted only two oaks, one on each side of the sandstone gateposts. Jason spoke into the intercom and the gates opened. They drove through to the main building.

The grounds looked deserted. They parked in the visitor's parking lot and entered through a side door. No patients or hospital staff loitered around. Walking down the musty corridor of the old building to the administrator's office, she expected to see mental patients wandering aimlessly or sitting in a catatonic state, like in *The Snake Pit*. The scene where Olivia De Havilland sits on the cold brick floor in the psycho ward, inmates all around her. In a dazed stupor she looks upward, out of the chaos, the walls become round like a tunnel, the dark, dank tunnel of a snake pit. Up, up it rises until she is a mere speck at the bottom.

Piper rubbed her arms.

The corridor at Triple Oaks was empty and quiet.

In the administrator's office, Jason informed an assistant they'd like to speak to the chief administrator.

"What does it pertain to?" the obese woman behind the desk asked.

"A homicide."

"What homicide?" Her eyes widened in alarm.

"Norma Knoller."

"My gawd, that happened ages ago."

"Yes."

"Mrs. Langacino would know about it. She was here back then."

"Would you please tell her we'd like to talk with her about it?"

She rose with effort, using the arms of the chair to assist her, and walked into the room behind her. Moments later, she was back.

"I'm sorry, but Mrs. Langacino refuses to discuss the incident." She sank into the chair. "She suggested you get what you need elsewhere."

Jason took Piper's arm and led her around the desk to the administrator's office. Without knocking, he opened the door and strode inside.

The woman behind the desk looked up in surprise.

"Mrs. Langacino, this is official business." He held up his shield. "I'm Homicide Special Detective Jason Bower. This is Piper Lundberg. We were told that you were employed here at the time of the Knoller homicide."

She came to her feet. "I told my assistant—"

"Your help in this matter is essential. Lives are in danger. Can we count on your cooperation? If not, I can get a subpoena."

"Detective Bower, how on earth can the details of a forty-three-year-old incident possibly be useful to the police now?"

"That's what we're about to find out."

She looked toward the door. When it was apparent no one was going to rush in and remove them, she rolled her eyes and waved a hand to the two chairs in front of her desk.

"Close the door, please."

Jason closed it and took a seat next to Piper.

"Yes, I remember it. You don't forget something that extreme. Creates an emotional scar for anyone even remotely close to something that horrific."

They sat on wooden chairs facing her desk, an uncluttered desk with a large green blotter and matching pen and pencil set. Through the window behind Mrs. Langacino, Piper saw about a dozen men and women in yellow cotton tops and pants sitting in a circle on the lawn, holding hands.

"If you'd asked me about the incident thirty or forty years ago, I wouldn't have been able to discuss it. It was so grisly. I'm still not comfortable talking about it."

"We appreciate your cooperation," Jason said.

"I was a student nurse in the ward next to the ward in question. What do you want to know?"

"Judith Avidon, was she a nurse here at that time?" Piper asked.

"Avidon? That's familiar. Avidon. Yes, I remember the name, but you're mistaken. I'm pretty certain that was the name of the guard who stopped the attack. Not the nurse's name."

Jason and Piper exchanged a look.

"Sorry, I don't recall the nurse's name."

"She would have been about nineteen or twenty. Brown hair, brown eyes."

"There was a young nurse on duty that day, in that ward. She was new to the hospital. Like me, a student nurse. She was the first person to come upon the attack and the one to alert the guard." Mrs. Langacino stared off into a corner of the room; she massaged the loose skin under her chin. "I vaguely remember her being a mousy thing. Quiet and shy. I didn't think she'd last one day in that ward, but she stuck it out. That is until that awful morning."

"What happened to her? Do you know where she is now?"

"Oh, goodness, I have no idea. She quit that very day. I almost quit myself. It was horrific. All that blood. Only a completely deranged person could do that to another human being."

"Who killed the inmate?" Jason asked. Piper was surprised by his question, surprised that he hadn't heard the story until she realized he hadn't been born when it happened. And not being obsessed with Sybil Squire like she was, he wouldn't know the minute details of her life.

"Another inmate. Wanda Berganstoff. The woman had had previous episodes of violence, but nothing like what happened that day. She and Norma seemed to get along just fine. Norma Knoller was Sybil Squire's daughter, you know? Sybil Squire, the actress."

"Yes, we know," Piper said.

"It was such a shock to everyone. It happened so fast. Norma'd had an awful cough, a bronchial ailment of some kind. It was getting on everyone's nerves. We think the chronic coughing sent Wanda over the edge. She was sensitive to loud or repetitive noises. Anyway, the nurse, the one you asked about, was bringing some cough medication to her, but it was too late, Wanda had already initiated the attack. The nurse was attacked too, but managed to sound the alarm. When I rushed in to help, it was all over. The guard was standing over Wanda, who was in the corner of Norma's room curled into a ball like a roly-poly bug, covered in blood and shaking like a leaf.

Norma was scarcely breathing. Poor thing, we did everything we could but... it was, well, too late."

"What did the inmate use to kill the victim?" Jason asked.

"Her hands, her head, the floor and walls and commode, whatever was handy. It looked like someone had thrown buckets of red paint around the room."

"What happened to her? To Wanda?" Piper said.

"She was transferred to the ward for the criminally insane. She died four days later. She choked to death on her uniform dress. Tore it into pieces and shoved it down her throat."

"Is that possible?" Piper asked.

"Anything is possible with the insane, Mrs. Lundberg. You wouldn't believe what they can do to themselves. The objects we find in their stomachs, and...well, every orifice for that matter." She added, "We can't keep them restrained twenty-four hours a day."

Outside, a man from the circle broke hand contact with his partners, jumped up and raised his fists into the air. He turned and ran away. The circle closed again, hand in hand.

"Are there any records from that day that might give us a name for the nurse and the guard?" Jason asked.

"Goodness, I wouldn't know where to begin to look for something like that. I'm sure you'll find everything you need in the newspaper accounts. The police took a report. The press was all over it, being that Norma was the daughter of a famous actress."

They thanked her. When they left the building and descended the main steps, Piper saw a large man in yellow charge around the side of the building, rushing at them. The man grabbed her arm and pulled her toward him, holding her in a suffocating bear hug. Too shocked to scream, she pushed at him. In an instant, Jason had the man in a headlock, twisted him around, and pushed him to his knees on the concrete walk. Several attendants appeared and attempted to restrain him.

Jason wrapped his arms around Piper, shielding her from another attack.

It was the man from the group circle. He struggled with his aides. Crying now. Calling out for Candice.

When they had calmed him down, one aide said, "His name is George. He thinks you're his daughter. He won't hurt you. He just wants to go home."

"Are you all right?" Jason asked.

She nodded. "He's very strong."

"You're not Candice," the man accused, as if she had tried to deceive him.

The aides led the man away. He shouted, "You're not Candice. You can't fool me."

Jason looked into her eyes, still holding onto her. "Do you want to file a complaint?"

"No. God no, I'm fine. He might file a complaint against me for impersonating his daughter. There's a lot of that going around these days."

He smiled, let go of her, picked up her purse and handed it to her. His touch still warm and tingly on her skin.

They drove to a branch of the county library in Los Feliz. Jason took over, asking the clerk in the newspaper morgue for articles on the case. Within minutes, they were viewing microfiche through the machine.

"Can't you find these reports at your precinct on a computer or a database or whatever it's called?"

"I could if I wanted to do this without you. You know the history. I need you."

Piper nodded, feeling pleased.

He found the article and they scanned it for names. Inmate Norma Watson Knoller—victim. Inmate Wanda Berganstoff—assailant. Nurse Judith Neely—eyewitness. And security guard Elliot M. Avidon—eyewitness.

"Looks like the nurse took the guard's name," Jason said. "An alias?"

"Or she married him. If Luke is Judith's son, he'd be about the right age. Early forties."

"There's something off about all this. The nurse and the guard were the only eyewitnesses to the actual attack. The inmate responsible for the killing, dies shortly thereafter. No confession. No denials. Case closed. And—"

"Then this same nurse takes a caregiver position forty years down the road to the mother of the murdered woman," she finished for him. "Why? A coincidence? A vendetta? What if—now indulge me here—what if the nurse had been the one to murder Sybil's daughter? The nurse, with the help of the guard? Easy enough to stage the killing and blame it on another inmate, especially an inmate with a history of violence. Judith Neely got a few lumps in the process. Lumps from the victim trying to defend herself?"

"But why? Why kill Sybil's daughter? And who is this nurse?"

"Whoever she is," Piper said, "death seems to follow her."

CHAPTER 23

JASON DROPPED PIPER OFF at the Vogt's house and said he'd be back at six. At six sharp, he called her on her cell phone.

"Sorry, Piper, something unexpected came up. I'll be tied up for at least two hours."

"That's okay. I'm going to get a bite and turn in early. We'll talk tomorrow."

"Where will you be, the guesthouse or the main house?"

"Main house."

"Call my cell if you need me, okay? Oh, by the way, I think I found our guard, Elliot Muney Avidon. He's living at the Tropical Palms on Broadway. I'll try to hook up with him ASAP."

"I want to be there when you meet with him."

"Pick you up in the morning."

She emailed Belle from the house computer and informed her she would be staying in the main house for a while. Belle called an hour later.

"Piper, what's going on? What's happened?"

"Someone broke into the guesthouse last night." She told her about the detective coming to her rescue.

"This is getting too bizarre, Piper. I knew you were getting in over your head. I told you so."

"I'm sorry, Belle, I don't know what to say."

"Maybe you should go somewhere safe. I don't like you being there alone."

"I'm not alone. Jason is on the case. He knows what he's doing. I trust him."

"Who's Jason?"

"Detective Bower. He's with the LA police and he has a gun and everything."

"Is he there now?"

"Yes," she lied.

"Well, okay, if you're sure."

"I'm sure."

"Don't try to be a hero and protect the home front. It's only *stuff*. It can be replaced. Except for Dr. J, that is. If anything else happens, if you don't feel safe, take my feathered baby and get the hell out of there."

"I will. I had the locks and the security alarm code changed this morning here in the main house. The man who was impersonating your handyman had a key."

"Good lord, the man's got balls. What if Luke would've popped in at the house while this cheeky bastard was pretending to be him?"

Piper wondered that too. With his smooth easy lies and cool bravado, she suspected he would have managed to play it out to his advantage.

"What I'd like to know is what happened to our handyman?" Belle said, breaking into her thoughts. "The real one is this little pipsqueak of a man. Very professional. Wears a blue uniform with his name on the shirt pocket."

205

"Nothing like the man I dealt with."

Before signing off, Belle added, "Good news and bad news. The shoot has turned around and things are going better between Mick and Zimmerman. Good for the movie, bad for you."

A week ago, Piper would have been disappointed to learn they wouldn't be calling in a new director and film editor. It now seemed inconsequential, like something from another time and place.

"VanRaven may have something for me. He said he'd call this week. In the meantime, I have feelers out at the studios."

"Fabulous. It doesn't hurt to have Lee there to champion for you."

The mention of Lee made Piper's stomach twist. She would call her the first chance she got. But not tonight. Tonight she would eat and go to bed.

"Gotta go, Piper. I'm off to Angkor Wat for a brief holiday. The temples, y'know?"

The Vogt's fridge had little to offer. She cooked pasta and red sauce from a jar she found in the cupboard. She ate in the kitchen to be near Dr. J. He was thrilled by the attention, and she was happy to have his company. He did all the talking, which was fine by her.

As twilight approached, the wind came up. Santa Anas, hot and dry. Piper went upstairs, sat at the window, and reached for the binoculars. As in the past, that part of the house remained dark, but she could hope for another sighting, another sign that Sybil was still alive. The wind rustled the trees and blew leaves into the air. She focused on the window where she had caught a glimpse of the burned hand, in the room where she thought Sybil was being kept. Something there caught her attention. She leaned in closer, wishing she had the more powerful telescope instead of the

206

binoculars. She made out bright red letters on the glass, letters that looked like they'd been written with lipstick. The tightly shut white blinds made the crooked letters more visible. W A L _____, the last letter disjointed and trailing off to the side, as if the writer had been interrupted or lost control. It had to be a message from Sybil. It just *had* to be.

Wal. . . ?   Was it part of a name, or just what it sounded like, a wall? Was that it, the word WALL?

Piper scanned the entire side of the mansion. Seeing nothing out of the ordinary, she tilted the binoculars down to the stone wall that ran between the two houses. The wall was covered with English ivy. The wind lifted large sections of it, flopping it back and forth against the stones. She panned along the top of the wall several times. Halfway through the third pass, what she initially thought to be ivy rustling in the wind, turned out, on closer inspection, to be something fluttering beneath the leaves--fluttering like pages in a book. She tightened the focus. It *was* a book, tucked neatly into the thick mass of ivy leaves and vines. The strong winds had freed it somewhat, allowing the top pages to flap lightly against the cover.

Grabbing the phone to dial Jason's cell, she looked back through the glasses at the ivy wall. The strength of the wind was picking up. The book inched toward the edge of the wall, the edge closest to the Squire property. She chewed on her lip. There wasn't much time.

She rushed downstairs, out the kitchen door and crossed the driveway to the wall. She ran up the length of it to where she thought the book would be, all the while praying she wasn't being observed from next door. By imagining an invisible plumb line from the Vogt's upstairs window, she reached up on her tiptoes and started patting the ivy at the top of the wall. She went ten feet in one direction before reversing direction and going fifteen feet in the other direction. The wind whipped at her clothes and hair, stinging her skin and eyes. Maybe the book had blown over the wall into enemy territory. She touched something not leafy. Filled with excitement, she snatched at it, breaking off several fingernails, and dragged the book off the wall, leaves and all.

Without looking at it, she clutched it to her chest. Like a fullback clutching the pigskin, she ran full-out back to the house. Inside, she locked the door and set the alarm. Her knees went weak. With her back against the door, she sank to the floor, her breath coming in heaving rasps, and opened the journal. The ink had run along the edges, but most of the writing was still intact and legible. The cloth cover of the journal was so grimy she couldn't determine its color or whether there had once been a design in the fabric. Crusted with dirt and grit, as if it had been buried in the ground or exposed to the elements for some time. The last hard rain had been the night the housekeeper died. There were no identifying details. No name signed the pages. Piper didn't need a name. Without a doubt, the journal belonged to Sybil Squire. The handwriting was unmistakably Sybil's. At first, she merely scanned the pages, catching bits and pieces, too impatient to read every word. There were no dates to indicate the year. Her mind flashed back to that period in Sybil's past, to the most monumentally tragic time in her life. Not one or two, but three tragedies to be precise. The deaths of two loved ones and the incarceration of her teenage daughter, Norma. When she spotted Norma's name, she read each word.

October 8. *Today, on her fifteenth birthday, Norma arrived home in America to live with Sam and me. Although Sam and I tried to make her feel welcome, she locked herself in her room and refused to attend her own party. What did I expect? After five years at boarding school in England, my little girl returns home to a new father and a new baby brother. Sam's such a happy go lucky person, always optimistic. His favorite saying, 'love and kindness conquers all.' He's sure she'll come around in time. He wants to make it work between them, especially since his relationship with his own daughter became shaky when Sam left Marlene's mother to marry me.*

December 22. *It's official. Norma Watson is now Norma Knoller! Sam adopted Norma. We all flew to Switzerland for the Christmas holidays. Norma was moody throughout the long flight. When we arrived at our chateau in the Alps, magical under the fresh white snow and clear blue sky, my spirits rose. It was perfect. Just the thing to bring her around.*

December 26. *On Christmas Eve, Norma exploded at the dinner table, calling us horrible names, scaring the servants and young Sammy, and screaming out that I had abandoned her and she wasn't* his *daughter. Sam was devastated. We returned to the States today.*

April 12. *Little Sammy's first birthday. We tried to have a quiet family party, but Norma's difficult moods have the household in a constant state of tension and anxiety. Sam's optimism is wearing thin. For the first time since she returned home last fall, he's hinting at sending her away. He wanted so much to love Norma and win her over. This is extremely hard for me. I'm not sure what to do.*

October 8. *Norma's sessions with Dr. Saunders are going quite well. She's begun to open up to us, little things like her presence at the table at mealtime. She's also taking an interest in her appearance, spending hours applying her makeup and styling her hair. Norma wants to be a film makeup artist.*

Today for her sixteenth birthday, we treated her to a day of beauty at Vidal Sasson's salon. Norma has never looked lovelier. At lunch at Chasen's, Norma even blushed when a young man at a nearby table complimented her on her stunning eyes and glowing skin. This gives me hope she may accept us again.

December 26. Christmas this year was filled with joy and good cheer. Norma has taken to Sammy like a genuine big sister. Oh how he loves Norma, clinging to her, calling her Noma. He always runs to her first, no matter what. I might be jealous of their close relationship if I hadn't wanted this for so long. We're a family. I am truly blessed.

Piper quickly rifled through to the end of the journal. The pages following the December 26 entry were blank. A yellowed newspaper clipping was taped to the inside back cover. She read the brief newspaper article.

The twenty-month-old son of screen idol Sybil Squire and her husband, Samuel Knoller, died in an accidental drowning at the couple's Hollywood Hills estate Monday afternoon. The child's mother discovered his lifeless body in an upstairs bathtub of their twelve room home. The half sister, Norma, collapsed and was admitted to Cedars-Sinai Medical Center. "It's all my fault," the tearful sixteen-year-old later told police. "I was running bath water. I left the room to answer the phone. I didn't know he had gone in there. I heard my mother screaming. It's my fault. Please, I just want to die."

A private memorial with the immediate family will be held at an undetermined date.

Scribbled next to the clipping were the words: **The rose garden**

That rainy night weeks ago, Sybil kneeling in the mud, hands covered with fresh dirt, she had been either burying journals or digging them up. Were there more journals buried in the rose garden?

Piper reread the entries. Samuel Knoller had a daughter. Their relationship suffered when he married Sybil. That was the first Piper had heard of Sybil's stepdaughter.

Piper knew nothing about the daughter, but she was sure she knew someone who did. She rose to her feet and rushed into Belle's office. She thumbed through the rolodex on Belle's desk until she found the number for Jane Hill, the Vogt's dinner guest who had been a friend of Sybil's long ago. She left a message on Jane's voicemail, telling her it was urgent that she speak with her as soon as possible. Then she left the same message for Jason.

CHAPTER 24

ONLY MINUTES AFTER PIPER left a message for Jane Hill, Jason called. She told him about the journal and read the notation about the stepdaughter. "I'm sure there are other journals, but this was the one she wanted me to see first, the one about the stepdaughter. Samuel Knoller and his daughter had a falling out when he married Sybil. He had a son with Sybil, then he adopted Sybil's daughter. It's possible this stepdaughter might hold a grudge," she said. "Stepdaughter, nurse, what do you think?"

He whistled softly.

"I think the other journals are buried in the rose garden. They could be the key to all of this."

"Look, don't do anything till I get there."

Piper hurried back upstairs, grabbed up the binoculars, and resumed spying. The outdoor lamp flicked on, illuminating the Vogt's driveway. She didn't have long to wait. Mr. Moto came out of the house lugging a large carton. He went to the carport, opened the trunk of the Lincoln, dropped the carton inside, and closed the trunk lid. Reminiscent of a scene from Hitchcock's Rear Window. The body in the steamer truck.

Moto backed the big car out of the carport and stopped. The nurse, wearing a chiffon scarf over her head, joined him inside the car. So much for Judith being on the east coast. By the time the Lincoln disappeared around the other side of the mansion, her palms were moist, her heart beat like a jackhammer in her chest, and her mind raced.

Mr. Moto and Judith were away from the house. But Sybil wasn't alone. Certain now that Judith's son stood guard over Sybil, she focused the binoculars at the back of the house, at the window where Sybil had written the message. She was surprised to see the blinds were open. Not just open, but pulled up. Light from behind, in the hallway, seeped into the room. The red letters were still there, but something else was there too. A man stood at the double window, on the far side of the message, a pair of binoculars to his face, the lens pointed at her. *Luke.* He lowered the glasses, grinned, then cupped a hand over his crotch. She dropped the binoculars and stumbled backwards.

Had he seen the message? It really didn't matter because she had gotten to the journal first. If there were more of them, they had to be buried in the garden. Sybil's message in the back of her journal "The rose garden" couldn't be clearer. Piper had to get the rest of them. He wouldn't expect her to go over there. The reasoning side of her brain told her to wait for Jason. The impulsive side said she had a better chance of succeeding now, with the other two gone.

Changing into a pair of Belle's black jeans and a dark hooded windbreaker of Mick's, she silenced her cell phone and dropped it into a side pocket along with a penlight she found in the desk drawer. She had forgotten the can of pepper spray in the guesthouse. Dousing all the lights in the house, she exited through the front door. The warm, dry, Santa Ana wind blew her hair into her face. She stopped to secure it inside the hood. With that break in her momentum, she almost chickened out until she thought about Sybil struggling to write those words on the windowpane. She continued. From the Vogt's tool shed in the rear yard, she grabbed a garden spade and hefted it. It could double as a weapon if necessary.

With a quick deep breath, she made a dash for the farthest corner of the ivy wall and slipped through the gap at the junction of the two walls. Staying close to the wall, she worked her way around the pool house. The rose garden was on the far side of the property, far from the ivy-covered wall where she had retrieved the journal. When had Sybil approached that wall and slipped her journal beneath the ivy leaves? Leaves crunched under her sport shoes. Olive and pepper trees flanked the garden to the rear and along the wall. She ran crouched down, making herself as small as possible. Even in the darkness, with the cover of trees and bushes, she felt exposed, vulnerable.

Before she had made it halfway around the shallow end of the pool, car lights washed over the ivy wall. She spun around, ran to the pool house, and ducked behind a pillar. She held her breath, waiting for the car to enter the carport, where she'd be out of their line of vision. The car slowed. *Don't stop there.* It stopped. Dropping to the ground, she crawled to the door of the pool house and slipped inside just as the Lincoln's engine died.

The room was pitch-black and smelled of mold and chlorine. Outside, two car doors slammed. A single pair of footsteps crossed the bricks to the house. She heard the sunroom door open and close. Only one set of footsteps. Where was the other one? With a trembling hand, she reached into the pocket of her jacket and found the penlight. She ran the beam over the walls. Across the room, farthest from the house, was a window. She prayed it wasn't painted shut.

214

The sunroom door opened and closed again. Voices. A man and a woman. Footsteps crossed the bricks again and came within several feet of where she stood on the other side of the door. The knob turned. She quickly shifted to the side of the door just as it opened. Through the crack between the hinges, someone stood on the threshold. The overhead light blinked on, nearly blinding her. She pressed herself against the wall and held her breath.

The female voice called out from across the yard. "Jack, over here! Come look at this!"

Mr. Moto stepped inside, his back toward Piper. He held a rolled up Persian carpet in both arms.

She continued to hold her breath, feeling a crushing tightness in her chest. She slid her hand into her pocket. Her cell phone was gone.

"Jack!"

"Wait a sec, I want to—"

She could see the vein in his neck pulsating. He dropped the carpet on the floor.

"Now!"

Moto stepped back and the room went dark. The door closed and the footsteps retreated rapidly.

Piper sank against the door. Her fingers grasping the garden spade and penlight ached from the pressure. She worked her way through the cluttered pool house, lifted the sash on the window and climbed out, dropping the garden spade inside. Just as she lowered the window, the door flew open, banging against the wall where only moments ago she had stood. The light came on, throwing shadows across the ivy wall. She heard an angry voice call out, "Check the whole damn place."

She ran the length of the wall, through the gap, and past the Vogt's tool shed. On the Vogt's front porch, her breath ragged and hoarse, she fumbled with the key in the lock.

A hand gripped her shoulder. "A little night reconnaissance?"

Piper spun around and collapsed against the door.

Jason took the key from her.

She wanted to throw her arms around his neck and hug him, so thankful was she that he wasn't Luke.

He opened the door. "Inside."

In the dark entry hall, her hand shook as she entered the security code. "I know, it was dumb of me, but I had to look for it. Judith and Moto left the house. It was the perfect—"

"No," he snapped. "There's no perfect time for you to go off half-cocked. Dammit, Piper, next time you wait for me."

Her only concern was for Sybil. But he was right—it was risky and stupid, and she almost got caught. Although she sure as hell wasn't going to tell him that.

The phone rang. She and Jason looked at each other. She patted her empty pocket. Stepping into the living room, she picked up the house phone receiver and said a tentative hello.

"Piper?"

"Jane? Jane, I'm so glad you called back."

CHAPTER 25

THE EVENING TRAFFIC ON Sunset Boulevard heading west was light. Rush hour traffic had passed, and 9 p.m. was still too early for the party crowd to be out. They drove by the Beverly Hills Hotel and made a right up Benedict Canyon past Chevy Chase Drive up the hill. Jane wore a Chinese-style, red satin lounge outfit. Considered seductive attire if not for the various stains speckled across the bodice. She frowned when she saw Piper was not alone.

Without asking, Jane poured them what she was drinking—brandy. After showing them into the den, where candles flickered and glowed around the room, she sank down on the sofa, scattering a number of small dogs and cats. The pets clamored over her, licking and nuzzling before settling down at her side and on her lap to sleep. Jason and Piper shared the loveseat, the only seat not occupied by an animal.

"What brings you here tonight? You were very vague on the phone."

"It's about Sybil," Piper said.

"Go on."

Piper and Jason told her what had been happening to Sybil, and now Piper. Jane listened with an occasional nod or sip of her drink.

When they finished, Jane said, "Heartbreaking. Will it never end for Sybil?"

"It doesn't seem so, does it?" Piper answered.

"What do you want from me?"

Piper handed her the journal, the pages in question marked with slips of paper. She read the one about the mysterious death of Sybil's third husband, Paul Winger.

"You want to know about Paul's suicide? About what happened that night?"

Piper almost said no, that she wanted to know about Sybil's stepdaughter, but Jane knew secrets and Piper wanted to hear all of them. She nodded.

"It was our secret—mine, Sybil's, my father's, and of course Norma. Norma witnessed the entire debacle. Daddy and I merely cleaned up the scene and swept the ugliness under the proverbial rug. Daddy was head of Transworld Artists at the time and, naturally, he had a lot of power. When I say power, I don't mean within the industry only, but with the press, the local law officials, and politicians. My promise to Sybil was to take what I know about that night to my grave. But—and I hope I'm doing the right thing—if it will help you to help Sybil, to help put these bastards behind bars, I guess I'm going to have to break that promise."

A white cat with a plaid collar leaped into Jane's lap, catching its claws on her pants, snagging the satin. Jane scratched behind its ear. "Sybil was on location in Havasu, filming *Delta Queen*. The movie wrapped up earlier than expected and she arrived home sooner than planned. She surprised Paul, who was in bed with his lover. The young man, a mere boy, actually, was naked and very very drunk."

"There was quite a scene. Paul begged her to understand. Yet how could she understand that the man she'd married, the man who pretended to be a caring father to her daughter, was a freak of nature? That's what she called him, 'a freak of nature'—in those days it wasn't politically correct to admit to being gay. She screamed at him, calling him every despicable name that came into her head. She threatened to tell the world that the great director, Paul Winger, was a flaming pervert. A queer and a pedophile. Her screaming frightened away his boy lover and roused Norma, who rushed into their room clutching a large kitchen knife in her little hands, terrified that someone was trying to kill her mother. Norma was ten at the time."

Jane looked from Piper to Jason. "Paul continued to plead and beg Sybil to forgive him. She refused. He went berserk, completely out of the mind. He snatched the knife from Norma and dragged her into the bathroom.

"That's where we came in, Daddy and I. Sybil was frantic. She called me. I called Daddy. Daddy could fix anything. He'd shielded her in the past. The studio would protect her again. Daddy and his assistant broke down the bathroom door and found Norma huddled in a ball in the corner, blood-spattered and in a state of shock. I'll never forget that awful sight. Paul, God rest his soul, lay nude, sprawled in a crimson bathtub. He was bleeding profusely from the crotch and a wide slit in his throat. He died in route to the hospital without uttering a word. It was horrible."

Piper shook her head. One gossip rag had hinted at a mysterious woman in the house, not a boy. "In the news reports there was no mention of a male lover."

"I told you my father was a powerful man," Jane said. "There was no reason for anyone to know what went on that night. No reason to make it public. Later Sybil admitted to me that their marriage of six months had not been consummated. His attempts on their wedding night, and the many nights following, had been clumsy, embarrassing failures. And now, of course, she knew why."

"So that's why Norma was sent to Europe?" Piper asked.

Jane nodded. "She was quite traumatized by the incident. She needed psychiatric help. The studio thought it best for her to get that kind of help...well, out of the country, away from the media."

"What did Sybil think of that?"

"She was heartsick about having to send Norma away. But in time, she realized that those of us who play an important role in this fantasy world called Hollywood must make certain sacrifices. Sybil's a strong woman, a survivor. She put it behind her, met and married Samuel soon after. That was probably the best period of her life. The birth of little Sammy was the happiest day of her life. She adored that boy. He was a sweet, beautiful baby."

Piper leaned forward. "Samuel had a daughter."

"Yes. Sam had left his wife and teenage daughter to be with Sybil. It was a bitter, harsh estrangement. Marlene— that was Sam's daughter—was especially heartbroken. She wanted nothing to do with Sam's new family. She went so far as to break into the house and threaten to kill all of them, to shoot them with a gun from her father's hunting collection. Sam was a big-game hunter in the days when killing a defenseless animal was considered macho."

"What did she look like?" Jason asked.

"Spitting image of her father. Fair complexion with dark hair and eyes."

Piper and Jason exchanged looks.

"Jane, do you have any idea where she might be now?" Piper said.

"I'm afraid not," Jane shook her head. "The last news I had about her was after Sam crashed his plane into that mountainside. Marlene had protested her father's will. Except for the small trust fund in Marlene's name and the Château in the Alps, the remainder of his estate went to Sybil. I guess you could say that her bitterness was justified. She blamed Sybil for her father's desertion, the loss of his love, and her vanished inheritance."

When Jane showed them out that evening, she pulled Piper aside and whispered, "Your Jason is a lucky man."

"He's not my Jason. We're not a couple."

Jane smiled. "Really? Have you noticed the way he looks at you when he thinks you're not looking?"

Piper felt her cheeks grow warm. She had caught herself stealing glances at him the past several days. He was an attractive man, after all, and he had rescued her. In the past three days, his arms had been around her three times. Each time protecting her. No one had ever protected her.

From time to time during the drive, she felt his eyes on her and thought of Jane's words. Piper had wanted Jason to believe her about the caregivers, and now he did. She had wanted him to help her, and he was. She wanted him to...Damn, *she wanted him.*

The traffic on Sunset Boulevard had picked up on the drive back. Just ahead, the cruisers packed the boulevard. That section began the over-the-top, always illuminated, giant billboards and digital screens on the sides of buildings—LA's version of Times Square. Fortunately, the road returning to the Vogt's was at the start of the chaos and not right in the middle of it.

"Knoller's daughter certainly had good reason to hate her stepmother," Piper said.

"I'll check her out," Jason said. "And that guard, the one from the asylum. We owe him a visit."

They made the left, heading up the hill.

Jason walked her to the front door of the Vogt house. When she opened the door and stepped inside, she said. "They have my cell phone. I dropped it in the Squire back yard tonight. They know I was there."

He followed her inside. "Lock up and set the alarm, I'm staying."

While Jason checked through the house, Piper closed all the blinds and then looked in on Dr. J., who wanted to play. Feeling guilty for leaving him alone all day, she indulged him by letting him out of his cage and scratching the back of his neck.

"All clear," Jason said returning to the kitchen.

Dr. J. greeted Jason with a series of animal sounds. Not the least bit frazzled by Jason's presence, Piper recalled how he had screeched whenever Luke entered the room.

"He must like you. He doesn't talk around new people." Piper fed Dr. J a piece of his favorite fruit, pineapple.

"He knows a bird lover when he sees one. Had a Green parrot in my college days. Now I have a BDD—big dumb dog."

That was the first personal information he'd offered. Was he married, engaged, divorced, gay? Not gay. That much she knew from the growing magnetism between them. Magnetism that grew by the hour. She could feel herself drawn to him by an invisible thread. She realized he knew so much more about her than she knew about him. In fact, she knew nothing about him. Maybe it was the brandy at Jane's, or his willingness to help her, or his obvious attraction to her, but suddenly she wanted to know all about Jason Bower, the man.

"I'm keeping you from your dog. Will he be okay?"

"Yeah. He has plenty of food and water. He just gets lonely when he's alone too long."

"Dr. J's like that. He sulks."

"Scooby Scooby Doo. . .where are you?" Dr J said and hopped back into his cage, his back to them. "Goodnight."

They laughed.

"Would you like something? A drink? Coffee?" Piper asked.

"Thanks, I'm fine." He looked away. "Which room were you in when you saw the handyman spying on you with the binoculars?" Jason asked.

She took him upstairs to the guest bedroom that faced the back of the house. In the dark room, with only filtered light from downstairs to see by, Jason looked through the binoculars at the window where Piper had seen first the scarred hand, then the message, and finally Luke. The blinds in every room across from them were now closed.

Piper took the binoculars. "The message is still there. They may not be aware that Sybil is trying to get help."

In the window's reflection, she saw Jason standing close behind her, his eyes not on the neighbor's window but on her.

Was it concern or duty that made him stand so close?

He lowered his head and touched his lips to the nape of her neck. A tingling wave of warmth radiated from her neck to her toes. She closed her eyes. His lips caressed a trail along her neck to the side of her face. She turned and lifted her face up to his. Their lips met and the kiss was soft and sweet. He kissed the corners of her mouth and then her eyes, his lips burning a trail down her throat to the hollow in her neck.

"Are you married?" she whispered.

"No."

"Attached?"

"No."

"Why not?"

He kissed her throat again. "Are you married?"

"Not for long."

"Attached?"

"No."

"Why not?"

He looked into her eyes and smiled. She smiled back.

The phone rang.

"Don't answer it," he said, his voice hoarse and low.

She glanced at the caller ID and gasped. Her name was on the display.

Jason saw it at the same time. "Answer it." He pressed the speaker button.

She lifted the receiver to her ear but didn't speak.

"Lose something?" It was Luke's voice. "I can return it to you. No trouble."

Jason disconnected and placed the receiver back on the base.

After the phone call from Luke that interrupted their intimate moment, Jason patrolled the house again, checking every window and door. Piper climbed into the guest bed. Jason pulled an overstuffed chair next to her bed. He kicked off his shoes, dropped into the chair, propping his feet on the bed, his service revolver across his lap. She fell asleep and dreamed of a safe place and tender kisses. Jason's kisses. His body close, his arms holding her tight, protecting her. When she awoke, Jason was lying beside her. She longed to feel his body curled around her.

CHAPTER 26

"TROPICAL PALMS," JASON SAID, looking around. "Why do they give rat holes like these such exotic names? I don't see any palms or feel the ocean breeze. We're miles from the ocean."

That morning Jason and Piper parked on Broadway across from the Tropical Palms Hotel. The neighborhood was every bit as seedy as he had said it'd be. On the fringe of skid row, rundown buildings with boarded up windows, hand-painted signs advertising twenty-five-cent X-rated movies, and GIRLS GIRLS GIRLS in neon blinked and flashed up and down the entire block. That morning Jason had suggested coming here on his own to make sure Mr. Avidon was the former guard from Triple Oaks Sanatorium. Piper insisted he take her with him. The homeless, the indolent, walking the streets or huddling in makeshift shelters confirmed to Piper this was no place for a woman to visit by herself. Even accompanied by Jason, a brawny officer with a .38 special, she felt apprehensive. Several young men openly dealing drugs on the corner glared at them.

Instead of getting out immediately, they sat looking at the depressing pea-green building. Along the second and third stories of the building, where the hotel rooms were located, faded and tattered curtains waved outside several open windows. The glass in every room was dull and streaked, the sills lumpy with mounds of pigeon droppings. In one window, an American flag twisted and flapped in the breeze.

"You and your husband, are you divorcing?"

"I filed the day I left him."

"Any chance of reconciliation?"

"None," she replied. "How about you?"

"Divorced."

"Children?"

"Two boys, eight and ten. I wanted a houseful, but my wife thought two was enough. The boys live with their mother in Oregon. I get them on school breaks and in the summertime. They just went back to school."

"You're lucky. I wanted children. Still do. Gordon didn't."

"You thought he'd change his mind after you were married?"

"He pretended to want kids. He used my desire for a baby against me, to keep me at home and under his control. He never intended to have children. Two years into our marriage he had a vasectomy without telling me. All the while letting me think that I might be sterile, not him."

"That sucks."

"Yeah, it does. Did."

His cell phone rang. "Bower here."

He listened, thanked the caller, hung up and turned to Piper. "Looks like we're on the right track. Just got confirmation that Elliot Avidon married a Judith Neely one week after the death of Norma Knoller. If this guy's our guy, he might have something to say. It's a long shot, but it's worth a try. Ready?"

Together they crossed the street to catcalls and hoots from the group of young men, which had doubled in size. Jason didn't hold her arm, but walked close beside her, their upper arms brushing occasionally.

They entered a closed-in staircase reeking of cat urine and feces. Graffiti scrawled boldly in black, red, and yellow spray paint gave the narrow space its only pulse of color. One flight up and to the left was the dim, windowless desk nook. No one was there. A stork of a man in a janitor uniform walked by with a plunger and a coiled metal drain snake.

"Excuse me," Jason said, "can you tell us which room is Elliot Avidon's?"

"Don't know no names. Gotta talk to Wyatt." He pointed to the empty desk-clerk nook. "But he don't come on until late afternoon. Come back then."

They returned to the car.

"What now?" Piper asked.

"We can go to my place. I'd like to shower and change and feed my dog."

"Of course."

He lived in Studio City, in the hills in a modest house just off Mulholland Drive. The view from the back of the house, looking down on Universal City, was spectacular. They stood at the side gate to the rear deck.

"Doofus jumps up on people when he meets them. He can be pretty overbearing. Let me put him out in the yard first. Kitchen's right inside. Help yourself to whatever. If you feel brave, join us the yard."

The dog burst out onto the deck and leaped down the stairs. He lifted his leg, made a huge puddle, and then ran straight for Jason. They roughhoused as Piper slipped through the gate, onto the deck, and into the house. The big black dog was a mix with no distinctive breed characteristics.

227

She smiled again. Damn, she was a real sucker for a man who loved animals. Gordon hated them. When they had been married about two years, she bought a goldfish. A week later, while she was out to lunch with Belle, he flushed it down the toilet, telling her it had died. That was when she began to mistrust him, and later to hate him.

On the wall in the dining room hung a small grouping of photographs, photos of Jason fishing on a boat with friends, Jason receiving a plaque from the Governor, Jason with a Boy Scout troop in the woods. A studio photograph of two boys and a woman held the center position. The boys looked like Jason. The woman was movie-star pretty. Blond hair, green eyes and a beautiful mouth with full lips. His sons and former wife, no doubt. They made an attractive couple. Piper felt a pang of envy. Jason hadn't sounded bitter or hardened by the split. He exhibited nothing but respect for his former wife, the mother of his children. Her picture graced his wall. Was he still in love with her? She glanced out the window. Jason was still in the yard, tossing a stick for his dog.

Spotting a bathroom at the end of the hallway, she headed for it. She passed a bedroom, probably the master bedroom, with a king-size bed, catching a glimpse of more framed photographs on the wall as she passed. She stopped. Stepped back.

She tried to see from the hallway, and then took a couple steps inside the room. Was that a picture of Thomas VanRaven and Clint Eastwood? Two incredible directors together in a snapshot that clearly wasn't a publicity shot. Why did he have photos of these movie icons on his bedroom wall? She ventured further inside the room. Then she saw a picture of Jason with an arm around VanRaven and Sydney Pollack, and was that Robert Redford, and Julia Roberts, and the president? There were also several shots of

Jason and some well-known television actors. The man at the wrap party sitting next to VanRaven in the theater *had* been Jason, not just a lookalike.

"You know what they say about curiosity—it killed the cat," Jason whispered in her ear.

She jumped. "Why didn't you tell me?"

"Tell you what?"

"That you know these people."

"They're not a big part of my life anymore. It wasn't important."

She pointed at the photo of VanRaven. "You were at the wrap party. Why where you there?"

"To see you."

"What? Then why did you duck out without talking to me? And how did you know I'd be there?"

"Because I figured your best friend and ex-husband, Lee, would be there to support her client, the leading lady. I hoped you'd show."

"How did you know I knew Lee?"

"I did some checking." He turned her to face him.

"I don't understand. I talked to you that day. I called you about Sybil and you brushed me off. You—"

He slipped his hands around the small of her back. "At the time there was nothing I could do about your neighbor. But I wanted to see you, and not on official business." He pulled her closer.

"That doesn't make any sense, I—"

His mouth came down on hers. The touch of his lips sent a shockwave through her. All morning she had thought about his kiss and wanted to feel his lips on hers again. His hands slid down, cupping her buttocks, and brought her against him. She felt herself responding to the warmth of his hard body and his kiss. He smelled of dog fur, fresh grass and clover.

Then he pulled away, peeled off his shirt, and said, "I'm going to take a shower." He pecked at her mouth and walked into the master bathroom, tossing the shirt onto the bed.

She stood there, her fingers touching her tingling lips. Her body aching for his touch.

She waited until she heard the shower water running, then she undressed and joined him.

They returned to the Tropical Palms and climbed the narrow staircase again to the second floor. The desk clerk, a bear of a man, sat talking on the phone while swiping a giant pretzel through a plate of brown speckled mustard.

He watched them approach, his eyes hard, unfriendly. "... and ten to win on seven at Santa Anita." He breasted the receiver. "Whadda ya want?"

"Elliot Avidon's room number," Jason said.

"He ain't in."

"Any idea when he might be back?"

"Nope." He put the phone back to his ear.

Jason stood, watching the man.

"Andy, I'll get back to you." He hung up the phone. "Hey, pal, this ain't no dorm, and I don't keep track of people."

Piper stepped forward. "Please, sir, it's a matter of life or death. A woman's life may be in jeopardy. Mr. Avidon hasn't done anything wrong. I swear. It's a personal matter. We need to talk to him about...well, about someone he knew a long time ago."

He glanced up at Jason and crinkled his nose in disdain. "Your guy goes out every afternoon. Don't know where. Most days he comes back around five-thirty...six." They all glanced at the clock on the wall. "You got at least half hour to go."

Jason pulled out his wallet and extracted two twenties. "Could you call when Mr. Avidon shows up? And maybe not let on to him that we want to talk with him."

The desk clerk reached for the twenties. Jason pulled them back. "One now, the other one after we talk with Avidon."

"What's yer number?"

They returned to the car to wait. The drug dealers from that morning had moved down one block. In their place stood a group of young boys smoking, passing around a magazine, and laughing—the drug dealers of tomorrow.

"Why didn't you tell him you were with the police?"

"Nothing shuts down the flow of information faster than flashing a shield to guys like him. Money talks. Besides, I'm sure he could smell cop on me. I look like a cop, don't I?"

She shook her head. "You look like someone in the business, the film business."

"No shit."

"What did you do?"

"Scriptwriter. TV mostly. LA Beat and others. I'm one of the few scriptwriters who went from the biz into law enforcement. It's usually the other way around."

"I thought your name was familiar. I just didn't make the connection."

"Why would you?"

"Do you like your job?" she asked.

"I must. It cost me my marriage. Well that and a few other things, like we had absolutely nothing in common except for the boys."

"I married my high school sweetheart." When he looked at her with a baffled expression, she added. "Oh, no, not Gordon. I wouldn't have looked twice at Gordon in high school. He was everything I hated back then. And resented. Ironically, after years of wild and crazy behavior, when I

231

thought it was time to settle down, he looked pretty good to me. My professional knight. I wanted a home, kids, stability. Only it didn't work out the way I hoped it would. My first husband is my best friend."

"I don't mean to pry, and you can tell me to take a flying leap, but isn't it kind of weird having your ex-husband become your closest female buddy?"

The last time Piper and Lee had been together it had been miserably awkward. Now it didn't seem such a big deal after all. Piper understood Lee's position. To Lee, Piper was still the same woman she'd loved in high school. Yet, they couldn't go back.

"Lee was a friend before she was my husband. Gordon, on the other hand, was never a friend. He had to be number one, had to control everything. I grew up in an easygoing, trusting, all-female environment. I didn't know how much I missed my independence until I saw it slipping away, year by year."

Piper pulled her knees to her chest and circled her arms around them. "When I edit a movie, I'm able to manipulate the scenes to the director or producer's liking, moving things around to get the best fit. I guess I need the freedom to express myself in my life. With Gordon there was no flexibility, no way but his way. Instead of taming me, he brought me down as subtly as a tiger brings down a wounded gazelle."

"If he did, he couldn't keep you down. You're one helluva fighter, Piper." Jason covered her hand with his.

"Gordon said I was a champion for the underdog. He considered it a flaw."

"He's an idiot. It's what I admired about you. You wouldn't give up on the widow. Not even when you knew that people thought you were delusional. You were willing to risk your own neck to save hers. That's not a flaw, it's a virtue."

232

Jason shifted and leaned forward. "There's a man coming down the street. He's walking very slowly."

She followed his gaze. About fifty feet from the entrance to the Tropical Palms a man with dirty blond hair combed straight back stopped at the doorway. He flipped a cigarette butt into the street, pressed a hand to his chest, and began to cough. The coughing fit went on for so long and with such fierceness the man had to lean against the front of the building. Red-faced and hunched over, he pushed himself off and walked another twenty feet before repeating the process. Finally reaching the hotel entrance, he used both hands to pull open the door, then disappeared inside.

"If that's our boy, he's got serious health problems," Jason said.

"Do we go?"

"We wait. If the desk clerk wants the rest of the money, he'll call."

The seconds ticked away. Piper realized she was holding her breath and exhaled. "How can you stand the waiting," she asked. "I'm a bundle of nerves."

Jason smiled. "I picture what he's doing, his progress. He's climbing those ten steps to the second floor. With his bad heart or lungs, it's a little slow going. He should be at the top now. He nods to the desk clerk, no words are exchanged. They don't have a speaking relationship. The desk clerk is watching him cross the lobby, or that open space that passes for a lobby, to the corridor. One…two…three…four…five. Five steps. Now he's out of sight to the desk clerk, who is staring at my phone number, debating whether to make that call or not. He's thinking about that second twenty, which of course, helps him decide. Also, like I said, he's no friend to the tenant. He picks up the phone on the desk, checks the number, and dials. It should be ringing just about…*now.*"

When his cell phone rang, she jerked slightly. Even knowing it might ring hadn't prepared her for Jason's prophetic talents.

"Yeah…" Jason said while reaching for the door handle. "Thanks, we're on our way."

CHAPTER 27

THE DESK CLERK TOOK JASON'S twenty-dollar bill without a word, jammed it into his pants pocket, and pointed to the corridor. "Two C."

The sour smell of urine continued, becoming stronger the farther down the windowless corridor they went. The gray carpet was bare in spots, the corded backing showing through. The door to 2A stood open. An obese man in his thirties sat on a metal chair looking out the window, the window displaying the American flag. As they passed, he glanced their way and saluted.

Jason tapped on the door of 2C.

"Yeah, who's there?" a male voice from inside called out, followed by a fit of coughing.

Jason waited until the coughing subsided before saying, "Mr. Avidon, my name is Jason Bower. I'd like a few minutes of your time, if you don't mind."

The door opened a crack. His ruddy face looked out. "What about?"

"About your wife, Judith, and your son."

"I don't have nothing to say about them. Not to you or anybody."

On reflex, Piper grabbed Jason's arm and squeezed. They had found their man. Now all they had to do was get him to talk to them.

"Mr. Avidon, it's a matter of life or death," Jason said.

"When ain't it with those two?"

Piper covered her mouth with her hand.

"Whose life you talking about?" the man said, opening the door a bit wider. His bloodshot eyes found Piper's. "Yours?" he asked her.

She nodded. "And Sybil Squire."

He snorted and coughed, but this time he quickly got the cough under control. "So she finally got there, huh? That was all she ever wanted, to get back at her. Took her sweet time, her and the boy, but she was never one for rushing things. 'Specially when it came to evening the score with the great Sybil Squire."

"Mr. Avidon, let us in, please. Talk to us," she said.

After a long pause he backed away from the door, leaving it ajar. Jason gently pushed it open. They entered, closing the door behind them. The room was small, the ceiling low and stained dark with water spots. It smelled of tobacco smoke, soiled clothing and sickness.

Avidon lit a cigarette. He offered the nearly empty pack to her and Jason. Jason refused. She took one. She had never wanted a cigarette so badly in her life. "Can I pay you for this? You're almost out."

"What's one less before I die? Cancer sticks. Coffin nails. They ain't kidding."

Jason lit hers. The smoke burned her mouth and throat. Suddenly, it didn't taste so good.

There was nowhere to sit except on the bed, a bed that was little more than a cot. She stepped to the open window and leaned against the sill.

"So whadda you want to know?" he said.

"What happened that day at the asylum?" Jason asked. "Who killed Sybil's daughter? Did Judith kill Norma and pin it on the inmate?"

Piper saw something in his eyes, a look of bafflement or surprise by what Jason had asked. It suddenly hit her. Like a montage in film, flashing before her eyes, she caught bits and pieces of the movies Sybil had mentioned, the ones she was sure contained clues. Murder, greed, insanity, and revenge by a blood relative—all were women. Her breath caught in her throat. It wasn't Sybil's daughter who had died that day. It wasn't Norma who had been bludgeoned to death, but someone else, and this man knew it.

"You don't ease into it, do you? Go right for the sixty-four-thousand-dollar question."

"We don't have a lot of time," Jason said.

Avidon licked his lips, sank down on the cot and said, "You're on the wrong trail. But I ain't surprised, 'cause that's what you're s'pose to think."

"Norma killed the nurse, Judith Neely," Piper said. It was not a question. "Norma killed her and took her identity."

Avidon's eye's stared into hers. "Okay, I'm gonna save you time and tell you what happened that day. I don't have a lot of time myself. You guessed it. Only took forty years for someone to catch on. I don't want no more people hurt or killed. I was in love with her. We was lovers in the sanitarium. When she told me she was pregnant, I knew I couldn't let her have my kid in no nuthouse. She planned it all out. Judith Neely, the new nurse, was a loner and perfect for the switch. She didn't have no family or friends to speak of. She was the same size and had the same coloring as Norma. Close enough to fit the bill, anyways. Soon as Norma laid eyes on her she knew what she was gonna do.

"Norma was good with makeup and hair. She got lots of practice making up the other inmates and even some of the nurses. Fact is, that very morning she dyed her hair the same color as that nurse's. She wanted to be a makeup artist for the movies, y'know, and there was no shortage of supplies. Momma sent her anything she wanted. Momma took good care of the nurses too, gifts and such. Anyway, Norma studied that nurse. Studied the way she walked and talked, those little things people do with their hands and body, right down to the way she blinked and looked away when talking to folks. When she was ready, she faked a chest cold and got this nurse to bring her some cough medicine. Norma ambushed her when she came into the room, knocked her out. She switched clothes, pulled her own hair into a ponytail, the way Neely always wore hers, then in cold blood she proceeded to do a real number on that poor girl."

It made sense, horrible sense. Judith Avidon was Sybil's daughter. After all these years Sybil was being held captive and terrorized by her own daughter, a daughter thought to be dead.

He looked at her with red, rheumy eyes. "I didn't have nothing to do with the actual killing. That was all Norma. But, hell, that don't matter. I'm just as guilty. I knew what was coming and I didn't try to stop it. Even did my part. Norma made me beat up her face, her eyes and mouth mostly, so they'd swell and make it harder for anyone to notice the switch. That was the hard part, hitting the woman I loved, and her being pregnant. Then she made me go get this other inmate from across the hall, a gal who'd picked on Norma a couple of times. Like I said, she always got even, always. Anyway, I dragged Wanda out of her room and into Norma's. She'd seen the whole thing and was too scared to do or say anything. Norma smeared blood all over her, and cracked Wanda's head and knuckles against what was left of the dead nurse's face, her teeth in particular, to make it look like she'd gone crazy with rage and beat a fellow inmate to death. When the scene was all set the way Norma wanted it, she sounded the alarm. It was a cakewalk. Nobody really questioned it. With a nurse and a guard as eyewitnesses, it was pretty much over and done with." He took a moment to rest; all the talking had made him short of breath.

"But why?" Piper said. It was all she could manage.

He cleared his throat. "Why'd I help her? Well take a good look at me. I ain't no Cary Grant. Norma was the most beautiful thing I'd ever laid eyes on. Looked just like her mother, she did. I was nuts about her. If she asked me to pop the Pope, I would've. Damn straight I would've."

Jason's eyes met Piper's. She saw disbelief in his expression. "No one noticed the switch? What about the hospital staff?" he asked.

"Not with her face all swollen and bruised. She played the hysterical witness to the hilt. Academy award performance. Like her momma, she could act. The next day she called in and quit. Who could blame her?"

"And you. Did you quit?"

"I stayed on for a while, so it wouldn't look suspicious."

Silence filled the room. She and Jason both trying to assimilate the information. Avidon lit another cigarette from the burning butt.

"Those two, my wife and son, are bad people. Psychopaths, I think they call people like them nowadays. She used me to break out of the asylum. We lived together on and off for about ten years—ten bad years. It got so I was

239

afraid to close my eyes. Beer bottle," he said, and pointed to a cut across his eyebrow, and one at the corner of his mouth. He unbuttoned his shirtsleeve, pushed it up to reveal a long white scar on his forearm. "Clam knife. She sometimes went off the deep end and when that happened, there was no controlling her. Lest ways, not by me. The only one who escaped her wrath was our boy, Tony. That one couldn't do no wrong. She spoilt him something awful. We never got along, me and that boy. But I loved her. I know that sounds stupid, but I don't know how to explain the spell she had over me. I wasn't the only one she could put a spell on. Men fell for her, young men, rich men. She had somethin' that drew em in."

"Did she leave you?" Piper mashed out the cigarette in a mound of dried bird droppings on the outer windowsill.

"Naw, that wasn't her way. If she wanted to get rid of someone, she made it more permanent. She tried to poison me. Damn near succeeded. I caught her lacing my orange juice with anti-freeze. Made me sick as a dog, almost didn't make it." He clucked his tongue. "Now I wish she'da killed me. It woulda been faster, more merciful than going out this way." He rubbed his chest. "Lung cancer."

"I'm sorry," Piper said.

He waved her sentiments away. "It ain't that I don't deserve it."

"Will you tell the police what you just told us?" Jason asked.

"No. If you can stop her, that'd be good. But I can't help you. Ain't no way I'm finking on her and the boy. I just ain't. If you go to the cops with what I told you, I'll deny everything."

"Without your statement, she's going to get away with another murder," Jason said.

"Then you best do what you can to stop her. I ain't spending my last days in the joint."

"Did Norma kill other patients under her care?" Piper asked.

"Don't know about that. I wouldn't put it past the two of them. She knows plenty about drugs and herbs and medicine that maybe won't show up in a dead body."

With Vera Wade's heart condition, she was an easy target. "Why is she after her mother?"

"She hates her. Blames her for everything bad that happened to her in her life. It goes way back to when she was a little girl. Back to when her fag stepdad went berserk and slashed hisself up right in front of her. She was sent away like it was her fault. Then her mother replaced her with a new kid. Her mother didn't pay much attention to Norma. She was only interested in her movies and getting new husbands, husbands that didn't want to be a daddy to Norma. All Norma wanted was for someone to love her. Her mother never questioned Norma's death in the asylum. Just closed the book on her." Avidon chuckled. "Norma went to her own funeral. Made herself up like a hospital nurse and even offered a personal condolence to Sybil. Sybil thanked her and walked away." He grinned. "Momma didn't have a clue."

Piper thought of Sybil's words at the pool that day she'd invited her over: '. . . *Family is everything. Love cannot thrive on deception and lies.*'

"Do you know what she intends to do with her mother?"

"If the woman's still alive it's because she wants to make her suffer for as long as she can. There's fifty-some years of payback behind that hate. You'd think killing the baby woulda' been enough for Norma, but it was only the beginning."

Piper felt numb. "What do you mean? What baby?"

"The little half brother. Norma hated that kid. Her momma walked in and caught her in the act. She caught her holding him under the water in the tub. Drowned him. That's when Sybil had her put away in that asylum. Everyone thought Norma had a breakdown from grief or misplaced guilt. Ha. That woman has no conscience. None."

Piper thought about that innocent little boy killed by the sister he adored because of hatred and jealousy. Norma might get away with her mother's murder, too, unless they could stop it.

He began to cough again. When the cough turned into an uncontrolled fit, she and Jason let themselves out of the room.

CHAPTER 28

"DOES SHE WANT HELP, Piper?" Jason asked when they returned to the car.

"What? Yes, she has to want help. Sybil tried to give me clues by way of her movies, four of them. I made the mistake of looking for specific messages in the body of the movies when I finally realized it was the content of the combined stories. As an editor, I should know I can't do my job unless I know the plot first. The plots all dealt with one or more elements—murder, revenge, greed, and insanity within a family. It hit me moments before Avidon confessed." She shook her head. "A confession that's worthless to us."

"Maybe not. If I can convince my captain that there's something suspicious about the Norma Knoller death, LAPD might request to have the body of the woman murdered in the asylum exhumed."

"Exhumed?" Piper asked, sitting up straight.

"He said the murdered woman was the nurse and not Sybil's daughter. He claimed that Norma took the nurse's identity. If that's true, the body in that grave should have no DNA components similar to those of Sybil Squire or any of her descendants—meaning the daughter and grandson. It could be the break we need to substantiate that Norma is alive and may be impersonating her own mother.

"I hadn't thought about *that* body."

"On the other hand, if the exhumed body does exhibit matching DNA, then Norma Knoller died in the asylum that day and there's no case."

"We have to try."

Jason nodded. "I agree."

After their visit to the Tropical Palms, Piper felt a need shower again, to wash away the ugliness of, not Avidon's deplorable living conditions, but his disturbing confession. What was happening to Sybil began fifty years ago, with the suicide of Norma's stepfather. No, long before that, when Sybil was born. This nightmare began with Sybil's mother who blamed her for everything bad in her life. First the mother and now the daughter. Sybil had been a victim all her life.

"I'm taking you to my place. I can't let you stay right next to them."

"I can't leave Dr. J there alone. I'm responsible for him. Belle would be devastated if anything happened to him."

"Okay, we get the bird and we're out of there."

Jason maneuvered through stop-and-go traffic. The sun was setting when they pulled up in front of the Vogt house.

His cell phone rang before they could exit the car.

"Bower," he said.

He grasped her upper arm, holding her back.

"He's still alive? Where? What hospital? Okay, I'm on my way."

Piper's pulse began to race.

"That was the desk clerk at the Tropical Palms. Avidon dove off the roof of the hotel. He's still alive, but barely."

"Oh my god."

244

"He left a sealed envelope for me with the desk clerk just minutes before he went up to the roof."

"A written confession?"

"That's what I'm thinking."

"Look, you go. I'll grab Doc and take him to your house. I'll need my car anyway."

He reached into his pocket, pulled out a house key, and handed it to her. "Call me as soon as you get there."

When she opened the car door to exit, he pulled her back, wrapped his arms around her, and kissed her. "No heroics. Don't go up to the guesthouse. Get the journal and the bird and get out. Pronto."

"Yes, sir. No heroics, I promise." She kissed him back.

"Where's the pepper spray?"

She patted her purse.

Piper didn't wait for him to drive away, she was already dashing to the front door. She rushed in, disengaged the alarm, locked the door, and headed for the kitchen. Dr. J squawked and screeched from his tree-like perch outside his cage. Good, she wouldn't have to coax him out to get him into his traveling carrier. Sometimes, when he was nervous or annoyed, he dug his talons in and refused to budge.

She grabbed Sybil's journal from the kitchen table and stuffed it into her purse. Then she rushed down the basement steps to where Belle kept an assortment of travel carriers. She chose the clear crystal shuttle, one she knew he liked and would go into easily. On the way back to the stairs something in the space under the staircase caught her eye. A toolbox that she didn't recall seeing there after Luke, or whatever his name was, had pumped out the flooded basement. She leaned down to read the name engraved into the metal. *Luke Monte*. Had Luke forgotten his tools in the Vogt's basement? No, not likely. They weren't Luke's tools. Luke wasn't the Vogt's handyman.

Not the man she knew as Luke. How had the phony handyman gotten his hands on the real handyman's toolbox? She straightened up and looked around. On the staircase step, at eye level to her, was a clump of moist dirt. Two steps down was another clump of dirt. Her gaze followed the clumps to the bottom of the staircase. The dirt trail led to the massive chest freezer directly in front of her.

She lowered the bird carrier to the floor and opened the freezer lid. Commercial butcher paper wrapped packages of frozen meat filled the entire chest from one end to the other. That was a lot of meat for two people. In the middle of the freezer, dirt marred a white package. She lifted it up, and then another and another, her heart pressing into her throat. Three layers down, she saw clear plastic sheeting with rivulets of dirt lining the creases and folds. Two more packages and she saw blue fabric. Buttons. A pocket. On the pocket was an oval patch. Stitched on the patch were letters. She leaned down closer. L-U-K-E. Luke. Her mind had difficulty grasping or making sense of what she saw. Maybe it was a bundle of clothes buried under the Vogt's prime cuts of steaks and chops. But it wasn't.

Upstairs, Dr. J squawked.

She removed another package. A pair of eyes, partially open and glazed over stared up at her. She breathed in the putrid odor that even the coldness of the freezer couldn't mask. She gagged. It was the real Luke.

That's when she heard him behind her. He caught her across the shoulders, smashed the chemical-soaked cloth against her nose and mouth, and held her tight against his chest. She couldn't move. She held her breath for as long as she could, but she was no match for his size and muscle. The last thing she heard before everything went black was Dr. J screaming like a banshee in the room above.

CHAPTER 29

HER HEAD WAS SPLITTING. The smell of chloroform filled her sinuses and burned the back of her throat. She opened her eyes to a spinning room and nausea. In the moments it took to regain her equilibrium, she tried to get her bearings. Her gaze settled on a pair of pale blue eyes. Sybil's eyes. Why hadn't she noticed how much his eyes resembled hers? How close his features were to hers, his own grandmother?

He sat on the bed beside her. He wore slacks. Except for the silver chain around his neck, he was bare-chested. His blond hair fell into his face. His hand was inside her shirt, caressing her breasts.

Piper stared back, expressionless, trying not to struggle. He wanted a reaction. He wanted her to fight him.

"She's not your type, Tony," said a female voice nearby.

Just past him in the doorway, Sybil stood in a nightgown.

"That's what makes it so much fun, Mom," Tony said. Although he appeared unruffled by his mother's presence, he pulled his hand away and rose up from the bed.

Not Sybil. Norma. The dark wig and brown contacts gone. Her pale blue eyes alive with indignation.

The woman held Sybil's journal and thumbed through it. "Is this the only one you have?" she asked. Piper nodded. "Where's your boyfriend? The cop?"

"I don't know." She fumbled to button her blouse.

"We'll have to move faster now."

They were in the master bedroom, the room she had seen Sybil pace in numerous times in the past. A birdcage sat on the floor near the bed. A yellow canary lay dead at the bottom of the cage. The room had the odor of death. The bird, she wondered, or Sybil? Was she dead too?

Within inches of her face, Norma said, "I can't begin to tell you what a pain in the ass you've been. You can't win now, so make the best of it." She gave Piper a hard shake and slapped her face.

Piper heard a low moan in the bed beside her. Slowly turning her head to avoid another bout of dizziness, she saw the thin, pale form of Sybil Squire on the far side of the mattress. Her white skin and hair blended in with the sheets, making her nearly invisible. Sybil reached out and touched her arm with icy cold fingers. The ring finger on her left hand was bent at an odd angle, the knuckle swollen three times its normal size. A circle of skin, where her beautiful diamond wedding ring had been, was bruised and raw.

These people were monsters. They thought nothing of torturing an old woman to get what they wanted. Sybil's breath no longer smelled of scotch and tobacco—the days of indulging their patient-turned-prisoner had long passed. Her breath smelled of neglect and decay.

Within the emaciated face, the sunken eyes remained expressive. They seemed to take over her entire face. Bruises and scabbed-over sores riddled her face, chest, and arms.

248

Sores the exact size and shape of a cigarette tip. Blood caked at the corner of her mouth, her pale feet poked out beneath her soiled nightgown. Piper's heart caved. Sybil became her loving Nana in her final days of terminal cancer, begging silently to be pain-free and at peace. Once again Piper found herself comparing this woman with her grandmother. She couldn't save Nana Ruth, but she could try to save Sybil.

"How touching," Norma said to Sybil. "A total stranger gets more affection than I ever got. Those frigging birds got more attention. Is it any wonder I have to be so tough on you? Is it?"

Tony pulled Piper from the bed and slammed her into a chair. A stabbing pain shot through her head, spots jumped in front of her eyes.

"All right, look, we're very close to finishing up our business here. You're going to help us, and then we'll leave you all and be on our merry way."

Piper seriously doubted they would leave them alive, especially after killing the handyman and stashing him in the Vogt's freezer. They had nothing to lose and everything to gain by killing them.

Norma opened Sybil's journal and rifled through the pages. "Listen to this," Norma said with her face in the journal. "Would you *listen* to this?" She began to read, "'Norma leaves for England tomorrow. I've no choice. They'll help her there. Sending my little girl away breaks my heart. I'll miss her terribly…they say it's for the best. But I wonder, is it?" Norma paused. Mocking sentiment filled her words. "'Jane says in time she'll realize that those of us who play an important role in this fantasy world called Hollywood must make certain sacrifices.'"

Norma Knoller whirled around, platinum hair flying, pale eyes flashing, to scream at the frail form on the bed, "You selfish bitch! You had no *choice*? It was for the *best*? Whose dirty secret was it, anyway? Not mine—I was ten years old. I didn't understand what was going on. The only sacrifice made was by me, *me*—your little girl. I was the one sent off to a strange country to live without family, to battle the bloody nightmares alone, because it was all for your perfect fantasy world. What did *you* sacrifice, Mommy dearest? Tell me! What great sacrifice did you make? You continued to star in your pathetic movies. You got married again and replaced me with your precious brat."

Sybil Squire closed her eyes, shutting out her daughter.

Tony leaped onto the bed, stood above the prone woman, his feet rocking on each side of her. "Grandmother, you were a rotten mother to my mother. My mother would never send *me* away, never. You owe her, y'know. Why don't you just tell us? Where is it? You owe us!"

Mr. Moto stepped into the room.

"Okay, if that's how you want to play." Tony turned to Moto. "Jack, your knife."

Sybil's eyelids squeezed shut tighter.

Moto extracted from his pants pocket a Mother-of-Pearl-handled pocketknife and handed it to Tony. Tony pulled out the nearly five-inch blade, testing the sharpness by shaving a patch of hair from his forearm.

"Now, Grandma, you have to open your eyes. It's important you see what we have to do to Piper Buttinski, your self-proclaimed protector. Because every slice made into her pretty body will be a black mark on your soul. You'll be responsible for her blood."

Tony leaped off the bed. He lifted the chair with Piper in it, carried it the five paces to the side of the bed and slammed it down. "If you don't open your eyes, Grandma, I'll have to slice off your eyelids. Is that what you want?" He pulled Sybil to the edge of the bed by her nightgown. He put his mouth to her ear and screamed, "Open them, *now*."

Sybil's eyelids opened. In a voice barely audible, she whispered, "Let her go and I'll…tell you."

"Oh, Grandma, it's too late for bargaining. We're beyond that stage of the negotiations. Besides, we have to punish your friend for being such a busybody. How much punishment I dole out, of course, is up to you." He grabbed Piper's wrist and pulled her hand toward Sybil, the palm facing her. "I used to read fortunes. Palms, actually. You'd be surprised what you can see in the lines of the hand. This line," he placed the tip of the blade at a spot under the index finger, and traced it to under the ring finger, "is the head line. It reveals your determination in life. We all know how determined Piper can be, don't we?" He retraced the line, only this time he pressed down, cutting. Pain shot up her arm. She strained to pull her hand away. He held it tighter. Moto held the back of the chair to keep her from tipping it over. A thin red line emerged. Tony wiped her blood on the sheets.

"Now this is the heart line. Emotions are involved here. Is that new boyfriend's name written all over this line?" He cut the width of her palm, from side to side. This cut was deeper. Piper cried out. Blood ran down her palm, wrist, and forearm to pool in the crook of her elbow. Again, he dragged her palm across the bedclothes, staining them with her blood. "This one, the life line, circles the thumb. If I press hard enough, I can take her thumb off." He brought the blade down on the space between her thumb and index finger. She closed her eyes. Her body trembled from head to toe.

"The pool." The voice was so soft she barely heard it over the pounding of her heart.

"What?" Tony said. "Grandma, did you say something? The key is where?"

"Swimming pool. Chained to the drain... bottom." Sybil let her eyes fall shut.

"Mom, Jack, watch them." Tony gestured to her and Sybil, then left the room, undoing his pants.

Piper wrapped a pillow around her hand to stop the flow of blood. The wounds burned. Her hand throbbed.

Norma paced from the bed to the window where Moto stood and back to the bed.

"He dove into the pool," Moto said.

Norma thrust her face into Sybil's face. "You better be telling the truth, old lady, or I swear I'll rip your heart out with my bare hands. And I'll make certain the world learns every sordid detail of that dirty secret you wanted so desperately to hide. They'll know what kind of depraved, twisted men you married. And what a selfish, uncaring bitch of a mother you were."

"You're sick, Norma," Sybil whispered. "You need help."

"Shut up!" Norma slapped Sybil across the face. Piper heard a bone in her face crack.

Moto said, "He's been at the bottom of the pool for a long time, I think she's lying. Wait, he's up. He's signaling." Moto opened the window and leaned out. He turned to Norma. "Wire cutters. He wants wire cutters. Where are they?"

"In the tool shed. Go help him. Hurry." Norma waved him out.

Norma replaced him at the window. "Looks like we won't need either of you anymore."

Piper scanned the room for a weapon, something heavy to charge Norma. The knife lay on the nightstand.

Norma turned and saw Piper looking at the knife. She rushed to the nightstand. She snatched up the knife and came at Piper.

Piper pushed the chair back and scrambled to her feet, deflecting the first stabbing thrust with the outstretched pillow. Norma's wild swing threw her off-balance, giving Piper a split second to shove her with all her might. Norma fell backwards over the chair. Her head hit the edge of the dresser with a thud. Norma tried to rise, but slumped to the floor, eyes rolling back into her head.

Piper snatched up the knife that had fallen from Norma's hand. As she came around the bed to help Sybil, she checked out the window. Moto was coming out of the shed with the wire cutters.

Piper pulled Sybil's legs to the side of the bed and lifted her into an almost standing position. Sybil was too weak and sank down on the mattress with a deep sigh. Sybil couldn't stand and Piper couldn't carry her. Piper had to get help. The phone on the nightstand was dead, the cord missing. Piper raced down the stairs to the phone in the kitchen. Keeping low so that Moto and Tony couldn't see her, she grabbed at the wall receiver. The dial tone was like heavenly music. She dialed 911. It seemed a lifetime before someone answered. "What's your emergency?" She gave them the address and said that she was being held hostage, someone was dead and the killers were about to take two more lives. Not waiting for a response, she turned and ran back through the house and up the stairs. In the bedroom she rushed to Sybil and kneeled at her feet. Something was wrong. It took her a moment to realize that Norma was no longer sprawled out on the floor.

"Where's Norma?" Piper asked, taking the limp scarred hand in her hand. The hand was warm, the palm moist. Sybil's head was bowed, her chin on her chest, her eyes closed behind an unruly mass of platinum hair. Then Piper saw it. Her gaze traveled downward to a naked foot and leg at the side of the bed, a foot with cigarette burns. She looked back at the woman whose hand she held. The woman lifted her head with great effort, turned her face toward Piper. Pale blue eyes stared into hers with pure loathing. Piper gasped.

Norma grabbed her around the throat and squeezed, pushing her down to the floor. Her body straddled Piper's and her knees held Piper's arms to her sides in a vise-like grip, her super strength fueled by rage. Amid screaming sirens, her thumbs pressed into Piper's windpipe and Piper knew that in no time, police or no police, she would be dead. She stared into those pale blue eyes and watched the world around her go red, then white. A brilliant white, like a bursting nova, and at the core, a vision of her grandmother fading in and out.

Suddenly the pressure on her throat eased. With a grunt, Norma fell away from her and toppled to the floor at her side. Sybil bent over Norma, both hands still gripping the handle of the knife, its blade buried in her daughter's back. Sybil's legs wobbled violently, her daughter's body the only thing holding her up. Sybil slumped to her knees. The two women, uncanny in their resemblance, seemed to embrace, bonding at last.

Piper eased out from beneath Norma and touched Sybil's shoulder. She had wanted to save Sybil, yet in the end Sybil had saved her.

She pulled herself to her feet, leaving a fresh trail of blood on the bed sheets. The room shifted and rocked. A sudden dizziness hit her. Dizziness she quickly blamed on lack of oxygen from her near strangulation. She fell to her knees. When the ceiling fan began to sway and items fell off the nightstand and dresser, she realized it was an earthquake. The ceiling cracked. Directly over her head a thick wooden beam split. She screamed. Her own scream filling her ears shocked her into action. Panic propelled her toward the exit with one thought—to get out.

On hands and knees, she crawled to the doorway, pitching to the side as knick-knacks and paintings crashed to the floor around her. She saw Jason charging through the doorway from the back of the house. The trembler tossing him from side to side, slowing his progress.

"Piper, hurry!"

"The pool! Tony—"

"We've got them."

She crawled another foot and stopped. The sight of Jason brought her to her senses. *Sybil.* She needed her help. She looked behind her. The beam creaked, shifted again, raining plaster down on Sybil's head. Piper crawled back into the room, glancing at the beam as she inched her way across the floor in what seemed like slow motion.

She lifted Sybil under both her arms and tried to drag her away from her daughter. Norma reached up, wrapped her hand around the handle of the knife buried into her upper back and tugged the blade out. She twisted around. The crazed look in those ghostly eyes frightened Piper more than the earthquake or the beam overhead. Norma raised her arm to plunge the blade into her mother's chest. Piper kicked at those wild eyes, her sandaled foot landing squarely across the bridge of her nose. She heard the crunch of bone breaking. With blood pouring from her nose, Norma pulled herself upwards, gripping the knife. Piper marveled at her superhuman strength. Norma turned to Piper, her mouth twisted into an ugly, triumphant grin. The blade rose above Piper's throat just as the beam gave way and came crashing down, seemingly powered by invisible hands. Norma looked up as it struck her in the face, a long sliver of wood pierced through one of those penetrating pale blue eyes, obliterating it completely.

Jason pulled Piper to her feet, lifted Sybil, and together they made their way down the stairs and out of the house.

The piercing sounds of sirens and car alarms filled the air. The neighborhood was alive with people running into the street, shouting. The entire world had suddenly gone mad.

CHAPTER 30

Los Angeles Times.

AWARD-WINNING ACTRESS VICTIM OF ABUSE:
Eighty-five-year-old Sybil Squire is recovering from injuries sustained at the hands of her daughter and grandson. The film star's daughter, assumed murdered years ago, resurfaced, and in a bizarre bid for revenge...

SYBIL SQUIRE WAS AGAIN headline news after nearly forty years. Three people were in the morgue, one was in the hospital, and two were in the county jail awaiting arraignment for a number of charges, Murder 1 heading the list. The earthquake made the front page as well, but took a backseat to the scandal involving the once-famous screen idol.

When Jason and Piper had exited the Squire house with Sybil, the ground stopped trembling as abruptly as it had started. Piper didn't remember much of what happened, or in what sequence, except that she was never so glad to be outside and to see the West Hollywood police.

Jason took Piper to the emergency room at County General where the cuts on her hand were stitched and bandaged. As he stood by, holding her other hand during the procedure, Piper thought how easily she could completely fall for his guy. Was he the one, Piper asked herself. The conversation with Belle played in her head: "Do I have a type?" "Yes, you just haven't found him yet." Maybe she had.

The police removed the body of Luke Monte, handyman, from the Vogt's freezer. A cadaver dog detected cadaver scent in Sybil's rose garden. Tony had killed the man, buried him, dug him up, and placed him in the freezer. To throw off suspicion from himself or maybe hoping to frame Piper for the murder, she wasn't sure which. The reference to the Rose Garden in Sybil's journal had been a clue to the whereabouts of the handyman's buried body.

The police found the key to the safe-deposit box chained to the drain at the bottom of the pool. Suspecting something sinister was about to happen, initiated by the unexpected visit from Mr. Moto and her grandson, Sybil had transferred a good deal of her fortune—cash, jewels and negotiable bonds—to a new safe-deposit box the day of the fire.

Avidon died from his leap off the roof of the Tropical Palms. The envelope left with the desk clerk contained a written confession to the murder of sanitarium nurse Judith Neely.

The body in Norma Knoller's gravesite was exhumed. Through DNA testing, it was determined to be the body of Judith Neely and not Norma Watson Knoller.

With his mother no longer alive to oversee his life, a devastated Tony Avidon—a.k.a. Anthony DeMille and more recently Luke Monte and Arnold Copeland—confessed to killing the Vogt's handyman on the day of the earthquake and conspiring with Jack Ling and his mother in the injection death of Sybil's longtime friend and housekeeper, Vera Wade. He went on to confess to charges of forgery, elder abuse, financial exploitation, and intent to kill his grandmother, Sybil Squire.

Sybil went to the private hospital in West Hollywood where a contrite Dr. Lowdell treated her for malnutrition, neglect and the physical abuse she had sustained while under her daughter's care. Her chances for survival were fair. When Piper visited her, a frail Sybil told her that to protect Piper, she had tried to discourage her from getting involved. "I should have known you wouldn't be deterred by anyone or anything. Your grandmother had those same strong principles. She would have been proud of you. As I am."

The earthquake, although it felt strong, of a magnitude that kills, was only 5.2 on the Richter scale—anything under 6.0 was considered a mere nuisance to Angelenos. Yet the quake's damage to the Squire house had been devastating, and it did kill. Investigators speculated that the structural damage had occurred during the earlier quake, weakening the overhead beam. The final quake had been significant enough to bring it down.

Sybil swore that only something as formidable as an earthquake could stop her crazed and obsessed daughter. If the beam had not fallen when it had, and where, Norma might have succeeded in killing her and Piper.

Piper had another theory about what happened that night. In part, she agreed with Sybil. She had seen that savage look in Norma Knoller's eyes. The beam's timely descent, in her opinion, was nothing short of a miracle, but the hand was guided not by God, but another. Piper didn't believe in guardian angels—until that night. She didn't tell anyone about the apparition that had hovered over her when

Norma was squeezing the life out of her and again when the knife blade was poised to plunge into her throat. No one would believe her. They'd say she had been hallucinating. But she saw what she saw and she believed.

"I saw them. I did," Nana Ruth told her that day in the clover patch.

"I know, Nana. I know."

Epilogue

IN THE BLACK-AND-white scene unfolding on the pearlescent screen of the small theater in Beverly Hills, Sybil Squire's flawless features literally glowed in the close-up. Young, beautiful, those pale blue eyes. . . .

She lifted the lid of the jewelry box. From beneath the small pistol, she slowly lifted the gold locket by the black satin ribbon. She opened the locket and gazed at the tiny photographs inside the oval frames. Tears welled up. Piper waited to hear Sybil deliver those final lines from *Black Ribbon*.

"Your light has gone out, my shining angels, and soon there'll be nothing left of you or me. Nothing."

The music keyed up and the screen darkened from the edges in, forming a circle that gradually swallowed the silver screen until there was only a pinpoint of light in the center. Then it too blinked out with the sharp crack of the gunshot. The credits of Mick Vogt's, *The Greatest Classic: Film Noir*, began to crawl up the dark screen.

Sybil's outstanding performance in *Black Ribbon*, showcased in the documentary, outshined her real life role as a tragic leading lady. Piper felt proud to have a part in that piece of history.

It all came clear to Piper. Moving next door to Sybil brought the loss of her grandmother, her only remaining family, to the forefront. She had become emotionally involved with Sybil, wanting to help her. To save her when she couldn't save Nana. In the end, the make-believe world of movies had given her a new family.

Piper thought back to that day with Sybil at poolside. Sybil's words, *"Family is everything. Love cannot thrive on deception and lies. If I had been more like you, my life might have been entirely different. . . At least your grandmother had you."*

"You have me," Piper whispered through the lump in her throat. "We have each other."

A cool, delicate hand pressed on hers. Piper turned to the woman beside her who looked straight ahead at the screen. In the light from the credit scroll, tears glistened in her eyes. A smile on her face.

About the Author

Carol Davis Luce is the author of many novels including *NIGHT STALKER, NIGHT PREY, NIGHT PASSAGE,* and *SKIN DEEP.* Four of her five novels are set in Nevada, from a small mining town to the majestic waters of Lake Tahoe. *NIGHT GAME* is set in the flash and neon of the gaming milieu. *NIGHT WIDOW,* a Hollywood flavor with shades of Hitchcock's 'Rear Window'.

She lives with her husband, Bob, and a psycho cat in Sparks, Nevada. Carol enjoys connecting with readers—visit her at:

http://imagerystudios.com/carol

https://www.facebook.com/pages/Carol-Davis-Luce/253106338074036?skip_nax_wizard=true

http://twitter.com/#!/CarolDavisLuce

Read other works by **Carol Davis Luce**

Novels:

NIGHT HUNTER (formerly Skin Deep)
NIGHT STALKER
NIGHT PREY
NIGHT PASSAGE
NIGHT GAME
NIGHT WIDOW

Short Stories:

BROKEN JUSTICE
FOR BETTER, FOR WORSE

www.ingramcontent.com/pod-product-compliance
Lightning Source LLC
Chambersburg PA
CBHW072225190626
46809CB00017B/551